SKYSWORN

Books by Eric R. Asher

Shop ebooks, audiobooks, and paperbacks at ericrasherstore.com

The Theme Park at the End of the World

The Steamborn Series

Steamborn

Steamforged

Steamsworn

Skyborn

Skyforged

Skysworn

Stormborn

Stormforged

Stormsworn

The Vesik Series
(Recommended for Ages 17+)

Days Gone Bad

Wolves and the River of Stone

Winter's Demon

This Broken World

Destroyer Rising

Rattle the Bones

Witch Queen's War

Forgotten Ghosts

The Book of the Ghost

The Book of the Claw

The Book of the Sea

The Book of the Staff

The Book of the Rune

The Book of the Sails
The Book of the Wing
The Book of the Blade
The Book of the Fang
The Book of the Reaper
Dreams of the Forgotten Dead
Garden Gnome Graves

The Vesik Series Box Sets

Box Set One (Books 1-3)
Box Set Two (Books 4-6)
Box Set Three (Books 7-8)
Box Set Four: The Books of the Dead Part 1
Box Set Five: The Books of the Dead Part 2

Mason Dixon: Monster Hunter

Episode One
Episode Two
Episode Three
Episode Four

Want to receive an email when one of Eric's books releases?
Visit ericrasher.com to get started.

SKYSWORN

THE STEAMBORN SERIES, BOOK SIX

By

ERIC R. ASHER

Edited by Laura Matheson
Cover typography by Murphy Rae
Cover artwork by Enggar Adirasa

Memory dwells in shadow.

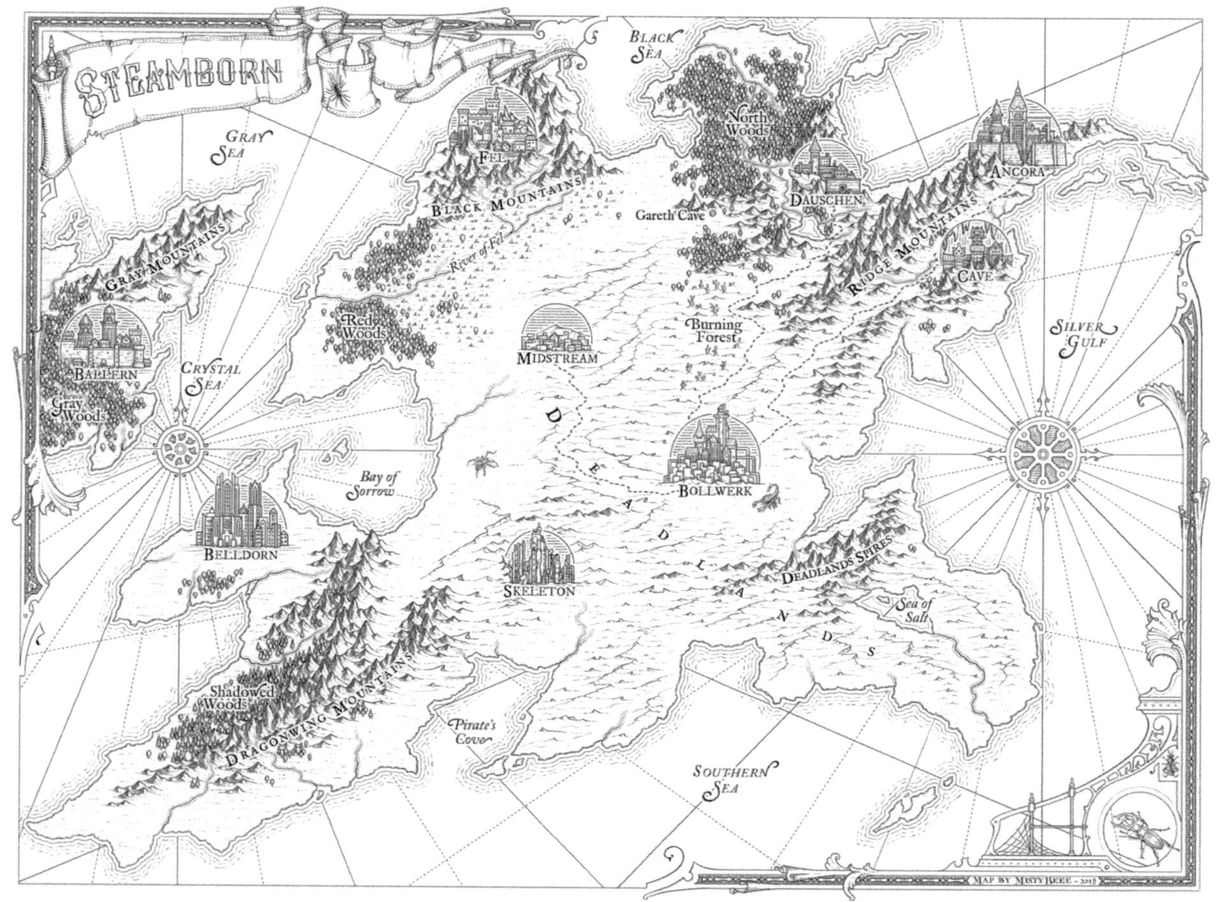

STEAMBORN
GRAY SEA
BLACK SEA
Fel
Black Mountains
North Woods
Dauschen
Ancora
Gareth Cave
Ridge Mountains
Cave
Gray Mountains
River of Fel
Burning Forest
SILVER GULF
Red Woods
Midstream
Ballern
Crystal Sea
Gray Woods
D E A D L A N D S
Bollwerk
Bay of Sorrow
Belldorn
Deadlands Spires
Skeleton
Sea of Salt
Shadowed Woods
Dragonwing Mountains
Pirate's Cove
SOUTHERN SEA
Map by Misty Beee - 2019

CHAPTER ONE

NEARLY A WEEK had passed, and time had given Jacob and the others a much better picture of what had happened in Fel. The lack of airships hadn't been luck. It had been Mordair's plot from the beginning. He'd abandoned Fel in full, leaving only a small number of citizens and skirmishers behind.

But there were other things that sowed confusion. Mordair's attack on the fisherfolk had been witnessed by too many survivors. They'd risen up against the remaining soldiers and imprisoned those found to be loyal to Mordair. More of Mordair's loyalists could be hiding among those who rebelled, and that left too many questions about the surrender of the city for Archibald to be comfortable.

In short order, Lady Katherine had her intelligence. For all the ships just south of Belldorn, Mordair had provided another blockade around Ballern. The only good news was casualties remained low in Fel up to that point. Those realizations brought an urgency to Lady Katherine's plans, and the split focus between reinforcing Belldorn and breaking the Ballern lines had everyone exhausted.

But exhaustion was something Jacob knew, and knew well.

Securing Midstream had been a simple day's work compared to Belldorn. Here they had the rubble of the outer city, where Ballern had come too close for comfort and destroyed the bordering villages. Many had escaped into the city, but many had died. To the west was the ocean, an open field Ballern's airships could strike from at any time.

It was a weakness in Belldorn's defenses that wouldn't have been an issue if not for the beachhead Ballern had established to the south. With the ability to refuel so close to the city, Ballern's forces had a plethora of inroads.

This led Jacob to his current predicament, and the cracked hydraulic hose spraying him in the face. "No! That's not it!"

"Are you certain?" Smith asked.

Jacob raised his face to glare at Smith, hydraulic fluid dripping from Jacob's hair.

"Ah, yes."

Smith crouched down and Jacob could hear him wrenching another valve closed, and the stream of hydraulic fluid finally cut off.

"That's it," Jacob said, grabbing a towel to wipe himself down. He was thankful for the stained apron and gloves they'd borrowed from the old tinker shop. The gear had mostly saved his shirt.

Smith drained the remaining fluid while Jacob watched. The braided hose they'd used to replace the broken one reminded Jacob of the reinforced tubing Smith now had in his biomechanics.

Jacob hopped onto the treads below and walked to the other side of their redesigned Titan Mech. The remnants of an armored crawler had given him the idea, and Smith had designed a new interface between the crawler and the Mech to make the idea work. Jacob wanted to make the Titan Mech amphibious, able to move with ease in shallow water or on land.

It wasn't as versatile as the two-legged design currently employed in Midstream and at four points around Belldorn, but it had other advantages. Or at least it would if they could get it working.

Alice cleared her throat, startling Jacob out of his thoughts as he spun to face her. "More of the skirting you asked for. Rin got it from their supplies in Canopy. Furi was right. It's what they line the Dragonwing saddles with."

"Fantastic, thank you."

Alice squinted, looking out toward the beach. "If you look close enough, you can still see the top of the last Titan Mech you sank into the sea."

Jacob grimaced. "And thanks for that, too."

Alice made her way around the Titan Mech, sporting a wide grin.

"Now, now, Alice," Smith called from above them. "Eva is going to haul it out today with a supply ship. In the meantime, we found the problem."

"Other than it sinking?" Alice asked.

"Well, no, that would still be a problem."

"He means we aren't trying to make this one float," Jacob said. "Two treads on the ground, or under the water, while the engines stay dry thanks to this." He patted the heavy rubber skirting.

"And the new smokestack is inside the ratchet, so, well, *that* should not happen again," Smith said with a nod to the ocean.

Jacob looked out toward the water where he could just make out the shoulders and head of the Titan Mech they had sunk. Poor positioning had folded the smokestack into the water when they pivoted. That was the end of that experiment. But Jacob noticed something else had wrapped around the Titan Mech's shoulders, a shiny carapace of dark maroon.

"Looks like a Sea Walker likes that Titan Mech." Jacob smiled at the docile giant. Sea Walkers didn't look so different from a regular Walker at first glance, and while they weren't known for trying to eat people, they did secrete toxins when hunting for fish. And it certainly wasn't something you wanted to get your hands in.

Smith frowned and looked down at Jacob. "I am not a fan of those creatures."

"Why not?"

"A close encounter in the Bay of Sorrow. A long time ago, when I first started apprenticing with Targrove. Although I believe the old man was somewhat amused at the rash that covered my entire body for a week."

"Ouch," Alice said.

"It did not hurt. But it itched. Oh, did it itch." Smith made a grasping motion with his hands, and Jacob didn't need to clarify what he was asking for. He passed a small, fluted jar of hydraulic fluid up to the tinker. "We are almost ready to test. Secure the skirting, and we will know in short order if this was a good idea."

"Want to help?" Jacob asked, turning to Alice.

She gave him an awkward smile that told him she'd like to do any-thing but help. Alice ran her hands down the finely woven gray and white fabric she wore. "This dress was a gift from Mary. Don't ruin it."

Jacob held out his hand, and she took it, hopping up the small pro-trusions on the treads before joining him at the base of the Titan Mech.

Alice eyed the frame of cables Jacob had anchored to the wall of the Mech. They tapered down to a gasket fastened to the floor. She took one side of the skirt without asking what needed to be done, and that alone told Jacob the design was good. Heavy clasps secured the skirt as they circled around the small compartment.

The second layer of cables didn't anchor any of the material but kept it from being sucked in too close to the chimney, or torn away by the engine itself. The most awkward part of securing the skirt was the gasket at the bottom. Jacob had to reach underneath and lift it so they could slide the skirt's edge inside, while using a portion of it as a glove so he could get his hand back out. After several failed attempts, and a few muttered curses, the gasket thumped against the floor.

Two arched clips pinned another layer of the skirting to the gasket itself, and Jacob gave the entire assembly a good smack with his leg. It trembled like the string of an instrument and offered a good resistance.

"That looks secure," Smith said, his voice muffled from his position above them. "Good thinking on the gasket. It is waterproof and heat resistant. I should have thought of it myself."

Alice turned to Jacob as she dried her hands off on a towel. "Do you need to test it? Or can we get lunch?"

"Why not both?" Smith asked from his perch at the top of the Mech.

Jacob grinned at Smith and turned his attention back to Alice. "How about it? Want to go for a ride?"

"You can swim, right?" Smith's question ruined most of the confidence Jacob had in their changes. Smith vanished inside the cockpit, and a burst of flame rose from the highest boilers on the arms.

Though Jacob couldn't see it, he heard the igniters fire behind the skirt, and it wasn't long before a small trickle of smoke escaped the chimney. He closed the access panel in the crawler base and turned back to Alice.

"Well?"

She ran her fingers through her hair and then started up the ladder just above the treads. "How different is this from the one we piloted in Midstream?"

"Almost the same," Jacob said. "But it has the traditional controls of a crawler as far as steering." He followed her over the edge of the cockpit and took his place beside Smith while Alice grabbed the harness by the controls to the cannons.

Smith moved one of the levers, raising and lowering the arms before pivoting the waist of the Mech around the ratchet.

"Already heated?" Alice asked.

Smith nodded. "Those flat boilers are something else. And it does not hurt we have incorporated the hydraulics into the base as well. You do not need nearly as much force to shift the hydraulic levers. Hold on.”

Jacob's harness wasn't quite tight enough when the Titan Mech lurched forward. He flailed for a moment before catching his arms on the console and leaning back to tighten the straps. It was nearly a straight shot to the water, but the streets weren't empty. A handful of soldiers and civilians danced away from the path of the Titan Mech. But the irritation on some faces turned to something else as their eyes rose to take in the towering form.

Jacob had been surprised when he first saw the treads on the Belldorn crawlers. They weren't shaped quite like those of Bollwerk's, which were more suited to the flat stone streets than the desert sands. But despite that, the crawlers of Belldorn had no issues traversing the loose sands on the beach beside the Crystal Sea.

It was easy to tell when they left the road, as the jarring clank of the treads on stone vanished behind the hiss of the engine and the rhythmic snap of the skirt below.

“Is it supposed to be making that sound?” Alice asked.

Smith leaned to his left and looked down at an access panel. It was too dark below the floor for Jacob to make anything out from across the cabin, but Smith nodded. “I can see it pulling the material in a bit like bellows. It is something we will need to test if they intend to keep these in service for long periods of time.”

“Add it to the maintenance plan,” Jacob said.

“Indeed.”

Alice took a sharp breath, and Jacob knew why. The shore was fast approaching, and beyond waited the gentle roll of the sea.

One thing they'd quickly realized in their initial testing was the base of the crawler was a little too buoyant to keep good contact with the sea bottom. Smith had the idea to repurpose the pressurized tanks once used for launching bombs. It had taken them nearly a day to refit the old crawler with ballast tanks, but as the treads dipped below the waterline and Smith opened the iris, the pumps engaged.

The whir of the motor soon vanished as the ballast tanks filled and the amphibious crawler slid through the water. They didn't go out quite as far as where they'd lost the last Mech, but the hair on the back of Jacob's neck still stood a little taller as the waterline threatened to reach the boilers on the arms.

Smith kept them dry by raising them into an elevated position, but Jacob still remembered the sound of burst metal the last time they'd tried this. He leaned over to get as good a look as he could of the skirting below. No water pooled inside the gasket, and he hoped the material would hold.

Smith pulled and pushed the levers in opposite directions to spin the Titan Mech in place before heading back to shore. It had some drag, and the treads spun on a loose spot of sand before they broke out of the water.

Jacob turned to look at Alice, who had her hands wrapped so tightly around her harness that her knuckles were whitening. "Fun, right?"

She gave him a sideways smile. "That was a little farther than I was expecting, and I didn't want to swim back."

Smith laughed. "A little farther than I was expecting, too. Between the scoops on the treads, and the tanks, this cuts through the water quite well. It could prevent a seaborn vessel from landing on the shore, no doubt."

A small cluster of Belldorn citizens stood and watched as the Titan Mech made its way down the street. Two boys cheered and clapped while their parents waved to Smith.

Jacob didn't recognize any of the faces below them until they made it to their worksite again. As Smith opened the gun pod canopy, a voice reached them.

"Come on."

Jacob undid his harness and peered over the side to find Mary. She offered him a brief smile as Alice started down the side of the Mech with Smith.

"Good news," Smith said. "We have a fix for the leaks. Even if a ballast cracks, I think that skirting can endure a full compartment."

"Good. Now come with me." Mary gestured for them to follow. "Theodosia is back for the day, and she wants to see us."

"Perfect!" Smith said. "I need to pass these plans along to the tinkers. She can send them to Frederick to have a proper barrier made, but for now, we have a Titan Mech that can survive the shallows."

Jacob thought shallows was an odd word for where the last Titan Mech was stranded. It was a good twelve feet deep, and Jacob didn't consider anything shallow if he couldn't reach the bottom with his feet.

Mary glanced back and eyed the pair of tinkers. "You might want to think about cleaning up those aprons."

"We can borrow some at the workshop. Lead on," Smith said.

CHAPTER TWO

W HILE JACOB THOUGHT he probably needed a bath more than just toweling off, that's all they took the time for. With a new apron around his neck, he smelled leather more than stench, and that would have to do for now.

Smith passed along a rough schematic for the design they'd used to alter the Titan Mech while Theodosia listened to his explanations. She rolled the papers up and handed them off to a tinker Jacob didn't know.

"Get these into production immediately," Theo said. "I want preparations made to station additional Titan Mechs along the western borders of Belldorn by day's end tomorrow. Replace one arm with long-range cannons." She focused on Jacob. "If the weight is distributed evenly, losing an arm shouldn't bother your creation, should it?"

"No, I don't think so. We used a single arm on one of the smaller crawlers to build a crane, so I think this should be similar. Sort of."

"Good," Theo said before turning to the other tinker. "Contact Frederick. See if he has anything to add."

The other tinker bowed and departed, letting sunlight into the workshop from the front door before it closed with a quiet thump. Theo turned her attention to the others.

"I've heard the stories of your visit to the Great Machine abandoned near the Skeleton. I've given some thought to it and discussed it with Targrove. There is more you need to know of what has come before. More you have yet to discover, but that I am certain is only a matter of time."

Jacob glanced at Smith to see if recognition showed on his face, but even the Biomech's brow was furrowed.

Theodosia rapped her knuckles on the arm of her chair. "Jacob, did Charles take the time to teach you how to read? Is that where you found your love of books?"

"What?" Jacob asked. "No, I already knew how to read."

"Oh, that's good. I'd heard the schools in Ancora had grown soft in the past decades."

Jacob crossed his arms and said, "Not that soft."

Theodosia smiled. "There were once other books in the ruins, you know? If we had known then what we know now, I would have saved them, but I am afraid they've long since rotted away." She paused and looked around the room. "I want to tell you something. Something I believe would be best if you kept to yourselves. I believe we know what the Great Machines are, those that Furi has spoken of. Legend tells the west was once a poisoned wasteland."

"Like the Deadlands?" Jacob asked.

"In a way, I suppose. But do not interrupt. I lose my thoughts too easily these days."

"No, you do not," Smith said with a slight raise of one eyebrow. "You only convince those around you of it. An odd ploy."

Jacob almost missed the small smile that flickered across the woman's face.

"In the age of the great wars, the same that left twisted ruins like the Skeleton, the earth itself was poisoned. Much of that history was lost but for a few books and writings that haven't turned to dust."

Jacob remembered the books Charles saw in the Skeleton. And remembered the pages he'd burned. Part of him wondered if Theodosia and Targrove hadn't saved more books for the same reasons.

"In the years that followed, not all the old knowledge was lost. Furi and Alice found references to it in the Crown Library, in fact. And some of the early tinkers are said to have built Great Machines to purge the poison from the earth. Targrove believed those Great Machines gave birth to the world we know now. It changed the air we breathe, the water we drink, the very creatures that live around us." Theo looked to Alice. "And what you found in the ruins only made him more certain. Over the centuries, the world rebuilt itself, and many forgot about the monsters in the west that never sleep. But you see, some never forgot and worship them to this day as gods."

"The Children of the Dark Fire," Alice said. "The church Furi told us about."

Theo grimaced and nodded.

"You say too much."

Jacob's heart almost stopped in his chest when the newcomer spoke.

He spun around at the words, further shocked to find Lady Katherine standing in the workshop.

"And you say too little, My Lady." Theodosia wheeled her chair toward Kat. "They must know what we know, or risk death in the unknown wastes."

"We aren't deploying into the wastes," Lady Katherine said.

"What wastes?" Mary asked. "What in all the hells are you talking about?"

"The wastes beyond Ballern," Theodosia said. "Or what once was. A great forest has blossomed on the lands once drowned in the madness of men. A place that saw the creation of the Great Machines and remains the root of the Children of the Dark Fire to this very day."

"Ballern is at our gates," Lady Katherine snapped.

But before she could continue, Theodosia's voice rose, cracking with an authority that almost had Jacob stepping away from her. "And who rules, Ballern? You face a war on three fronts with some allies who cannot be trusted to serve anyone but themselves. You risk plunging Belldorn into an age of darkness by ignoring the poison that brought down an empire. And I will not stand idly by."

"Stories." Lady Katherine threw her arms up in disgust. "You have stories and theories and little proof. And if you are right? If it was the old wars that reshaped the world? What then? This isn't the same world anymore, Theodosia. This is our world, and we have to do the best we can in it."

"For it," Theodosia said.

"What?"

"We have to do the best we can for it. If Targrove is right—"

"*If.*"

"—then the days of our world are numbered. The Great Machines will never stop until the air of all the world becomes like that of the Burning Forest, and life as we know it dies in fire."

"Proof, Theodosia. I have to have proof."

"You already have it in the existence of the Burning Forest. But in that regard, it matters little. This war will take you to Ballern. And when the war reaches Ballern, you will face the Children of the Dark Fire in all their power. Believe or do not believe, you will not end this conflict without destroying the Great Machines."

Lady Katherine grimaced and looked away. "The Porcupines from Fel will arrive in three days' time. There will be no pause once they cross the bay. Our remaining Porcupines will join them as they reach the city, and we will bring Ballern to their knees. Do what you must to be ready. And tell no one. There are few who know, and those that do have been told small variations on our plan. Should we identify a traitor, they will regret crossing Belldorn."

"We will be ready," Theodosia said. "I only ask that you be ready to strike when the time comes to cross the sea."

Lady Katherine eyed Theo before turning to Smith. "What of the Titan Mechs?"

"We resolved the major issues. Theo has forwarded the plans to Frederick and we should have more in place in a day's time."

"Good. Should our front lines need reinforcement, keep them at the ready. In the meantime, I need you and Jacob working with the local tinkers."

Mary rose from her seat. "What do you think you're doing, Kat?"

Kat stood her ground despite the anger on Mary's face, but she didn't reply.

"*She* says too much? Talking about traitors? Refusing to acknowledge that a cult who overthrew a monarchy *might* be a problem?" Mary stepped closer to the Lady of Belldorn and leaned toward her. "What aren't you telling us?"

Kat let out a harsh breath and turned away. "I'm stressed, Mary. You understand that? Ballern has a foothold on our shores for the first time since the Deadlands War. And even then, they never had this many airships successfully make the journey across the sea."

"And what's this talk about traitors?"

Kat's gaze flashed back to Mary. "How did Fel build those tunnels without *anyone* knowing? The area is fished regularly. Someone knew. Someone didn't report back. We have traitors inside Belldorn."

"Or spies!" Mary said. "You have your own spies in other cities. You have spies in Ballern and Ancora and even Bollwerk!"

"Ancora?" Jacob asked before Alice shushed him.

"Look at me, Kat." Mary didn't speak again until the lady met her gaze. "You can't crack like this. You have to keep it together for your people. Things are bad. Fine, we all understand that. But you're a symbol of the strength of our city, so pull yourself together and inspire your people."

Kat took a deep breath, started to say something, and then reached out to hug Mary. She turned away to hide the tears, keeping her back to the table for a time. When she spun to face them, there was only steel on her face. "My apologies. But if you hear anything, please report it."

"We will do our best, My Lady," Theodosia said. "Be well."

Kat nodded before leaving through the front door.

Mary and Smith exchanged a glance before the whole group went back to planning the deployment of Belldorn's defenses. The fleet and crawlers were fairly self-sufficient, but there were other aspects to consider, and Theodosia had more experience defending the streets of Belldorn than anyone else in that city.

"Come on, Smith," Mary said. "It's time for another patrol."

CHAPTER THREE

S AMUEL DRUMMED A quick beat on the back of his Dragonwing, and the beast shot forward, weaving between the towers of Belldorn with terrifying speed. Only when he reached the sea did he slow, hovering to watch a supply ship drag one of the Titan Mechs out of the water.

More worrisome were the shadows in the distance. Ballern's flight paths had come closer to the city, and unless Samuel missed his guess, they'd eventually turn directly into the city itself instead of visiting the temporary docks to the south.

"Probably not a good sign," he muttered.

He turned his mount back to the east and flew at a more reserved pace. It wasn't long until the bustling streets of Belldorn vanished into a grassy plain, and the stables came into view. He signaled the Dragonwing again, and the beast circled the ring of perches before dropping onto an empty one.

"Metal perches seem to be working a bit better," Samuel said when he saw Rin two stalls down.

Rin glanced up from the Spider Knight to the long perch that was currently home to over a dozen Dragonwings. "Yes, I think the sounds of the city and the battle were bothering them. I didn't expect them to chew through the wood so quickly."

Samuel slid off the back of the Dragonwing, taking a short ladder down to the platform where Rin stood. "Tatsu definitely had a good idea."

"He is occasionally good for something," Rin said with a smile.

Samuel had found Tatsu far more than occasionally good for something. He'd engineered the new frame for the stables in a matter of hours, and had the first perch erected that same evening. Of course, it was the next day that the Dragonwings had chewed through it, but nonetheless, it was impressively fast construction.

"Was he a tinker in Ballern?"

Tatsu's head popped up from the stable behind Rin. "A tinker? Rust it all, Spider Knight. Why would I ever be a tinker?"

Samuel gestured to the perches. "It's a great design. Keeps the Dragonwings divided from the Walkers below. Although, I admit that doesn't seem to be a large issue." And even as Samuel spoke, a Walker in the pasture beyond calmly let a pair of Dragonwings ride on its back.

Tatsu blew out a laugh. "I was surprised to see that too. We don't have many Walkers near Canopy, so in a way, I guess this is new to the Dragonwings."

"It's new to all of us," Rin said. "Did you see anything on your flight?"

"Not much. I think Ballern's fleet is a bit closer, but nothing that has me too concerned yet. Belldorn has deployed more Titan Mechs and fished one out of the sea."

Rin nodded. "Are you ready for our patrol? Satisfied with the new mount?"

Samuel looked up at the Dragonwing. "I can say yes to both of those questions."

"Good, the Skysworn should be in the air in the next ten minutes. We'll meet Mary on the north side of the city and start the patrol. Tatsu, are you good here?"

"Fine. I have more work to do on the back of the stables."

"You're welcome to join us if you'd like."

Tatsu shook his head. "We need the Dragonwings rested and fed. Not to mention I need myself rested and fed."

Rin cast Tatsu a grin and started pulling his gloves on. He turned to Samuel and said, "See you in the skies, Spider Knight."

Samuel stretched before making his way up to the Dragonwing. Once he was mounted, he clicked the transmitter Smith had installed in his collar. "Mary, you there?"

Static came back before Mary's voice answered. "Don't use my name on this channel, Knight."

"We're just leaving the stables. Should be to the docks in about five minutes."

"Perfect. Disengaging now. See you out there."

Samuel pulled down his goggles and took a deep breath before giving the largest plate on the Dragonwing's back two quick taps with the guide sticks. The creature's wings buzzed to life, and they rose into the air. Once they were at speed, Samuel wouldn't be able to hear the transmitter. He could barely make it out when they were hovering, so he wouldn't hear from Mary again until they reached the Skysworn.

He returned Tatsu's wave as they left the stables. The Dragonwing soared to the north, leaving the perch behind in a flash. Samuel watched the mountains to his right, smiling at the snowcapped peaks as he skirted the edge of the city.

He'd expected Drakkar to join him for the patrol that morning, but Furi had persuaded the Cave Guardian to join her at the Crown Library. She'd found some old literature about Cave, and probably had more questions for Drakkar than Drakkar wanted to answer.

But the Cave Guardian needed time away from the chaos too, Samuel had no doubt. The Spider Knight could have gone for more rest himself, and a quiet library didn't sound bad, even if he would just use it for a nap. Drakkar spending some hours with someone who was turning out to be a valuable ally was far more productive than any nap.

The heart of Belldorn was far busier than the outskirts. Armored crawlers and soldiers marching in formation were the only residents of Belldorn outside the city proper. Samuel could understand why. The farther north he got, the more damage he could make out on the blocks closest to the bay.

They might have stopped Mordair's progression at the tunnel, but they had not spared all the city. The line between those streets that had seen battle, and those that hadn't, was a stark thing from above. One of the smaller towers of Belldorn had fallen to the earth, its structure burned out and blown apart. Around it lay the charred remains of several homes.

Samuel watched a handful of people sifting through the rubble. It might be weeks or more before they knew if they had found everyone who had died in the attack. By then, Samuel was sure there would be more bodies on the ground.

For a moment, the sight reminded him of what had come to Ancora in the Fall. But while there had been fire and battles here, the Lowlands had been a vision of absolute destruction. Few buildings had survived, and a terrible number of people had not escaped.

Samuel closed his eyes for a moment to clear the thought before guiding the Dragonwing toward a bronze shadow near the horizon. The Skysworn was halfway between the bay and the city when Samuel caught up to them. The Dragonwing didn't hesitate as he signaled it to land, almost pouncing onto the railings of the Skysworn. The Spider Knight unfastened his leggings and hopped down to the deck. He hadn't made it to the cabin before Rin joined him, detaching from his mount in a fraction of the time it had taken Samuel.

"So, this is the Skysworn," Rin said, looking around the deck as he followed Samuel.

"Do you know Mary?"

"Only by reputation."

Samuel grinned. "That's probably for the best. Whatever you've heard, assume it's worse."

Rin's brow wrinkled.

Inside the cabin, Smith leaned over the console, muttering to himself as he ratcheted a lever into place. "There. It should not stick again."

Mary turned toward the door. "Samuel. Rin. Welcome aboard."

"Captain." Rin nodded to Mary.

Mary narrowed her eyes. "I know you. I had no idea you were from Ballern."

Rin raised an eyebrow. "Truly?"

"Well, I assumed some part of your family had come from the area, but not that you had lived there. I've seen you around the docks, never far from the gaming parlors."

Rin let out a small laugh. "It is one of the few places that reminds me of Ballern. Though I wouldn't trust the tables at Ebenezer's."

Mary nodded. "Then you have some sense about you. That man's an old pirate, and some habits are hard to kill."

"Are you supposed to tell me he's a pirate?" Rin paused. "Isn't that, I don't know, a secret?"

"Not many secrets left on the docks. Unless you know where to look, and what to avoid."

Smith slid a wrench back into his apron before ruffling his hair. Samuel was glad to see much of the color had returned to the tinker's face after his brush with death.

"You look better."

"I feel better. I can go for a couple hours without falling asleep now."

"And that's a good thing," Mary said. "Our patrol has been assigned to the beach from the docks to the mountains and back. Get this over with so you can get back to Jacob, and I can make sure Eva isn't doing anything stupid."

Rin took a step forward. "Is Eva a pirate too?"

Smith held his hands up in a warning gesture. "You are treading in personal territory there. Best to keep that in check until the second date."

Mary snorted and spun her chair around to face the windscreen. "It was a good decision to defend the pass. They turned away a company of crawlers, and I wouldn't be surprised if they returned with air support."

"We can fly ahead if you'd like," Samuel said.

Mary shook her head. "Eva's ship patrolled before us. Two of their scouts saw something in the mountains but couldn't confirm what it was. I'd rather have you on the chaingun."

"A chaingun?" Rin asked. "Like those monstrosities Bollwerk fitted to their warships?"

"The same." Smith crossed his arms. "Would you like to see?"

Rin gave a series of rapid nods as if that was the silliest question Smith could have asked.

"I'll be on the horn if you see anything." Mary glanced back and met Samuel's gaze. "You see or hear anything out of the normal, you tell me."

Samuel wondered why Mary had mentioned hearing anything out of the ordinary if they were inside the ship. But in a moment of clarity, he realized she was asking him to keep an eye on Rin. So perhaps she knew more about Rin than Samuel did, or her years as a pirate made her more cautious.

Samuel followed Rin and Smith out of the cabin and over to the hatch waiting behind it. A short ladder took them below deck and into the golden glow of the small lights Smith had installed close to his workbench. It wasn't far to another hatch that led down into the gun pod. Smith held it open and gestured to Rin.

"Are you sure?" the Dragonrider asked.

It was Samuel who answered. "Smith is a tinker. If he has a chance to show off one of his creations to someone new, trust me, he's sure."

Rin cast Samuel a smile as he climbed down the narrow hatch into the seat that hung inside the gun pod. Samuel didn't miss the hesitation as Rin realized there wasn't much more than glass between him and a long fall to the ground.

Smith proved Samuel's words true. He went through the controls on the gun pod in excruciating detail, as if he was explaining them to Jacob, and Jacob would then need to rebuild them rivet by rivet.

He made it sound far more complicated than it was. Samuel had sat at those controls more than once, and their intuitiveness was a testament to Smith's skills. But watching Smith smile even wider than Rin as the Dragonrider spun around in a tight circle before raising and lowering the chaingun was a light moment in a dark week.

"And that is why you must always close the hatch." Smith tapped on a length of the glass that had blocked part of the hatch. "If you get an arm or a leg stuck in that gap, it will not be stuck very long." He thumped on the biomechanics of his chest. "Then you will be a Biomech like me and Jacob."

Rin looked to Smith. "Jacob's a Biomech? I had no idea." He didn't say it with disgust or any kind of judgment.

Samuel nodded. "Tree Killer near the Skeleton. Took his leg clean off."

Rin blinked.

"Lucky they only got his leg," Smith said. "A whole swarm of them came down from an ironwood tree. Never seen the like, I tell you."

Rin shuddered. "I hate those things. I don't kill things I don't have to, but those are a plague in the forest. They don't blend in well near Canopy, so they're easy enough to avoid, but we still lose people to them every year."

"Sorry to hear that." Samuel rubbed his hands together to fight off a sudden chill.

He lost his focus as Smith delved into some of the finer mechanical details of the chaingun. The story about the relic hidden in Gareth Cave kept his attention for a time, but his mind wandered to Ancora, wondering how the reconstruction was going and how Bessie was faring without him.

He knew the Spider Knights would take care of her, but it was rare for him to spend so long away. It wasn't until Rin asked if he could fire the chaingun that Samuel snapped back into the conversation.

"It was recently disassembled and cleaned, so it likely needs to be fired, anyway. Wait until we are over the mountains."

Samuel recognized the smile on Rin's face, like a child given permission to do something normally forbidden.

"Please aim for the clearings," Mary said. "If Lady Katherine has scouts on the mountain, I'd rather not explain why we attacked them."

Smith actually laughed.

Samuel eyed the tinker. "How is that funny?"

"It reminded me of an old smugglers' run. When Mary and I made it a very long time ago."

"Smith …" Came Mary's warning voice over the horn.

"I'd heard you were smugglers," Rin said.

Smith stood up a little straighter. "So we are known in Canopy. It is an honor. Especially to be recognized by a thief, for one."

Rin narrowed his eyes. "And where did you hear that?"

A small smile flitted across Smith's face, and then it was gone. Smith continued as if he hadn't heard Rin's question. "We lost a good contact in Pirate's Cove. Mary greeted him with a bolt from a wrist launcher instead of the package we were supposed to deliver."

Mary groaned. "I've told you a million times that was an accident."

"I serviced that bolt thrower not thirty minutes before you shot him."

Samuel could just make out Mary's sigh. No one spoke for a moment until Mary came back over the horn. "As to your question, Rin, we learn a lot of interesting things working with smugglers."

Rin nodded to himself as if that had answered his question. Samuel wasn't sure if that was the case, or if Rin simply realized prying into what Mary and Smith knew might not be his best course of action.

"We're over the foothills if you want to test out that chaingun," Mary said.

"Guard off the trigger," Smith said.

Rin flipped small metal cages off the triggers.

"Whatever you want dead, put it in the center of that circle."

Rin didn't say any more, only spun the gun pod slightly to the south and lowered the angle of the barrels. He pulled the trigger, and bursts of fire exploded just outside the pod. Moments later, the earth churned in a clearing not far below them. A lone tree lost a branch to the burst before Rin released the triggers.

The smile on the Dragonrider's face when he looked up made Samuel laugh.

"That good?"

"Sir, I would like one of these mounted on a Dragonwing." Rin slapped the side of the chaingun mount.

Smith grinned. "Too heavy for that, I am afraid. But it is an interesting request. Maybe when this war is over, I can build something to suit your mount."

"I'm sure we can come to an agreement," Mary said. "A trade of services, perhaps?"

Rin's smile broadened. "And to think a couple like-minded pirates had been living so close in Belldorn."

Mary's next words cut off the lighthearted exchange. "Two foothills over and then west to the mountain pass. What is that?"

Samuel and Smith both stuck their heads down into the gun pod to get a view of what Mary had seen.

"Rust it all," Rin said. "What …"

Samuel blinked as he tried to understand what he was looking at. Smith cursed and ran down the corridor. Samuel followed, climbing up onto the deck to get a better view. But once he was at the railing, he was sure his eyes weren't playing tricks on him.

A large section of the mountain's face had moved. And not as an avalanche might, but a slow, deliberate shift like a door the size of a building. Rin joined him a moment later before they both made their way into the cabin.

"Is it ours?" Mary asked.

Smith shook his head. "I have no idea."

"It can't be Fel," Mary said. "Not this close."

"What if it is?"

Mary cursed and reached out to the transmitter. She turned the dial to a frequency Samuel had never seen before and pressed the button. "Kat, come in."

"Skysworn?" a familiar voice answered.

"We are over the mountains. We just saw something that looks like a huge hangar open in the mountainside. Do you know anything about that? Or has Fel reached us with another tunnel?"

"Stand down, Mary. That installation is one of ours."

The tension in Samuel's shoulders relaxed a hair. "What is it?"

"Who is with you?" Lady Katherine asked.

Mary glanced back at the rest of the cabin. She hesitated before she answered. "Smith, Rin, and Samuel."

"The Dragonriders?"

"Yes."

"Very well. I suppose it was only a matter of time before Rin was aware of it. The base is ours, and the installation is home to a great many Emerald Needles. It will be a stronghold should the worst happen. Within the mountain is the source of our Emerald Needles, those that will follow the bait to the targets we set."

Rin rubbed his forehead. "You raised them for us, didn't you?"

Lady Katherine didn't answer. But she didn't really need to. Samuel knew the Emerald Needles were one of the Dragonwings' natural predators. If they were sent into Canopy, they could wreak destruction much like that which had fallen upon Ancora. His stomach soured at the thought.

"How long have you been raising them?" Rin asked.

This time Lady Katherine did respond. "Nearly three years now."

Rin hesitated. "Then the last skirmish we had, you could have unleashed them. That was two years ago."

"I could have, yes. But I do not want open war with Canopy. We have found an understanding, and I would very much like to keep it that way. Tell your council if you must, but please share those words with them as well. I want no part of war with your city."

Rin rubbed at his chin. "Strange times."

"Sometimes strange times require extraordinary alliances."

Mary turned the Skysworn away from the mountains and started back along the beach. It was there at the edge of the city that Samuel caught sight of another Titan Mech. A lumbering monstrosity that straightened a damaged home so a group of tinkers on the ground could reinforce it.

It reminded him again of Ancora's reconstruction, and not for the first time that day, Samuel wished he was home.

CHAPTER FOUR

FURI WAS STILL absorbing Drakkar's stories about the early days of Cave while she flipped through another Mokuskrit book she'd found deep in the archives of the Crown Library. Drakkar was a warrior, of that she had no doubt, but he wasn't like the fighters she'd known in Ballern.

When she was young, she'd enjoyed the arena and the war games, as the monarchy called them. It wasn't until she'd grown old enough that Kura told her the truth. The warriors in those games were one of two types: a person of violence so pure they'd kill their own family for sport, or an enemy to the monarchy.

It had been quite a jarring revelation when she'd been captured by Belldorn. They hadn't sentenced her to death, or isolated imprisonment, or some archaic war game. And while some from Ballern might consider all from the eastern lands to be an enemy, she'd learned different from Kura.

But Drakkar's stories spoke to her. The idea that his people had been driven from Fire Island by the same forces Ballern feared, and yet Cave had become a sanctuary. A kind of neutral place that often remained hidden from the rest of the continent. Fortified, dangerous, and filled with a kind of wild freedom.

Furi wanted to visit Cave one day and see the underground world Drakkar had described to her. She'd lived so much of her life on the docks, a Skyborn in the clouds, that the idea of a city underground was a thrilling concept.

She looked up from her translations to find the Cave Guardian lean-ing over her shoulder. "Almost done. It's an interesting section, to be sure."

"And you think this contains more of the legends that surround the Great Machines?" Drakkar asked.

Furi nodded. She didn't think that. She *knew* it. "This symbol here, that's hooked and ends in a flourish arching back over the top? That's the Mokuskrit symbol for gods."

"But that could relate to almost any religion in the west, could it not?"

Furi tilted her head from side to side. "Not really. Well, yes, but this is from before the Children of the Dark Fire overtook Ballern. Before the Great Machines were called Great Machines, I think this was their name." She pointed to the translated section.

"Gods of Iron and Steam?"

"It's not a literal translation, but I think that's as close as I can get. It's more like Gods *made* from Iron and Steam, but this fits better."

"We've seen the Great Machines, Furi. They were not forged of iron. Iron would have long crumbled. That was steel, and steel of a kind I have never seen produced by a modern smith."

"I know, but I don't think the people who wrote this had a word for steel. This book is from one of the villages that used to exist far to the west of Ballern."

"Used to exist?" Drakkar raised an eyebrow as he walked around to the other side of the table.

"Yes, they attacked Ballern. I mean, they attacked a new colony Bal-lern had sent to the edge of the forest in the northwest."

Drakkar let out a sad sigh, as if he already knew how this story would end.

"It's farmland now. They killed everyone and churned their bones into the soil."

Drakkar let his head bow forward and closed his eyes. When he opened them again, he smiled at Furi. "The hands of those in the east are no cleaner than those of Ballern, Furi. We have all done terrible things. There are sometimes not enough who remember what befell the losing side in the old wars. We claim victories and sanctuaries, only for wars to fall upon the same fields and streets in later decades. But it is a rare thing what Fel and Ballern have done. An alliance that has crossed the sea and brought ruin upon so many."

"I know," Furi said, a small tremor in her voice as she looked away. "Drakkar, I just, it's hard. It's so hard. I have friends in Ballern. Skyborn I would trust with my life. But they might never understand. I think Kura would fight, at least help us recruit those who would fight."

"Allies behind walls are never a bad thing, Furi. No matter their number, knowing more than your enemy can be a key to ending a conflict." He gestured around them at the sealed glass vaults and carefully preserved books. "It is why we are here, and it is why Jacob and Alice gave me such hope for Ancora."

Furi leaned forward. "Hope for Ancora? What do you mean?"

Drakkar pulled out a chair and sat down. He smiled, but it never reached his eyes. "Jacob was apprenticed to Charles von Atlier. For decades, we in Cave knew Charles only as a threat. A monster of war who was responsible for countless deaths."

Furi frowned at those words. "Alice and Jacob were friends with a war criminal?"

Drakkar laughed quietly. "In a way. But that man changed over the years. Became something else, something more, until war finally came to claim him. I see some of him in Jacob, and I worry he could walk the same path."

Furi glanced down at her translation, scribbled a few more characters, and then looked back to Drakkar. "You mean the Titan Mechs."

"Yes. Archibald and his tinkers may have been able to revive them without Jacob, but he has a keen understanding of Charles's work. It is a legacy I am not sure the tinker would have wanted."

"Jacob's trying to defend his home. His friends. And I don't think you can say different, can you? Why else would you be here fighting?"

"There is no other reason anymore. You are right. I fight for my city, and my friends. But there is a darkness in all who are touched by war and conflict, Furi. A small part of us never truly recovers. It could lead some into your arenas. And others into darker places. So we fight for peace, a paradox in itself. We cannot have peace without strength, and few who have strength are willing to control it."

Drakkar's gaze grew distant, as if he'd stepped into another memory from a different time. Furi wanted to hug the Cave Guardian. His words rang true, and she hated the fact they had. She didn't have to ask to know he'd lost people, just like she had. Maybe, in the end, they could stop the wars. Even if it was only for a while. A decade of peace was worth much.

ANOTHER HOUR PASSED while Furi finished translating the Mokuskrit. Drakkar was deep into the history of the second empire of Ballern, a time when the city had been rebuilt from the ruins of a forgotten one. Furi wondered if it had been as bare as the Skeleton or the Great Machine in the Deadlands.

Footsteps sounded in the hall, and they both turned their attention to the door.

A girl with a halo of red hair came through, followed by a young tinker carrying a large pack.

CHAPTER FIVE

"Jacob, Alice," Drakkar said. "What brings you here?"

"We have a gift for Furi." Alice nudged Jacob forward.

He held the pack out, and Furi took it with some confusion.

"For me?" Furi asked, turning the pack over between her hands.

"In case we ever shoot you out of the sky again," Jacob said with a sideways smile.

Alice elbowed him in the ribs, and he grunted.

Furi's brows drew down, and Alice started to explain before the Skyborn jumped out of her seat.

"You mean this is a glider?" Furi bounced on her heels.

Jacob rubbed at his side and smiled. "It is. See? I told you'd she'd get that joke."

Alice blew out an irritated breath.

Furi slid her arms into the straps and tightened them against her back. "I've wanted to use one of these ever since you talked about it. And Alice's story about jumping off the wall in Fel? You know what would be amazing? To jump off the docks and sail down to the city."

"The docks in Ballern?" Alice hesitated. "As in the docks that are above some of the *clouds*?"

Furi nodded enthusiastically and slid back out of the glider pack. "Thank you." She sat down and opened the rear flap to look at the mechanism inside. "This looks different than the one you showed me before."

"I made a few small updates to it. It should be easier to control than the older ones. Smith had the idea to use larger gyros, and they worked really well. It's still Charles's concept, and mostly his design, but with a few more changes."

"Charles," Furi said, trailing off. She closed the pack and frowned when she saw what was on the outside of it. She ran her fingers over the embroidered patch. "What is this?"

"It's a Shadowwing," Alice said, stepping closer to her. "I read some more of your notes from the last book you translated. It sounds like Shadowwings are in the Great Machines across the sea too."

"They are, and there are quite a few that live in the woods."

"Do you like it?" Alice asked.

Furi nodded.

"Oh good. It's something for the Skyborn to wear. A symbol to stand by. We have the Steamsworn Fist, and it resonates with the Steamborn. But the Skyborn and Steamborn together. We're something else, something new. I don't know. It just felt right. I know it's a little abstract, but I think you can make it out."

Furi smiled and lifted the patch to get a closer look at the cluster of triangles and polygons that formed the outline of a Shadowwing, its wings spread wide. "It reminds me of Fel's flag. With the Tail Sword?"

"Oh." Alice wrung her hands together. "We can change it. We can definitely change it."

"No, no, that's not what I meant. It's just, you have these hard lines and edges, but they form a gentle creature. A Shadowwing lives a peaceful life. But if you look harder, it could almost be an Acidwing."

"Acidwing?" Drakkar said. "I thought those died out long ago."

"Not across the sea," Furi said, perking up immediately. "They're beautiful creatures, brilliant greens and reds with thick black bodies. They only nest in the southernmost woods, but they're still around."

Alice looked down at the patch in Furi's hand. "An Acidwing. They were once the harbingers of the great storms. Huge hurricanes that could swallow entire continents for a week at a time."

"We have that story too," Furi said.

Jacob glanced at Alice. "Miss Penny used to talk about that in school." He turned to Furi. "You learned the same thing in Ballern?"

"Not in school," Furi said. "The fisherfolk on the docks have always told old stories." The small smile on her face widened. "Actually, Jakon has quite a few stories too. You should see him at his stand someday. He's like a street show and a chef all in one. Anyway, most of the stories from the docks are nonsense, you know. But a few are more than that."

"My dad used to tell me stories like that," Jacob said. "Stuff my great grandfather had passed down. He lived through the Deadlands War, might have even met Charles at some point, or maybe even Targrove. But most of that was lost when the old house burned down. It's a part of our family story we just don't know anymore."

Furi nodded. "A lot of the Skyborn are like that too. Sometimes a ship will burn up, and no one can get it off the dock. The damage can be severe, even raining fire onto the city below. But we lose our homes, our family homes, and sometimes the people we love. It's … I just mean I understand."

Drakkar leaned forward. "We all understand."

Furi spread her hands across her latest translation. "But that's why things like this are so important. This was someone's story. And it lasted longer than they did. Maybe it will last longer than us. Kura taught us the importance of remembering these things. I only hope the stories we leave behind have a happier ending."

Alice rubbed at her eyes and took a deep breath. "You two hungry? I could really go for a snack."

Furi started packing up her notebooks and stuffing them into the small pack she'd brought herself. She hesitated when she looked at the glider pack leaning against the chair.

"It has clasps on it for whatever pack you want to take with you." Jacob crouched down and flipped the canvas cover off the bottom half of the glider. "Just clip it in here, and you're set."

"Perfect," Furi said, slipping the straps from her backpack into place before hefting the glider pack over her shoulders. "Drakkar, are you coming?"

"I ate before I met you here. I should get back to help at the stables."

Furi huffed. "I ate too, but that doesn't mean I'm not going to drag all three of you to the candy store down the street."

Drakkar looked up from the vault where he'd replaced one of the documents he'd been studying. "A candy shop? I do not indulge very often."

Furi grabbed the Cave Guardian by the bracer on his forearm and dragged him toward the stairs. "Consider this not very often."

Jacob laughed and followed them through the Crown Library and out onto the streets of Belldorn. The oddness of the city hit him in that moment and reminded him of Ancora in the brief time after the Fall and before the Butcher came for him.

There was dread in the air, but the lull in the battle stretched on. Some walked down the streets, clearly armed and ready for anything that might strike at them from the shadows, but others went about their lives. As if a sense of normalcy was the best defense against the power that threatened their city.

And maybe there was something to be said for that. A small bit of normalcy in the chaos around them. He took Alice's hand as they walked past a handful of closed shops before coming to a garishly colored storefront that looked like something out of the children's stories Miss Penny told the younger students.

A simple sign hung above them, hammered from copper and inlaid with bronze, if Jacob had to guess from the discolorations.

Belldorn's Fine Teas and Candies

It wasn't so much a bell that sounded as they pushed through the red and white striped door as the delicate notes of a chime. Jacob glanced up at the small device, a series of keys extending down into the path of the door, each sounding a delicate note as it sprang back into position.

There weren't many patrons inside, but Jacob only noticed that in passing. Against the far wall, from floor to a ceiling some twenty feet above them, sat gallon jar after gallon jar of teas and candies. There was almost nothing in the shop in front of the counter, only that sweeping wall of glass containers.

An elderly woman finished handing an order to a customer before she gestured for Furi and the others to come forward.

"A Cave Guardian?" She let out a small laugh. "This city never ceases to amaze me."

Drakkar pulled his hood down and smiled at the clerk. "At your service."

"Not today, my friend." She leaned against the counter and flashed him a brilliant smile. "It is I who am at *your* service, dear. What can I get for you? Tea?"

"No," Furi said. "We're here to celebrate. I need chocolate."

"Well, take your pick." She gestured to the wall. "Every kind of bean and every kind of candy you can dream of is on that wall."

Alice leaned closer to Jacob. "Do you think they have Cocoa Crunch?"

It was the shopkeeper who answered. "Cocoa Crunch you, say? Hmm, can't say I've heard of that …" Her eyes narrowed. "Wait, that's what Ancorans call Crunch Nuggets. Are you an Ancoran, dear? I would have sworn you were a pilgrim." She shrugged and turned to the wall.

Only then did Jacob notice there wasn't a ladder against the towering wall. Only a vertical beam that stretched from floor to ceiling, and some kind of platform by the shopkeeper. She pushed two small knobs across a gridwork of positions and then pulled a long lever.

A puff of steam rose from the platform's anchor before it sped up some ten feet, rolled to the right, and gently plucked a glass jar from above with delicate care. Claws held the jar on the platform as it returned to its original position.

"That's amazing!" Jacob said. "How does it know where to stop? Does it ever drop the jar? How do you keep it maintained? I mean, I think it looks pretty old and—"

The shopkeeper held her hands up. "Mercy, boy. I don't need to ask if you're a tinker, do I?"

Alice burst into laughter, and Jacob could feel a small flush on his cheeks.

The shopkeeper kept speaking while she scooped out a cluster of uneven chocolate that didn't look much like Cocoa Crunch. "Now, if you're a tinker, you'll probably know of the old tinker Targrove, yes?"

Jacob nodded, and the shopkeeper smiled.

"Well, Targrove built this old girl." She patted the platform. "It's never broken down. Not in fifty years. Needs a little grease from time to time, and some oil on the pistons, but it runs like a dream."

She passed a small paper tray across the counter. "Now, you lot try this and tell me if it's not better than anything you've had in Ancora."

Alice raised a skeptical eyebrow.

"Try it first, child."

Drakkar laughed, reaching over Jacob's shoulder to pick up a nugget of chocolate. The others took a piece of their own.

Furi glanced back at them. "To better days ahead."

"Better days," they echoed.

Jacob popped the candy into his mouth and bit down. It still had that same chocolate richness he was used to from Cocoa Crunch, but the cluster inside almost exploded in his mouth. Tiny air pockets gave way in a bite that was both crispy and smooth.

Alice turned to look at him, both her eyebrows quite high. "Okay, that's one of the best things I've ever eaten. Better than Festival, though?"

"It's different," Jacob said. "But I like how light it is. Cocoa Crunch in Ancora is more like a fudge."

"Ah," the shopkeeper said. "They must break up the molasses and cool it in the chocolate. I'm familiar with that, but I prefer to dip it, myself." She turned back and looked at the wall. "I don't think I have anything quite like that here, though. I'll have to add it. We just ran out of Needle Tea from the North Woods. I'll use that jar next week.

"What else can I get you?"

After they'd sufficiently indulged in enough snacks to ruin any chance of dinner, Drakkar also purchased a strange cluster of balls that looked like dirt.

"That's … tea?" Jacob asked.

"The *best* tea," Furi said. "You don't have pressed teas in Ancora?"

"I guess not."

Drakkar held out a gold piece when the shopkeeper gave him their total. "Will this be acceptable payment?"

Jacob recognized the coin from Cave. Cast from an alloy of gold and platinum, the simple concentric circles on the obverse could survive the harshest environments.

"Drakkar, you don't have to pay for all of this," Furi said. "Let me help."

The shopkeeper shook her head. "Don't disrespect a Cave Guardian's offer, dear." She took the coin and slid it into her pocket instead of the register. "As the owner of this establishment, I can keep what I like, you know?"

Drakkar smiled. "An old tradition to accept an offer. One I am glad to see is still known in Belldorn."

"Enjoy your tea. Should you have need of more, my shop will always welcome a refined palette." She glanced down at the other three. "And less refined palettes, if they have need of chocolate."

Furi grinned at the shopkeeper and waved as they made their way back outside.

CHAPTER SIX

THE DAY PASSED faster than Jacob expected. It wasn't long until his work back in Theo's shop bled over past dinner time. After their trip to the candy shop, that worked out well. He split a strange dish of crispy kebabs and fruit with Alice when she returned from visiting Samuel at the stables.

It wasn't until he sat down to eat that he realized how tired he was, and how much he needed a break. Thankfully, Alice had the same thought, and they made their way out onto the streets and walked for some time with the thin crowds and fading light.

It was nice, walking in silence with Alice. Jacob didn't feel a need to fill every moment with words or thoughts of everything happening around them. It was a comfortable silence until they reached the beaches of the Crystal Sea.

"A shadow falls across the moon as surely as the darkness of war," Alice whispered.

"What?"

She shook her head. "Just something I read that Furi translated from one of the Mokuskrit books. Archibald didn't write like that, you know? *The Dead Scourge* is almost cold next to those old words."

"I know what you mean, but sometimes I just want the facts as fast as I can read them." He realized what had prompted the quote from Alice as he looked toward the horizon. The distant silhouettes of airships cut across the rising moon.

But it wasn't only facts Jacob needed with speed. Sometimes it was help. And sometimes, it was people he missed. "I wish Charles was here to help."

"So do I. But I think Theo is up to the task. I'm beginning to think she might know even more than Charles did about what happened in Ballern."

Jacob nodded. "Pretty sure you're right. But what about the Children of the Dark Fire? Do you think he knew about them?"

Alice shrugged. "To some degree, I think. Look what he did in Ballern."

"Yeah …"

"It sounds like some kind of mad cult, doesn't it? A whole religion based around some myth of machines?"

Jacob grimaced. "Only problem is, the Great Machines aren't a myth. I mean, I'm sure some of what their cult says about them is a myth, but you've stood inside of one."

"It's like they worship something a tinker created. A divine gadget." Alice said the last with a humorless laugh. "I think Charles would have been amused at that idea."

"I think so too. But look at the history, Alice. We're talking about a scale that changed the entire continent."

"The ruins Mary showed me looked as big as Bollwerk itself. Those machines changed more than a continent, Jacob. They changed our entire world."

Jacob sat down on the beach and crossed his legs. Their enemies might be sailing in the distance, given away by dim lights that could have been stars other than the fact they were moving, but there was calm in the crash of waves and gentle lapping of the sea.

"Why do you think they haven't attacked yet?" Alice asked when a series of flashes told them the airships were communicating.

"I think it's Ballern's last push. I think their queen has decided that either Belldorn will fall or Ballern will."

"Do you think they're really that reckless? They poked at each other for decades."

"How long can they wait, though? It has to come down to this, eventually. Every war has to end."

"If Belldorn wins here, Lady Katherine will move against the city itself." Alice didn't say it as a question. It was a statement of fact. And in that, Jacob thought Alice was very much right.

"And Fel is waiting for them at Ballern." He gestured to the lights on the horizon. "But how many of those are Fel warships? Can Belldorn stand up to them? Dauschen didn't. They never even set foot in Ancora and still destroyed our homes."

"It's going to get bad, isn't it?"

"Always does," a voice boomed from behind them.

Jacob startled and jumped to his feet, spinning around to find a familiar face. "Smith?"

"You two are difficult to find this evening. Theo said you went for a walk. Figured you would either end up here, or at Mary's."

"We could have been at one of the stores," Alice said.

Smith shrugged. "Stores are all closed. The Crown Library is closed. I suppose you could have wandered to the stables, but why go there when the sea is so close? Not a sight so common in Ancora, I think."

Smith was right about that. The outskirts of the Ridge Mountains and the city walls blocked much of the view from Ancora. Citizens could catch a glimpse of the water from the highest towers in the eastern wall, but the wall was rarely open to the people from the Lowlands. Even those who lived in the Highlands were not given access often.

Jacob wondered if that would change after the Fall. And if Archibald succeeded in building an airship dock where the Lowlands once stood, what would the view be like from there? He shook himself out of his thoughts and looked up to Smith.

"Why are you looking for us?"

Smith scratched at the back of his head. "You two know about my history, and Mary's." He glanced over his shoulder as if someone were waiting to hear his words. "Belldorn is an old city, but it was built on the ruins of an older one. Near the outskirts, where Ballern bombed the edge of the city, some of the old tunnels collapsed."

"What's in them?" Alice asked.

"Mostly groundwater. But there are a few nests in the dark."

Jacob raised an eyebrow. "Nests of what?"

"Nothing too bad. The worst we have encountered under the streets were miniature Stag Beetles. They do not grow much longer than a foot in length and have no venom to speak of."

But Smith's words weren't all that reassuring to Jacob. He knew what liked to lurk near underground rivers and bodies of water. If the groundwater was similar to what stood below Ancora, there was likely far more than miniature beetles.

Smith continued. "The bugs are not the problem. The access to the inner city is. If you follow the tunnels long enough, they will take you from the edge of the city nearly to the Crown Library. We need to secure them and be sure no infantry from Ballern can cross our lines."

"From the edge of the city to the Crown Library is over a mile, Smith." Alice turned her back on the sea and looked to the city. "That's not something we can handle on our own."

"I know. But the three of us can go underground to see what our options are."

Alice pursed her lips. "That sounds like a very easy way to get lost."

Smith shook his head. "Mary and I know the southern tunnels. We used them regularly to hide goods smuggled off the docks. There was a brief time I lived there when Mary and I had a … disagreement.”

Jacob blew out a small laugh. “Well, if you lived there, I feel a little bit better about what we might find. I need to get my air cannon from Theodosia’s shop. Alice?”

“I have my bolt glove with me, but I’d rather have the wrist launcher too.”

“So you will join me?”

Alice scowled at Smith. “Of course we will. We haven’t forgotten how important Belldorn is to the defense of our own home. Even if we didn’t have friends that live here, we need Lady Katherine’s strength to endure.”

Smith turned and started toward the city. “If I had your understanding of politicians when I was your age, I might not have gotten myself blown up.”

Alice exchanged a grin with Jacob, and they followed Smith back into the city.

CHAPTER SEVEN

AS REASSURING AS Smith's description of the underground had been, when the tinker walked out of Theodosia's workshop with a chaingun strapped to his back, Jacob's reassurance vanished. Jacob asked him why he was carrying such an unwieldy weapon, and he didn't much enjoy Smith's answer.

"I like to be prepared. In case I am wrong."

The words stuck in Jacob's mind as they made their way south through the city. Most of the citizens had retreated to their homes or shelters as evening closed on them. The majority of people they encountered now were well armed and dressed in the blue and gold uniforms of Belldorn's fleet.

But even in the looming shadows, they were still greeted with short nods and the occasional wave. These weren't people Jacob and Alice knew, and he was certain Smith didn't know everyone they'd passed. It spoke to a kindness in the people of Belldorn. Something ingrained in the city that reminded him of parts of Ancora. Like the Highlands, where Lowlanders were often shunned, there were pockets of warmth. The Wild Horse and the candy shop by the hospital, and the hospital itself, all came to mind.

Jacob expected Belldorn, so much larger than Ancora and even overshadowing Bollwerk, to be far colder than it was. But maybe he should have seen that warmth sooner, a warmth that hid between the towers and arched windows and jagged skyline. Not even Ancora treated its prisoners with the kind of welcome and forgiveness as Belldorn.

And what had it gotten the city on the sea? An alliance with the forest city of Canopy. A power in its own right, and the only fleet of Dragonriders known in the world.

They reached the edge of Belldorn, stepping out from the narrow alley Smith had led them down. Jacob understood why when they exited. Even with the sun still casting the last rays of light in glinting bursts of fire on glass, they stood in darkness.

Far to the south, past the shattered homes and burned-out husks of crawlers, a swarm of lights played near the forest. Ballern was truly at their doorstep. Jacob feared the battle to come would bring a toll that surpassed even the Fall of Ancora.

"This way," Smith said, calling Jacob's attention away from the dread in his gut. "I did not believe the Carrion Worms would return to the sands that surround Belldorn so quickly."

They circled the first collapsed home, and in the distance, the rubbery white flesh of a Carrion Worm compressed and stretched forward, its scythe-like mandibles extending and retracting as it searched for the dead. But it wasn't only the dead that would appease a Carrion Worm.

"What if they're in the tunnels?" Alice asked.

"Then Jacob will make a mess with his air cannon, and we will be done with it."

The confidence in Smith's proclamation bolstered something in Jacob, but it didn't change the fact the Carrion Worm he was watching now was the largest he'd ever seen. Whatever it had been feeding on had sustained its terrible growth.

Charred wood crumbled beneath their footsteps, sending ash up in small puffs as Smith circled a well that had collapsed in on itself. The deeper they walked into that ruin, the more the scent of charred wood and aging rot assailed them. Beyond that, where one of the Ballern airships had crashed into the city, leaving a tangle of melted metal and soldiers, the ground opened in a gaping shadow.

Whatever had once stood over that place was unrecognizable. Jacob couldn't tell if it was a home, a tower, a shack, or something else. But the stairs were plain to see, and Smith strode down them with confidence. Shortly after he disappeared inside, a golden glow came to life.

"You will want your lanterns for this area. Deeper inside, we will have glowworms, but not for some time."

Alice trailed Smith inside, and Jacob did the same, glancing back once at the lights of Ballern's fleet to the south.

The first thing Jacob noticed underground was the bowed ceiling above them. "Smith, how stable is this place?"

Smith followed Jacob's gaze. "It has had that appearance as long as I can remember."

The dust drifting down from the cracks wasn't a salve for Jacob's worries.

"Do not be concerned. Should it collapse, there are a dozen more exits from the underground."

"As long as we aren't under the part that collapses," Alice muttered as she followed Smith.

Jacob trailed behind them as the corridor narrowed and started to weave outside of a straight line. They'd been walking for almost five minutes when it looked like they'd reached a dead end. But it wasn't until Smith vanished that Jacob realized it was a trick of the light, and the bend in the corridor had hidden a path.

Another set of stairs waited beyond, but these were not roughly hewn stone. These were polished and rounded as if they belonged in front of Parliament back in Ancora. The dark walls lightened until the gently marbled stone stood in sharp contrast to the shadows below.

Smith stepped out onto a landing and paused until the others reached him. Past the tinker, another set of marble stairs ascended, but what was revealed in the other direction froze Jacob in his tracks. Massive steel beams punched through an earthen ceiling, stretching at least thirty feet from top to bottom where they vanished into the marshy earth.

Scattered between those impossible forms were homes and buildings long since fallen to ruin. But it wasn't one or two, it was an entire town, and in the distance, glowworms lit the ceiling like a webwork of stars.

"Some of the oldest documents in the Crown Library came from these ruins," Smith said. "Or so the stories say."

"I don't understand," Alice said when they reached the bottom of the stairs. "Did they build this underground on purpose?"

"Oh, no," Smith said. "They built it before the great floods. Some think it is older than the Skeleton itself. Targrove told a story of the sunken city once. Built before the great floods created the Bay of Sorrow."

"I doubt a flood created the bay," Alice said.

"Maybe, but it was a good story. What is not in doubt is that this city flooded." Smith pointed to the watermarks at various points in both the buildings and the steelwork. The homes had watermarks higher than any on the beams themselves, which told Jacob the worst floods came before Belldorn was built up.

The angled braces and platforms high above them reminded Jacob of the caves beneath Dauschen. For a moment, he was back with Charles before the end. Jacob shook the thoughts away and studied their surroundings, looking for any signs of movement of what might be lurking nearby.

Smith started down the stairs, glanced back, and laughed. "I do like Ancorans. Always wearing your boots."

Jacob looked down at the tall boots that came most of the way up his shins. He wondered why Smith had mentioned that until the large tinker stepped onto the ground, and sank into the marshy floor. That certainly explained the humidity permeating the air.

"Eww," Alice muttered. But for her small complaint, she didn't hesitate when she reached the marsh, striking out across it right behind Smith.

Jacob followed, somewhat unsettled at the spongy footing. Each step sunk slightly into the ground before coming free with a quiet pop. Alice was light enough she still moved in relative silence, but every step Smith took sounded like a suction cup popping off a metal surface. There was no way for the group to move through the marsh in total silence, and Jacob began to understand why the smugglers would sometimes shelter there.

"Smith?" Alice said. "What did you smuggle down here? The halls are so narrow I can't imagine it was anything large."

"For the most part, you are correct. But there are other entrances, as I mentioned before. This is not the only cavern beneath Belldorn, though all the western tunnels lead here."

"You wouldn't be able to store anything here long," Alice said. "It would mold and rot in no time."

"This is the lowest chamber in the underground. You'll see when we reached the other side. But if Ballern finds the tunnels, this will be where they come."

Most of the wood in the marsh had long since decayed. But Jacob caught sight of the occasional log, as thick as a city street where it hadn't been fully devoured by weevils. And that thought gave him pause.

"Are there weevils here?" Jacob asked.

Smith glanced back at Jacob and followed his line of sight. "That is an old ironwood. No weevil could chew through that. Given enough time, and enough desperation, the Stag Beetles will consume it. But ironwood can last nearly as long as steel, given the proper conditions."

"I hardly think these are the proper conditions," Alice said.

"One day, you will see the cousins of the old ironwoods. And you will understand how tall that tree once was and how strong its trunk once stood. The rot you see is the passage of centuries."

But what Smith said made some sense. What few buildings had retained their integrity were built of thick steel. There were no timbers that remained, no framework or roofs to speak of except those formed from stone tiles. And Jacob slowly realized the lack of an angled roof on many of those ruins was not because it was flat and out of sight, but because they had long rotted away.

Their path across the marsh took them close to another fallen ironwood, only this one was not so silent in its death. The wood churned with the glint of chitin and the slow red crawl of Fireworms.

Alice stepped closer to the log, leaning in beside the giant curved growth of a flat orange fungus. "Look at the beetles. They aren't bothering the Fireworms at all."

"And neither should you," Smith said. "If one of those worms calls out in distress, I would prefer not to meet its parents."

Jacob remembered Samuel's story about the giant Fireworm in the caves not far from Dauschen. The thought of one of those giants turning on them the way it had turned on the Stone Dogs was an unsettling prospect.

Jacob stepped closer to Alice, and with the two standing together, the miniature Stag Beetles swarmed to the edge of the fungus. They raised curved black mandibles that were nearly half the length of their bodies. He understood then why the dim light reflected so well. Each of the beetles wore shimmering armor of iridescent green, so dark as to almost be black until they were caught in the lantern light.

"They sense your warmth," Smith said. "It is why they stay so close to the Fireworms. That is also why you see some of the platforms above you. It is hard for the beetles to navigate the steel. And to sleep on the marsh floor is to awaken covered in them. Which wouldn't be a problem unless you accidentally smashed one, and the rest decided to bite you." Smith said that last bit with an edge of annoyance.

"Speaking from experience?" Alice asked.

Smith grunted. "More experience than I care to admit."

Alice held her hand out and let one of the iridescent beetles climb onto her palm. It immediately stopped moving and flattened itself as much as it could into her warmth. It was a strange thing to see a creature so small, like a tiny Jumper, hiding from the light. Alice plucked the beetle off her hand and gently set it back on the fungus before they continued on.

The cavern slowly closed in around them, narrowing until they reached another set of stairs, not so unlike the pristine marble ones they'd entered from. But on the other end of the cavern, broken and jagged steps threatened their footing as pieces of them crumbled away, pinging off the lower stairs.

"This is where we need to stop them if they come," Smith said. "Every other exit into the city is behind this passage. If they breach Belldorn's lines, even a handful of them, it could turn the tide."

"How could they possibly know about this place?" Jacob asked.

Alice turned to face him on the cracked landing. "Because they have spies in Belldorn."

"Not only spies," Smith said. "But think about the pirates who trade between the cities. Everything has a price. And information is no different."

Beyond the broken stairs waited a long passage. It bore some similarity to the mines in Ancora, except for a few obvious differences. Instead of wooden frames to prevent cave-ins, metal beams arched overhead, decorated with intricate vines and birds like nothing he'd ever seen. If they were to scale, they were at least the size of a Sky Needle.

Perfect paving stones formed an overlapping pattern in shades of gray and gold and blue, polished beneath a layer of dust and preserved to a point Jacob could scarcely guess at their age. But he understood Smith's concern because the passage was spacious enough for a company to march through it.

"It's wide enough for a crawler," Alice said. "Not that they could get one down here, but still. It's huge."

Smith nodded. "This is where I want to lay traps. There is another tunnel to the north large enough to bring crawlers in." He leaned down and worked a knife between the paving stones, lifting one with some effort. "We can install traps here to keep infantry out."

"What kind of traps?" Jacob asked.

"Traps like you made for the crawlers. But make them for people."

Jacob winced at the idea. Not only at the idea of killing, but making a trigger sensitive enough to fire at a footstep.

"We can do this, Jacob. It will not take much to adjust the pressure plates."

Alice reached out and squeezed his arm.

Jacob blew out a breath. "Okay. I don't like it, but I like the thought of this being unguarded even less."

"Good," Smith said, brushing off his hands. "Let us return to the workshop before it is too late to get anything done."

CHAPTER EIGHT

S AMUEL WAS NEARLY ready to collapse when the transmitter in his collar hissed. "Mary, come on. Do you realize how late it is? I'm going to sleep at the stables. You should turn in too."

"Spider Knight, this is the Lady of Belldorn."

"Sure, Mary. Try again."

Drakkar cleared his throat beside Samuel. "I think that truly is Lady Katherine."

Samuel could feel the color drain from his face. "Ma'am, Lady, Kat, Katherine, I am so apology. I mean, I apologize. I mean—"

"Samuel, stop talking," Lady Katherine commanded.

"Yes. At once."

"Are you aware of the underground?"

Samuel glanced at Drakkar. "I'm not. Are you?"

Drakkar nodded. "I am familiar with the fact there are ruins beneath the city, but I do not know much more. A common hideaway for smugglers and those who do not wish to be seen."

"There is more to it than that," Lady Katherine said. "But I admit, that is the bulk of what you need to consider now. To the south, there is a bronze archway, now scarred and scorched from Ballern's attack. Meet me there in half an hour."

"Do you know where that is?" Samuel asked.

Drakkar shook his head.

"I do," another voice said. Samuel turned to find Rin standing there in the deep blue and brown of his Dragonrider vest.

"Is that Rin I hear?" Lady Katherine asked.

"Yes," Samuel said.

"Good. Rin, please escort these two to the southern arch. Bring Tatsu, if he is available."

One of Rin's eyebrows crept a little higher. "Of course, My Lady."

With that, the transmitter went silent, and Samuel groaned. He realized that sleep was much further away than he had hoped.

"Tatsu!" Rin shouted. He waited for a time, and when no one responded, he raised his voice again.

This time he received a groggy response. "Rin?"

For a moment, Samuel was jealous of the bleary-eyed Dragonrider who appeared before him. Tatsu had clearly found the opportunity to get some sleep. He rubbed at his eyes and pulled a hay-covered blanket tighter around his shoulders.

"Tatsu, get your armor. We're escorting these two down to the arch."

Tatsu narrowed his eyes and yawned. "Wasn't that bombed? Or is there another arch?"

"There is another arch, but we're going to the one that was bombed. Get your *armor*."

Tatsu slid the blanket off his shoulders, revealing that he was still wearing the thick leather hide of the Dragonriders. "I'll grab my spear." He vanished back into the stable for a moment before reappearing with something Samuel would not have called the spear. A wide blade sat on either end of the long wooden staff, and it looked as ready to slice something in two as it did spear it.

Rin blew out a breath as he eyed Tatsu's weapon. "You're going to carry that all the way through the city?"

Tatsu studied the spear tip that was slightly taller than he was. "It's not that far. And if I can carry this on Buzzer's back, I can carry it on the streets.

"Buzzer?" Drakkar asked.

"It's what he calls his favorite Dragonwing. Most of us aren't that particular about our mount, but Tatsu has always been a little different."

The other Dragonrider smiled. "And Rin has always been a little judgmental. Ever since we were kids."

"You grew up in Ballern too?" Samuel asked.

Tatsu nodded. "One of the Skyborn. And you are a Spider Knight." There wasn't a question in Tatsu's voice. It was a simple observation, or a statement of something he'd already heard before.

Samuel no longer wore the simple armor that had helped them blend in at Pirate's Cove and Fire Island. It had felt good to slip back into the leather and polished steel of his old armor. But it certainly stood out, as no soldier in Belldorn wore the like.

"Come," Rin said. "I would prefer not to be late meeting the Lady of Belldorn."

At that, Tatsu's back stiffened. "We're going to meet Lady Katherine? At this hour?"

Rin only answered with a smile and then struck out to the southwest.

✧   ✧   ✧

THE VILLAGES AROUND Belldorn reminded Samuel of Ancora far more than the city itself did. Or at least it reminded him of the Lowlands before the Fall. Large timbers framed the houses, many of which were stacked on top of each other to create the appearance of two-story homes. The jarring transition between colors and flags and even flowers told Samuel different families occupied the same buildings.

There had been a few multifamily homes in Ancora like that. More of them existed in the Highlands, where rules governed much of the decor along the streets. But Samuel rather liked the mosaic of color that stretched out through the village, an unruly pattern, if one could even call it a pattern.

A huge mural graced the side of a tall building, home to at least three businesses Samuel could see signs for. He didn't have to ask to know it was a portrait of Lady Katherine, the brilliant flag of Belldorn waving above her, and the wreckage at her feet that of a Ballern warship, the crest easily identifiable.

But beyond that, where the streets of the village met the outer bands of Belldorn, the scorched earth and ash told a different story.

"Rust it all," Tatsu whispered. The village simply stopped, with nothing but rubble stretched out before them for nearly an entire block. It was another sight that reminded Samuel of Ancora, but in a much darker way.

"Come on," Rin said. "I can see the arch on the other side of the street."

"What street?" Tatsu asked. "There's nothing left."

Tatsu was right, they couldn't see the stone beneath their boots, and the debris they walked across threatened to roll their ankles. In the distance, where the fire hadn't burned away the bodies completely, a pair of Carrion Worms feasted. The rot was already setting in, and Samuel knew the stench would only thicken.

One corner of the stone and metal arch had escaped unscathed, the polished bronze gleaming in the light of the small fires still burning in the area, obscured only by the occasional bits of ash drifting through the air. Samuel could make out the Belldorn airships and soldiers placed in honored positions on that monument. But many more disappeared beneath a layer of soot and char.

A pale, hooded form stood at the base of the arch, turned toward the lights on the horizon to the south. Ballern's forces, gathering to raid Belldorn. Gathering to break the alliance that had Ancora and Dauschen's fate bound to it.

The closer they came, the more detail Samuel could make out on the cloaked form. It was clean but for a trace of ash along the hem and embroidered with precious metals. It was a technique he'd rarely seen outside of royalty and Parliament, and cast little doubt on the fact Lady Katherine had beaten them to the arch.

A scorched length of wood snapped beneath Samuel's boots, and Lady Katherine turned to face them.

"Welcome. Thank you all for joining me."

"Why here?" Drakkar asked. "Would not the stables have provided better protection?"

"I was not concerned with protection, Cave Guardian. I trust the four of you more than most outsiders. And, if I am being honest, I trust you more than some of my inner circle. Or those who believe I consider them part of my inner circle."

"You honor us," Drakkar said, bowing slightly to the lady.

Lady Katherine dismissed his gesture with a wave. "This is not the time, Drakkar. I appreciate your sentiment, but I must return to the tower to coordinate this evening's efforts. Smith, Alice, and Jacob ventured beneath the city. I have asked them to sabotage the area in case Ballern attempts to infiltrate the ruins."

"You want us to help?" Tatsu asked, his lips curling slightly. "Underground?"

Lady Katherine let out a small laugh at Tatsu's disgust at the idea of going underground. "No. I have another task for you. One that could save us if the sabotage fails, and one that could spear the heart of Ballern's fleet regardless of what happens underground."

Tatsu's expression evened out. "That sounds better already."

Lady Katherine produced a large leather satchel from beneath her cloak, holding it out to Rin. "Only your Dragonriders can do this. These are the transmitters that will summon the Emerald Needles."

"My Lady," Rin said. "I thought we had agreed this was a last resort. Only if the ships could not return fast enough from Fel."

Lady Katherine gestured to the ruin around them. "Do you know what this was, Master Dragonrider? These were not the outcasts or shunned of Belldorn. It was an enclave of our greatest artisans. Painters who could make you believe their brush strokes gave life to the unliving, writers who could color the world with their words, and scholars who spent their days in the history of our city when they weren't in the bowels of the Crown Library. And what is this place now? A graveyard."

Rin's hands clenched into fists. "It's terrible, I know, but you're asking us to unleash a plague."

"I am asking you to defend the city that defended you, Skyborn. Do not think Ballern would look kindly on the refugees in Canopy. Do not think they would spare those who shelter inside Belldorn's city proper either. You lived on the docks long enough to know what they will do."

Rin's eyes widened, but he did not answer.

It was Tatsu who turned to the other Dragonrider. "You know what they'd do, Rin. They'd execute them in the town square and spike their heads. I know you remember what they did to my dad." Tatsu grabbed Rin's vest and leaned closer. "If you won't do it, I will."

Rin shook himself, gently pulling Tatsu's hands off his vest. "I will. For the Skyborn. For the Ballern that should be."

"For the Ballern that *will* be."

"Wait until they strike," Lady Katherine said. "It will force them to cluster as they move on the city. And it will be their undoing."

Rin pulled one of the transmitters out of the sack. It looked like a bolt, nothing more. "How does it work?"

"Fire it into the ship. The head of the shaft has an actuator built into it. Once the signal activates, move to the next ship and *do not* wait to see if it is working. Do not return to any ship that has been targeted, because once the Emerald Needles have been released …"

"I know," Rin said, squeezing the bolt in his fist. "I know."

"What about the docks to the south?" Samuel asked. "You can't leave those standing."

Lady Katherine smiled, and it was the least friendly expression Samuel had ever seen on her face. "I have other plans for the docks."

CHAPTER NINE

MORDAIR HAD ALWAYS enjoyed his trips to Ballern, a city that had kept its love of seagoing ships alive as much as its love for airships. It was one of the few places he'd been in the world where simply saying "the docks" could leave a question about where you were going.

"Mister, is that your ship?" a small child asked at the pier.

Mordair's hand sprang out to stop the Red Hand from pushing the child away. A stern glance backed her away as he crouched down to talk to the youth.

"It is, young one. Do you like ships?"

"I like your ship, sir. It's huge! I've never seen anything like it."

Mordair glanced back at the towering ocean liner and the massive ramp that stretched down half the pier. "It is a grand ship. It brought us across the Gray Sea, you know."

"Wow, and the seas are rough this time of year, sir."

Mordair smiled at the child. A child who would soon enough be one of Mordair's peasants. If he'd broken the will of Fel, he could do better in Ballern. It was only a matter of time. "Patrice, see that this child and his friends have a thorough tour of the ship. Any who would like to join, see they are cared for and no injury befalls them."

For a moment, the Red Hand stared at the use of her proper name. Then she bowed to Mordair and led the child away.

Patrice meant well, Mordair knew, but her constant presence could be suffocating at the best of times. What she perhaps didn't understand was that they had little risk in Ballern. Belldorn and Bollwerk were occupied elsewhere, which gave him time to mingle with the citizens of Ballern.

The strange looks from those who knew him from Fel brought a smile to his lips. It was a rare thing for him to be seen without the spiked breathing mask he wore in public. A reminder of where his family had come from, and the mines that had stolen so many of their lives.

Rumors had long lived that Mordair was weak in a physical sense, reliant on a breathing mask, among other things, and he entertained those rumors at his amusement. Because an enemy who underestimated you was an enemy who could be broken at a whim.

Impressions were important in Ballern, and he needed the stories of his arrival to be disarming. He needed a veneer of generosity and kindness; one he could maintain until their plans were unleashed in full.

A young man in a gray and faded gold vest caught Mordair's eye. A Skyborn, the lowest class in Ballern, Mordair had no doubt.

Mordair raised a hand in greeting. "Young one, where might I find something to eat?"

"All around. Are you blind?"

Mordair's smile didn't crack. "Allow me to rephrase my question. Where might I find the best food on these docks? And would you join me? I would be pleased to offer you a meal. As much as you'd like. Tell me more of the docks and what Ballern is like outside the walls?"

The boy's eyes flitted from side to side before he nodded and led the way into the crowds. Mordair could feel his guards at his back, but they'd been instructed to keep their distance.

"You want the best food on the docks, there's only one cook to see," the boy called over his shoulder. He wove between a pair of stalls selling vases, armor, and more trinkets that seemed to have no unified relation.

It took them to the widest path of vendors, where a small white tent fluttered in the breeze, and steam billowed off an aged copper pot that looked like it had seen more battles than Mordair himself.

"Jakon!" the boy called out.

A slender man glanced up from beneath a slouching chef's hat and smiled at the boy. "Walter, what brings you here? I thought you'd be watching the ships still."

"The biggest of them is tied up now. But this man asked what the best food on the docks was, so I brought him here."

There was surprise on the chef's face, a surprise that told Mordair he knew exactly who the King of Fel was. That was … interesting.

Mordair sat down on a stool and gestured for the boy, Walter, to join him. "Walter? That doesn't sound like a Skyborn name."

Walter frowned at that. "A Skyborn name? We have names from everywhere, you know? We aren't all from Ballern. At least not our families. Some of us escaped Fel in the old wars. That's what my pop says."

Jakon laughed as he dished out a generous helping of stew. "Walter, that's the King of Fel you're talking to."

"Sir! I had no idea, sir! I'm so sorry, sir!"

Mordair smiled, and it was genuine, but perhaps not for the reason it seemed. Even this boy, a Skyborn halfway across the world, knew to fear him. It would make securing the city so much easier that way. "Think nothing of it, Walter. I'm just a visitor to your fine port."

"Sorry, sir, I just heard bad stories. But sometimes stories is just stories, I guess."

"Very wise of you, Walter," Mordair said.

"What brings you to Ballern?" Jakon asked.

"You've not heard of the attack on Fel?" Mordair took the bowl when Jakon offered it with a shake of his head. "It is a rather recent development. Belldorn attacked us, and you know how evil that city can be."

Walter nodded, his eyes widening. "They're scum, sir. Murderers and pirates and nothing more."

"Your father taught you better than that, Walter," Jakon said, a sternness to his words.

"Oh?" Mordair asked. "You believe them to be something more?"

One of Mordair's guards leaned in close to his ear, whispering something that made a violent smile crawl across his face. "A smuggler, you say?"

Jakon stiffened for only a moment as he handed another bowl to Walter. Apparently, he wasn't used to being identified, least of all by a king from another city. But for his moment of surprise, Jakon was a quick thinker, like any good smuggler.

"That was another life," Jakon said. "When Ballern wasn't doing so well. Some reputations are hard to shake, you know."

Mordair looked around at the local people. Their worn clothes and shuffling pace didn't speak to him of a city doing well. They looked more broken than the citizens of Fel he had brought to heel. It told him the Queen of Ballern had not been honest about the situation in their city.

This was not a place of unity and singular purpose. This was a place rife with division, and if pressure was applied in the right places, it would bow to his will.

Mordair smiled at Jakon. "An excellent stew, chef. Excellent stew." He turned to Walter. "I must be off to visit your queen, young one, but perhaps we will meet again one day, should the fates align." Mordair dropped two golden coins onto the countertop, far more than any stew could cost, and then walked away.

✧ ✧ ✧

MORDAIR'S ASSUMPTIONS ABOUT the unspoken divide in Ballern solidified when he walked into the palaces of Ballern. Tall spires hid the excess that dripped from every wall within. Enough gold to feed its citizens for a decade had instead been formed into a grand statue of a woman in a sweeping gown. Mordair recognized the name. The Lady of Ballern had died in the Deadlands War, or shortly before. Accounts were muddled.

But the presence of wealth was reassuring. Finding a way to support those most loyal to him, those who had followed him all the years in Fel, would be a simple enough matter with such waste on full display. What would the Queen of Ballern think of Fel? With its cracked walls and stone throne that looked out over the sea?

Mordair made his way past the statue to the door manned by two guards. "I have business with the queen. She is expecting me."

A pair of poleaxes crossed in front of Mordair's face. Long weapons that were difficult to do anything but thrust in close quarters. The display wouldn't keep him out. Three strikes would disarm both guards and leave them vulnerable to a killing blow, but instead, Mordair smiled. And waited.

"Let him in," a voice boomed from beyond the doorway, echoing in an odd fashion that Mordair didn't understand until he passed the guards, and was disgusted by the golden obscenity that was the room.

While the columns flanking the throne might not have been solid gold, as they would have fallen under their own weight, the gold leaf coating every inch of that room was near blinding. But there were hidden bits of wear, flakes missing from rotundas, and the intricate mosaic in the ceiling needed more than one gem replaced.

But the effect was striking, and the four steps that led to the dais were large enough to look intimidating, even at Mordair's imposing height.

"Welcome, King of Fel. May our alliance bring prosperity to all our peoples."

"You honor me with your welcome, great queen." Mordair bowed and let none of his disgust rise to his face. "My people grow tired, Queen. May we find rest among your residents?"

The queen nodded. "At your leisure. You may keep your ships docked and live upon them as well. I am sure the vendors would be quite happy."

"Yes, I have had the pleasure of meeting some of them. They are an outspoken and somewhat rambunctious lot."

The Queen of Ballern laughed. "So long as your people are peaceful, they are welcome in all parts of the city, Mordair."

"Belldorn joined Bollwerk in the attack on Fel. The plan has done well."

The Queen of Ballern frowned and looked away for a moment before returning a hard gaze to Mordair. "We have not forgotten the horrors and death delivered upon us by those who call themselves Belldorn. My grandfather, a king, dismembered and his head mounted upon our gates. We threw down our oppressors, Mordair. Threw them down into ruin and scattered them across the sea. Generations will be given their vengeance. For your aid, you may shelter in our city for two weeks."

"Two weeks," Mordair said. "That is not what we agreed—"

"Two weeks if you cannot join in the attack."

Mordair's smile faded.

"Join the attack on Belldorn, or retreat to the Great Machines. The choice is yours, but you will not stop us in our moment of triumph. And your people will not sap our resources."

Mordair stood a little straighter. The Queen of Ballern meant to crush Fel at her earliest opportunity. He had little doubt of that now. She saw the mighty ocean liners as a weakness and not the fortresses they were. She thought her airships to be superior to Fel, and in that regard, she might have been correct. But the queen had shown too much transparency. And while he still had die to cast, Mordair would use more caution dealing with the queen.

But he didn't hesitate even a moment before saying, "Of course we will join your efforts in Belldorn. Those who would show you no loyalty must be crushed." The Queen of Ballern could not have known what the smile on Mordair's face truly signaled. Their alliance would last so long as it was beneficial to Mordair and his people, or so long as he could tolerate her pedantry. Whichever came first.

CHAPTER TEN

"A RE YOU SAYING you don't trust Helena to take care of Midstream?" Gladys asked. "She has Theo and her, umm, assistant."

"Of course not, Princess." George rubbed at his face. "I only mean it would be good for us to appear to be defending our own city, instead of traipsing into another."

"Traipsing," Gladys said, snorting a laugh. Perhaps there was some truth in what George was saying, but the opportunity to climb aboard a Bollwerk supply ship and ride it north to Fel had been overwhelming. And besides that, there had not been more than a handful of soldiers spotted in the desert around Midstream.

"I suppose it is a rare thing to see inside the walls of the fortress city."

Gladys's steps slowed as they cleared the edge of the airship docks to the north of Fel. Even those bore armor that obscured their view out into the ocean and east toward the mountains. They were nearly to the lifts before the gaps in the armor grew wide enough to offer a sweeping vision of what lay beyond.

Fel sat at the base of a small bay, a sheer drop to the rough waters waiting below the docks. To the east, the Black Mountains rose against the sky, and airships sailed in and out of the docks. Small beaches of black sand hid the line between the sea and the shore, as if the ground itself moved with the waves.

The snowcapped peaks softened the overwhelming vision of gray. Gladys turned away from that landscape and continued down the path to the gatehouse that would take them into the city. There was no fight in the citizens on those docks. They didn't rejoice at the arrival of Bollwerk's ships, but neither did they shout insults or threaten those who disembarked from them.

Instead, it was as if the entire situation was routine. The dock hands went about their daily tasks, securing ships and helping unload when that offer of help was not turned away. Gladys found it unsettling, and she always kept a hand near the hem of her cloak, within a snap of her wrist of a throwing knife.

The stark gray turrets of the fortress city rose before them, a soiled red banner rustling in the breeze, so it almost looked as if the Tail Sword emblazoned on it was alive.

They passed into the darkness of the gatehouse and out the other side. There wasn't much in the way of defenses inside that gatehouse, and Gladys supposed she knew why. The chance of ships arriving unseen on the docks was slim, and there was no other way to reach that gate.

George paused at the edge of a broken crenellation. "Archibald said he would speak to the people himself. I thought him half mad. Maybe that remains to be seen."

Gladys followed his gaze to the warship hovering over Fel. Bollwerk's monsters could cow the fiercest enemy, but the strange acceptance of those on the docks made her think many of the people who remained in that city did not need to be threatened to be controlled. They'd already been broken.

"This way," George said, guiding her to the left and the narrow, arched walkway that kept them in the sky above the courtyard far below.

George's words came back to Gladys's mind as they reached the entrance to the highest tower. Inside waited an iron lift and a spiral of stone stairs that climbed far above. There had long been stories about the throne room of Fel. Some of those stories had shaped Midstream and the rise of the warlords. No one Gladys knew had ever seen the throne room and survived, so when the opportunity arose, she seized it.

As aged as the iron was, betrayed by rust stains on the platform and the chains that held it, the mechanism moved silently to a stop. George slid the gate to the side and stepped inside, holding it open for Gladys.

There was only one lever in the lift, and when George pulled it, the cage climbed to the top of the tower. What waited beyond chilled Gladys to the bone.

A sweeping hall with smooth black columns that soared up to meet the ceiling of deep arches and domes greeted them. Their footsteps didn't echo in that place, as there weren't enough walls left to trap the sound. But ahead of them, atop a dais carved of the same gray stone of the Black Mountains, sat the throne of Fel.

A monstrous thing, like a fang ripped from the maw of some great beast, wrapped in chains and framed by a tattered red tapestry. No Tail Sword waited on that cloth as it rippled in a gentle breeze, only the discoloration from rusted chains and the dagger-like stone surrounding it, as if the room had been carved from the very mountains themselves.

George cursed and stared for a time, while Gladys started poking around the room. There weren't many places for things to be hidden, and it was behind a towering column that she found what she was seeking, and perhaps what she had most feared.

She tried to choke back the cry on her lips, but the sudden appearance of George told her she'd failed.

Nestled on a shelf between the masks and bent crowns of ruthless desert warlords and the loot of royal rings sat a simple wooden mask. It was not made to be a threatening beast like so many of the warlords, but instead had wide eyes and teeth that showed strength, but could also be seen as a welcoming smile. A protector. A benevolent king.

Gladys remembered the face that went behind it. She didn't know if she remembered it more from paintings and photographs, or if she remembered it more from the short time she'd had with him. But the crack in that mask and the dark stains along the edge crashed into her as if she'd just lost her father all over again.

"So it is true," George said, wrapping Gladys up in a vast hug. "It was Fel who brought the warlords."

Gladys pulled away from George and took the mask off the shelf. A mask she had not seen in many years. The mask of her father.

✧ ✧ ✧

AFTER A BRIEF time studying what Gladys could only think of as a grisly trophy room, she followed George back to the lift, where they made their way to the bottom of the tower. She would not soon forget the trove of broken swords and masks and mangled jewelry that still bore the stains of their wearers' final moments. It was a grim display of Fel's prowess in war, and one Gladys wasn't sure had been abandoned in a panic.

"I think they left it on purpose," Gladys said.

"Hmm?" George asked.

"The masks. The treasure. All of it. It's made to look like they left so fast they couldn't take it with them. But I think they left it as a statement to anyone who came into Fel afterwards."

"You may be correct, Princess. Mordair had more than enough time to mobilize his airships. And you only need to look at the piers in the bay to know how much he managed to take with him."

"What do you mean?"

George smiled. "Mordair has a fleet of seaborne vessels greater than that of his airships. None of them remain. Not a single ocean liner that belonged to the king himself. The airships that remain are merchants and traders. It appears the military that defended this place has moved on."

The royal guard didn't keep his voice low, even though they were now surrounded by small clusters of Fel citizens. They had offered little resistance, and Gladys wasn't entirely sure why. It was one thing to be broken by a king, but it was another not to defend one's own home. If there was one thing she was sure of, it was that more had befallen those inside Fel than they knew.

Despite the weight of her father's mask in her backpack, Gladys felt sorry for those citizens who hurried away from them, averting their eyes, and only catching short glances from an exhausted people. Perhaps part of that exhaustion came when they saw Archibald's forces penetrate the wall, crumbling the myth of the city's invulnerability.

But the small child, carried in his mother's arms, who asked only if the soldiers were there to save them, and the mother's whispered refrain of *please,* told Gladys much.

It wasn't long before they reached one of the main streets that ran through the center of Fel. Brilliant red banners hung from the buildings at regular intervals, creating a garish hallway where the cloth could have been mistaken for blood.

"There," George said, pointing off to a gathering crowd down the street.

Above them, retracting back into the giant warship, was an empty platform. It wasn't until they came closer to the crowd that Gladys could make out Archibald standing on a slightly elevated stage. She wondered if Archibald had been pompous enough to deliver that structure himself, but once they were close enough, she could see the red and black colors of Fel staining the stage all around him.

Four guards. That was all Archibald had come with. And two of them were distracted, assembling a large, curled horn pointed into the audience. Gladys had seen similar tools used in Bollwerk. Not so unlike the horn a symphony might use, but made to amplify the voice of a single speaker.

The guards stepped away from Archibald, and he walked closer to the curled horn. "Citizens of Fel. I come to you as the Speaker of Bollwerk, and to reach out to you in these dark times. Your king may have abandoned you to the northern seas, but we will not."

Gladys caught the whisper that rolled through the crowd. Disbelief and conjecture about what had truly happened to Mordair. She heard them mention the bodies still hanging from the wall, and there was no stronger symbol of Mordair's iron fist.

The desert princess looked around, trying to find what the crowd was talking about, and eventually her gaze caught on a distant horror. She was glad they weren't closer. The decay was terrible enough at a distance. Bodies strung from crenellations like meat at a butcher shop.

Archibald showed his prowess as Speaker in that moment, and his guards proved to be more than simple protection. One whispered into his ear, and the Speaker barely missed a syllable. What came next reminded Gladys the Speaker could be as ruthless with his words as he was with his warships.

"Today is the last day you will look upon your family and country-men on those walls. Today we, the people of Bollwerk and Belldorn alike, will release them into your care. Bury them as you see fit. For those unclaimed, a ceremony will be held on this dais at dusk. They will be burned with honor and remembered for more than the atrocities suffered at the hands of Mordair's rule!

"I do not ask for your trust in this time—only your patience. Patience for us to find any of Mordair's loyalists who have stayed behind to sabotage you in these desperate times. Patience for us to bring you doctors and supplies you so desperately need."

"We have fish!" a man cried out. "We don't need help from desert trash!"

Some voices rose to agree.

Gladys felt George's hand on her shoulder. He squeezed twice, his unspoken signal to be ready for anything. As if she wasn't already.

More voices shouted down the dissenters. And some of them broke Gladys's heart.

"That's my son on that wall!" a man screamed at the first protests. "You let my boy die for *nothing* while you hid in your damned cave, coward!"

One nod of Archibald's head sent the guards into the crowd. Both men tried to pull away, but the guards escorted them to the stage.

"I am not here to take your voices," Archibald said. "You have been deceived. Deceived so thoroughly you hate your own brethren with a passion meant for outsiders. Meant for people like me. But what you fail to understand is we are extending a hand, a chance to break free of a tyrant and form your own house of rule. Tell us your stories."

And with that, Archibald stepped away from the horn, and the shell-shocked citizens were pushed toward it by the guards. The man who lost a child spoke first, and Gladys could not move, did not dare look away—because this was the evil they faced.

"They took my wife a year ago," his voice cracked. It looked like he was going to say more, but he choked on the words. He moved on. "My son, my son still served in the guard. Some of you knew him. They took his name and burned it. He became one of the many. He didn't call me by name anymore, only 'citizen,' and when I asked him why, I could see the fear behind his eyes.

"You all saw it. In your sisters and brothers. Mothers and fathers. We lost them all to Mordair. The fleet became more of a cult than anything else. My son told me Mordair meant to deploy the warships. Take them all to Ballern." The man shook his head. "I didn't believe him, and like a fool, I asked another soldier on the street. A day later, my son was hanging from the wall. Another day and those ships were gone. Mordair didn't retreat. He abandoned us."

The man spat on the ground and walked off the stage. No one tried to stop him. No one tried to stop any of them as one by one the citizens of Fel stepped up and recounted the horrors inflicted on their families. But Gladys could see the web of truth that connected all of them. Either they, or someone in their family, Mordair had perceived as a threat or a traitor.

He'd abandoned every single person he didn't think was absolutely loyal. She turned back to the dead along the wall. Her own family had suffered at the hands of Mordair's lineage. She'd never really stopped to consider how many thousands of others had suffered the same.

She put her arm around George's waist and listened to the stories of a broken city.

CHAPTER ELEVEN

"Y OU ASLEEP?" JACOB whispered.

"Not even close." Alice rolled over and he could just make out the silhouette of her face. There wasn't much room on the slatted cot, but there wasn't much room left in Mary's house at all, with so many of them staying there.

Furi snored in the corner, and Jacob was extraordinarily jealous of her dead sleep.

"So," Alice said. "Do you think the traps will be adequate? You heard the same transmission I did between Mary and Kat. Raids are starting in the ruins."

Jacob hesitated and then ran his fingers through the fringe of Alice's hair. "I don't know. Smith seemed confident about the changes to the pressure plates, but I don't think we got enough installed."

"It sounded like they'll be working through the night. It'll have to do." She squeezed his hand and took a deep breath. "I guess we'll know in the morning."

For a time, they didn't say anything more, only remained still in the darkness. More than once, Jacob heard footsteps in the house. They weren't the only ones with troubled sleep. Maybe one day he'd be able to sleep through the entire night again, but it wouldn't be while Ballern was within striking distance.

Eventually—they couldn't be sure when—Jacob and Alice fell asleep to Furi's snores and the hushed conversation between Mary and Eva in the other room. The last thing Jacob remembered was wondering how Samuel could possibly be asleep with all that talking.

✦　✦　✦

MORNING CAME WITH thunder and screams.

"Jacob! Jacob, wake up!"

He startled awake, almost cracking his forehead against Alice's as she shook him. She was already dressed, and not just dressed, but armed with her wrist cannon and bolt glove.

"Let's move!" Mary shouted from the other room.

"What's happening?"

Alice threw Jacob's boots at him.

"Ballern," Furi said from the corner. "Early morning strike. Long-range cannons. I should have gone with Samuel."

"What? Where's Samuel?" Jacob asked.

"Headed for the stables to meet Drakkar. They'll be gone long before you could get there."

Jacob rubbed his eyes and slid his boots on. "What about the raids in the underground?"

"Javelin traps wrecked them," Mary said as she hurried in and out of the room. "I'm heading to the Skysworn to meet Smith. Furi, with me."

Furi hopped up, following Mary toward the front of the house.

"Jacob, Frederick sent new plans to Kat. A few of the larger schematics will fire ballista bolts. They're setting up close to the bay where you and Smith finished the amphibious Titan Mechs."

Jacob nodded. "I'll head that way."

"I'm coming with you." Alice slid into her glider pack and leaned Jacob's against the wooden cot.

At first he wanted to say something about not needing gliders on the ground. But what if they ended up on a supply ship? Or the Skysworn? Or even a tower they needed to escape from? Jacob thought Alice might be thinking more clearly than he was.

"Keep an ear to your transmitters. We'll come to you if things go bad."

"And what if things go bad for you?"

Mary didn't answer. The front door slammed, and Jacob and Alice were the last to leave.

"Let's go!" Alice said.

Jacob slid into his vest before hoisting the glider pack and grabbing his air cannon. He checked for the hand cannon before he saw it holstered on Alice's hip. Good, they'd both be as ready as they could be.

Alice grabbed a case of compound bombs and they hurried to the front door, snatching a handful of biscuits Mary had left on the counter. Outside on the street, the familiar sounds of cannons and crawlers echoed in the distance while soldiers marched by.

"Hurry," Alice said, and they took off at a jog to the west, heading for the shores of the Crystal Sea.

They'd barely made it a block and a half before a string of crawlers started to pass them on the streets. Jacob knew how fast those machines could move, but this company did not cross their path at high speed, likely due to how crowded the street was with soldiers and crawlers.

"Let's catch a ride," Alice said, and she switched from a jog into a sprint.

Jacob didn't have time to ask her what she meant and instead followed as fast as he could. He'd grown fairly accustomed to his biomechanics, but running flat out still sent a spike of pain into the cap on his leg. He didn't let it slow him down.

Alice leaped onto the rear armor of the nearest crawler, grasping the back seat and turning to look at Jacob. "Come on!"

Jacob hopped up to the narrow platform beside her, his hands slamming onto the back seat hard enough to draw the attention of the soldiers riding inside.

The soldier narrowed his eyes. "What do you kids think you're doing?"

"Heading to the beach," Alice said.

Jacob raised his head and smiled, repositioning his feet on the rear support to better secure himself. "Do you know where the javelins are?"

The soldier frowned and then nodded slowly. "Not far from those monstrosities they deployed."

"Monstrosities?" Alice asked, curiosity plain in the question. "Do you mean the Titan Mechs?"

"Aye."

"That's where we need to go. How close are you going to those?"

The soldier turned around and said something to the driver before leaning back where Jacob and Alice could hear him again. "Not far from it. Captain says you're a tinker."

Jacob squinted into the shadows of the armored crawler, trying to see who the captain was he was talking about. But he didn't recognize the man, which made Jacob wonder how he could possibly know who he was.

"I am. Do you know Smith?"

The soldier nodded. "The mechanic who flies with Skysworn Mary. Aye, I know Smith."

"Frederick and Smith helped me design those Titan Mechs, but I want to be in the sand to make sure everything is working."

"Anyone helping us in this fight is welcome. You have our thanks." The soldier shouted to the driver again before turning back to Jacob. "We'll slow down at the beach. Be ready to jump."

Alice and Jacob both nodded and watched as the distant ocean grew ever larger.

"You lot need to be careful on the beach. It's more than airships closing on the city."

"What do you mean?" Jacob asked.

But it was Alice who answered, tugging on his sleeve, and she leaned out to the side of the crawler and pointed toward the water. Jacob frowned and looked into the distance. There on the water were massive steel ships like nothing he'd seen before. He'd heard stories of the power Mordair's fleet held over the sea.

"They can't come all the way to the shore," the soldier said. "But they'll send landing barges, and they're heavily armed."

Jacob took a deep breath. "It's always something."

Alice glanced at him and laughed. "We should be used to it at this point."

"Get ready," the soldier said. The crawler slowed so suddenly that it almost knocked the wind out of Jacob as he slammed against the back of the vehicle.

"Thank you!" Alice called out as she hopped down into the sand and sprinted out of the path of the crawlers. Jacob followed her, turning to watch as the entire company shifted to the south and raced toward the front.

Two of the amphibious Titan Mechs stood to either side, nearly half a mile between them. As Jacob looked out into the Crystal Sea, he feared they wouldn't be enough. They could fire javelins at the airships above, but Jacob didn't think the Titan Mechs could penetrate the steel warships from Fel.

If they were lucky, the incoming landing barges would have no idea the Titan Mechs could enter the water. Lately, it felt like they were anything but lucky, but as Jacob sprinted across the sands with Alice, he tried to tamp down the worst of the fears that gnawed at the back of his brain.

Something like relief swelled in his chest when he recognized one of the men standing at an unburied trap. "Frederick!"

The man's head of graying hair, pulled back into a neat bun at the base of his neck, turned toward the voice. Frederick raised a hand in greeting as Jacob and Alice closed on the older tinker.

"What are you doing here?" Jacob said as he slid to a stop in the sand.

"I came with these," Frederick said, patting the oversized trap. But it wasn't quite the same as what Jacob had helped design. This trap had additional levers and a switchboard that looked like it belonged in a factory more than a trap.

"What is it?"

"It's your trap! A few modifications, as I'm sure you noticed. This one isn't made to be buried." Frederick turned a wheel set in the back of it, and the entire grid of springs and bolts tilted toward the sea. "Should have made a stand for it, though. A bit awkward on the ground, I'd say."

Jacob looked down the beach where he saw more than one of Theodosia's tinkers, given away by the leather aprons they wore on top of polished armor. "You have your apron on still?"

Frederick glanced down. "Of course, my boy. We're still tinkers, are we not? Need the pockets, you know. Ready to test those Titan Mechs? Trial by fire, eh?"

"Are you mental?" Alice asked. "Did you see the ships coming this way?"

"Hard to miss," Frederick said. "The adrenaline gets to me before a battle. Always has, you know. Makes me talk too much, Targrove used to say. May've had a point."

"So these traps aren't meant to be buried?" Jacob asked, bringing Frederick's focus full circle.

"Oh, right! Yes, let me show you. Each switch arms a launch tube, as I've taken to calling them. It can fire a standard javelin, or it can use these." Frederick leaned down and slid a long steel bolt from a barrel in the sand. At first glance, it looked like a javelin, but instead of the solid fins, it had a spiral bulb at the end with smaller fins placed at an angle.

"Different stabilizers," Jacob said, taking the two-foot length of steel from Frederick.

"Indeed. Less weight, more range, but far more accuracy. Don't need it if the enemy is close, but at a distance…" Frederick smiled. "It's loaded. This lever primes the air cannons."

Jacob moved the large lever from side to side, and he could hear the sudden inhalation of bellows above the chaos beginning to unfold around them.

Frederick pointed to three sights at the edge of the trap. "Range finder, javelin, short javelin. You'll need to compensate for wind on the longer targets."

"How did you build these so fast?" Jacob asked.

"We stole the parts," Frederick said with a laugh. "The control panels were meant to replace the worn ones in the lifts all across Bollwerk. The inspectors won't be happy with the delay, but I suspect they'll be happier than being dead."

"That's not a very high bar," Alice said.

Frederick nodded. "No, it's not."

"What's it aimed at?" Jacob asked.

Alice crouched down to look through the sights and turned the wheel to focus the trap's aim. "The nearest of the landing barges."

Frederick flipped an arming switch and gestured to Jacob. "First shot is all yours."

Jacob threw the lever down and the crack of compressed air and springs fired a bolt skyward. At first, it looked like it would sail past the barge entirely, but as the air caught the fins and spun it violently, the bolt slammed into the hull of the barge and bounced away.

Frederick blinked. "Well, that was unfortunate."

CHAPTER TWELVE

FREDERICK HELD HIS arm straight up in the air before dropping it forward. The signal was repeated down the beach, and flames leaped from the shoulders of the amphibious Titan Mechs.

Alice cranked the lever to refill the pressure as high as it would go and armed another launch tube. This time she raised the arc of the sights far above the landing barge and fired.

The javelin whistled as the wind caught it, spinning it up into a buzzing missile as it cut through the air.

"Think you might have aimed a bit high," Frederick said. "Next time—" But his words cut off as Alice's shot found its target. A clipper, rushing through the air toward them, caught the bolt through its front windscreen.

The small airship trembled and then dove. It crashed into the water not far from the landing barge, and when the water hit the boilers, it ruptured in a magnificent display of steam and shrapnel, cutting into the landing barge like a bomb.

"That part wasn't on purpose," Alice said.

Frederick gaped at the sight of the landing barge, now stuck in a lazy circle as though its rudder had been destroyed. "Jacob, I think it best if we let Alice aim."

"Me too," Jacob said with a rapid nod.

The Titan Mechs surged forward as the nearest landing barges closed on the shore. They didn't stand a chance as the arms grabbed entire ships, twisted, and simply plunged them beneath the waves. Jacob was worried about the boilers contacting the water and rupturing, but whoever the pilots were, they knew to be careful, bending their arms at ninety-degree angles to keep them relatively dry.

Alice took aim at another airship, but this time the javelin sailed past, splashing down harmlessly. Jacob cranked the bellows again and armed another tube.

"Be sure to disable the last tube," Frederick said. "Otherwise, you'll get less pressure."

Jacob nodded and flipped all the switches but one. This time Alice's shot pierced the gas chamber of a clipper. It didn't fall immediately, but the vessel turned and fled out to sea, likely returning to whatever ship it had deployed from.

The air filled with smoke and fire as the nearest of Fel's destroyers launched a salvo of explosive shells across the sea. They missed the Titan Mechs and managed to sink one of their own barges. But Jacob and Alice's luck faded with the second salvo.

Two embankments of traps along the beach were there one moment, and a smoking ruin the next. The Titan Mech nearest them caught the shrapnel from another explosion, and one arm went limp, crashing into the water, where the boiler ruptured. Jacob had designed them to be thin, so when the pressure escaped, it didn't destroy the Titan Mech in full. It was able to fight on with one arm, and the traps mounted on its shoulders fired back with a vengeance.

"Keep firing!" Frederick said as he sprinted away, angling for one of the installments that had been bombed.

They found a rhythm soon enough, with Jacob arming and taking care of the bellows while Alice aimed and fired. More than one javelin found its mark. And in an accident, when Alice was aiming for a nearby clipper, the arc took a javelin through the top of a barge. They hadn't thought much of it at first until the vessel slowly sank, scattering its soldiers into the water.

But no matter how many barges they hit, or airships they crippled, the soldiers still marched on the shores. Jacob saw the foremost of them reach the Titan Mechs, and he might never escape that vision of blood and gore dripping from hands he helped build.

"Don't watch," Alice said, pulling him back into the moment. "Prime the cannon again!"

And so he did.

Round after round found its mark as the enemy grew closer, but as Alice's shots gained accuracy with the shorter distance, so did those of the barges and clippers. More ships passed overhead, too small and too fast to identify. Jacob didn't focus on those. He couldn't if he was going to keep up with Alice.

She hammered another salvo that pierced the armored hull of a landing barge. But even that wasn't enough to stop it. They'd need something larger to do that. Something … Jacob's gaze trailed down to the case of compound bombs at his feet.

"What are you doing?" Alice shouted as Jacob dug out a Banger and its outer shell. He tested the fit between the fins of the javelin. "The weight is going to unbalance it."

"Maybe a little." Jacob cleared the launch tube before clicking the igniter, slamming the shell closed, and forcing it into the cage of the javelin's fins.

Alice didn't wait once the assembly was settled in the trap. She tweaked the aim a little higher, and let it fly.

At first, the added weight did exactly what Alice warned him about, dropping the end of the shaft a hair before the wind caught it and spun the entire mass into a wobbly spiral. It crashed into the edge of a barge and somersaulted over the armor.

There was a moment as if the entire world had taken a breath, and then the bomb detonated, sending fire and shrapnel all across the Crystal Sea. Even as the boat sank, they could see it descending in the clear water, and Jacob could see the bodies too.

But they'd passed the point where he could mourn every loss of life. The mass of ships near the shore had thickened, and as they watched, another Titan Mech took a cannon shot from a destroyer straight into its canopy. It didn't fall, but it stilled.

"North," Alice said. "They're on the beach. We have to go."

"We have time," Jacob said, loading another bomb into a launch tube.

Alice aimed and fired, sticking the javelin into the hull of a slow-moving landing ship. The bomb took too long to detonate, and Jacob cursed as he realized the landing ship was heading toward them.

"Run!"

Alice and Jacob sprinted back toward the city as the bomb detonated. Shrapnel and fire rained down across the beach, and the shriek of rent metal filled the air around them.

Two crossbow bolts thunked into the sand at their feet. Jacob didn't know where the shots had come from, but Alice tackled him as another cut through the air by his head.

He rolled and came up with the air cannon, sweeping it across the street until he found the man in the shadows, reloading. The shot took him in the chest and sent him to the cobblestone alley in a bloody heap.

Alice's wrist launcher whipped a series of bolts toward a low roof a moment later, resulting in a sharp cry and a loud thud. "They're already in the city. We have to *move.*"

Jacob didn't argue. He knew the bulk of Belldorn's forces were entrenched to the south. If they were caught from behind, unaware of the extent of what was happening on the beaches, they'd be overrun as surely as that Titan Mech had been.

"We have to reach the south. They have to be warned and we don't have the frequency for those units!"

Alice didn't answer, only spun into an alley and ran flat out. It was half a mile to the southern front, and they'd be exhausted if they kept up the pace, but the consequences if they didn't were far too dark to let that stop them.

CHAPTER THIRTEEN

Part of Furi thought the battle over the Crystal Sea would be like the slow, drawn-out chaos when the Nightingale went down. She couldn't have been more wrong.

Swarms of clippers flanked every destroyer, and while one of Belldorn's Porcupines exchanged fire with them, the clippers would target a single airship until it crashed to the sands below. Furi strangled the harness in her jump seat as the Skysworn shook with a nearby explosion.

"Mary!" Smith shouted. "Two clippers on our back."

The captain of the Skysworn cursed, and the ship lurched to the side, a more aggressive flight pattern than even the smaller ships could follow. "Taking us up!"

"Mary, you need to fire the front chainguns."

"Smith, this is hardly the time to be testing some new gadgetry!"

"As soon as we even out, I'm heading to the gun pod."

"No, I need you on the engine."

"I will be literal steps away, Mary."

"Unless the gun pod gets hit, you oaf!"

"I'll go," Furi shouted over the argument. The Skysworn's nose dipped as they punched through a low cloud, evening out as they lost sight of the clippers.

"We do not have the time," Smith said.

"Rin told me all about it. Just give me the basics!" Furi unlatched her harness and raced to the cabin door. She didn't clip onto the safety lines, instead holding on as she leaned into the wind. It felt like minutes had passed before she reached the hatch to the hold below, but she was familiar with adrenaline.

Smith's voice echoed around her through the horn as she sprinted down the hall, going over the function of the controls, giving her more detail than Rin had. And by the time she dropped into the pod, she almost felt like she knew what she was doing.

"Gunship ahead," Mary shouted.

"Furi, focus on the aft. Those clippers are still on us."

Furi spun the chainguns around, shuddering at the sight of nothing beneath her but clouds and a very, very long fall. She flipped the trigger guards off both handles and squeezed.

She wasn't sure what she'd expected, but the bone-rattling shake of the chaingun wasn't it. She tracked the clippers through the sky, raising the chaingun's arc as she went, until the path of her fire crossed with the path of the clipper, and everything went sideways.

Briefly, the flash of sparks and explosion on the clipper had her celebrating, but the moment was lost in a black flash outside the gun pod. A thunder threatened to deafen her as she saw the panels fall away from the Skysworn. Vaguely, she could hear Smith and Mary above the calamity, understand they'd been hit from below.

It drew her attention away from the remaining clippers as she pointed the chainguns as low as they'd go, finding a strange ship beneath them that couldn't have been large enough for more than one person. It mattered little as the fire from the chaingun tore the tiny airship in half and sent it careening into the sea.

But her new angle of sight gave her a vision of a destroyer, its flags brilliant red against the morning sky, and its metal as dark as the heart of its king. A Fel destroyer, a beast to rival the worst Ballern had to offer. But they were supposed to be on the other side of the sea.

Two panels opened at the front of the Skysworn, and Furi could just make out the spinning barrels before they spewed fire across the clouds.

"The cannons!" Smith cried. "Take out the cannons!"

Furi raised the chainguns after a glance behind showed her the clippers had scattered. She joined in the hail of damage roaring from the Skysworn's bow. Small fire and bolts sailed past the Skysworn, but Mary's minor course deviations kept them guessing, switching their patterns enough to avoid being hit, but also enough they couldn't maintain constant fire on the cannons.

Furi leaned back in her seat as she realized how close they were to the destroyer, and Mary's evasive patterns stopped. She ran down the throat of that cannon after its last round, and Furi could see the shower of sparks all around it. Then that shower became a fireball, and that fireball dropped the entire battery of cannons through the destroyer's deck.

"Engaging thrusters!" Mary shouted.

Furi fumbled with her harness while Smith cursed repeatedly and at great length over the horn. Less than a second after that satisfying click, the Skysworn shot forward, skating below the destroyer as black smoke rose from the decks, and they vanished into a cloud bank.

"Kat! Kat, this is Mary. Answer me now!"

Silence punctuated by the occasional thunder of distant explosions echoed around them.

"What? I'm a bit busy, Mary."

"Fel is over the Crystal Sea. We just engaged a destroyer. They're going to take the western beaches if you don't get that other Porcupine in the air *now*."

"Understood," Kat said with far less irritation in her voice. "Deploying destroyers and Porcupine."

"Look at that," Smith said.

Furi leaned over to the side. From their current vantage point, they looked down on almost the entire fleet over the sea, and one terrible ship at the center of it all.

"What is that?" Mary asked.

"Carrier," Furi said. "One of Ballern's, but I've never heard of it leaving the northern seas. That's how they got the ships across the Crystal Sea. I thought it was the supply ships, but it was more than that."

"Kat, there's a giant ship above the Crystal Sea." Mary read out their bearing and waited.

"Understood. What is it?"

"Furi called it a carrier. Apparently, it's like a giant supply ship that can transport a great deal of smaller ships. I think … it might be bigger than Bollwerk's warships."

"Send the other Porcupine out over the sea. High altitude, full armament. I don't want anything larger than a toothpick left of that vessel."

"Look at their formation," Furi said. "Fel's already securing the beach while Ballern comes in from behind."

"What about the southern front?" Mary asked.

"With the aid of the Dragonriders, we are holding, but they've taken most of the bombed area and moved underground. It is only a matter of time before they make their way through and into the city."

"Then we have to cut off the head. Keep any more from reaching the underground."

"Get to the south, Mary. I'm sending the fleet to the sea, and you do not want to be in the path of what is coming."

"Understood. Furi, Smith, hold on!"

CHAPTER FOURTEEN

DRAKKAR STOOD ON the stirrups of his Dragonwing, cutting between two of Ballern's clippers as he squeezed the handle of a crossbow and let another bolt fly. The wide barbs struck the windscreen, and it collapsed. Drakkar didn't have to see the pilot to know they hadn't been wearing goggles. A properly fitted pilot wouldn't have run.

The small vessel tilted from side to side and veered out to sea, circling back to Ballern's beachhead.

Drakkar angled for Samuel, chasing down the Spider Knight and signaling him to slow down.

"What is it?" Samuel called out.

"Another company is moving to secure the blocks near the underground."

Samuel shook his head. "We can't stop them all. We can do damage to the ships, or we can stop the ground troops, but we can't do both."

Rin's Dragonwing came to glide above them.

"Rin," Drakkar shouted. "It may be time to use the bait."

"No," the Dragonrider said. "I won't unleash a plague like the Emerald Needles unless our survival demands it."

Drakkar looked down at the conflict below them as Belldorn's soldiers exchanged volleys with Ballern's. He had little doubt what would happen if the underground was taken in full. "You may need to come to terms with it, Dragonrider. The hour grows late."

"Tatsu is targeting the dock while the rest of us protect the line," Rin said. "Perhaps it is time we join him and draw those from Ballern back to protect their own."

Drakkar nodded. "A good strategy." He pulled a quiver off his own mount and tossed it to Rin. "You need to manage your ammunition better, Dragonrider."

Rin cast him a smile and clipped the quiver to the saddle. "Thanks, Drakkar." He shot forward, with Drakkar and Samuel in close pursuit.

The Cave Guardian felt a knot loosen in his chest at Rin's suggestion. It showed forethought and strategy, and a strategy not so different from one he would suggest himself, for that matter. And where there was measured thought, there were not often reckless strikes.

But even a measured attack and solid strategy on that battlefield could end in disaster. The bodies and hollowed out crawlers strewn across the dirt and ash below spoke to that fact. Rin had not seen the ruin wrought on Ancora with his own eyes. Had not seen the bodies hung from the wall in Dauschen. Drakkar feared Rin might not fully understand Fel's ruthlessness.

Ballern was a poison, to be sure, but Drakkar had yet to see the sheer violence and unrelenting torment reflected in their society like he'd seen with Fel. It mattered little with the airships and crawlers bearing down on Belldorn. The battle would be fought, and the survivors left to sort through the wreckage.

Soon the ash of the battlefield was behind them, and the villages turned to grasslands before Ballern's temporary docks rose to greet them. Drakkar lifted a spear into his hand, watching the wall for any sign of guards, but he found none.

Rin signaled to dive lower, and Samuel and Drakkar followed him in. All three Dragonwings lit upon the highest rails at the top of the dock. A handful of workstations stretched out before them, rich with tools and food, but little else remained.

But Ballern had made a simple mistake, outside of leaving the docks so poorly secured, and Samuel noticed it as soon as Drakkar had.

"Look there." The Spider Knight pointed to the center of the docks, where dried brush and long-dead timber sat in a chaotic pile, as if a bonfire had been planned. Close by was a neatly stacked supply of coal and firewood, and Drakkar had little doubt it had been harvested for Ballern's forges when the area was cleared of underbrush. But it would be their undoing.

The Cave Guardian slid a pair of Burners out of a pouch inside his cloak. The igniters gave a satisfying click, and flames sprouted from the holes surrounding the orbs as he tossed them through the air.

Rin cast a smile back at them. "A signal fire."

"It will be," Drakkar said. "Find what you can and toss it in. Fuel for their torches would be best."

"Intruders!" a guard shouted, finally spotting the Dragonriders.

Rin released a bolt from his crossbow faster than Drakkar could raise his own. The guard fell with a scream as Rin took aim again. The Dragonrider grimaced and glanced at Samuel. "Leave him. He'll draw attention away from us."

From the look on Samuel's face, he didn't like the idea any more than Drakkar did, but they followed Rin into the air and then split. Each returned to the burgeoning fire with fuel and tinder. Drakkar was last to return, a canister of torch fuel clutched in his hand.

He cast it down on the flames, and the Dragonriders took to the air, leaving a towering fire and choking black smoke in their wake.

✧　✧　✧

LADY KATHERINE PORED over the map on the bridge of her Porcupine. It was the largest of their airships and even eclipsed the size of the other Porcupines due to an extra layer of armor. It made the beast slower in the skies, but it stabilized it as well when the main cannons fired, and the bursts barely shook the markers she had placed on the map.

She'd gambled in letting Ballern establish their small beachhead, hoping to gain intelligence of what their enemy had brought to their shores. But that gamble had become a disaster. Now they were facing a carrier in the Crystal Sea, a new vessel they'd never seen, and more than one report of incredibly small and fast airships had reached her, capable of firing bombs of their own.

Lady Katherine pressed a transmitter anchored to the table, a direct line to one of the Porcupines they'd loaned to Bollwerk and Midstream. "Captain, status."

"Aye, My Lady. Crossing the Bay of Sorrows now. Destination?"

"Continue on your current heading. We have more to the west than anticipated, but the southern lines must hold."

"My Lady," a commander called from across the bridge. "I have another report that more infantry have penetrated the underground."

Lady Katherine slammed her fist into the map. "Root them out. And if we can't pull them out, then we bomb the entrances they've breached."

"My … My Lady? That would destroy more than the southern front if—"

"You heard me! Belldorn has stood against Ballern for centuries, and they will pay for their trespass. They will pay dearly."

"At what cost?"

Lady Katherine heard his question, but she didn't acknowledge it. If Rin refused to use the bait for the Emerald Needles, they had few other options. Mary might be able to deliver a handful of the bait bolts from the Skysworn, but they needed the agility of the Dragonwings to sweep through the ranks of airships.

Their last Porcupine would arrive soon. Brute force would bring down some of their own buildings, but it would save countless others.

War brought sacrifice. A rule to which there was rarely exception.

CHAPTER FIFTEEN

FURI WATCHED THE slow turn of a swarm of something to their north, a cold dread rising in her gut. "No … it can't be."

"What the hell are those?" Mary muttered.

"Strikers," Furi said. "*Strikers!*"

Mary cursed, and Furi took that as a good sign. It meant she knew what they were, and Furi didn't have to explain the tiny assault airships that would be on them in seconds. The short-range strikers could never cross the sea on their own, but onboard a carrier, that was another story entirely.

Furi braced herself against the seat in the gun pod as the Skysworn nosed up and then dove.

"Almost as fast as us," Smith said. "And I don't like the look of those harpoons." Even as he spoke, one glanced off the Skysworn's armored underbelly and detonated, rocking them hard enough to put Smith on the floor and almost throwing him into the gun pod with Furi.

"Are you okay?" Furi called up to him.

He nodded and hopped back to his feet, showing a better recovery from his previous injuries than Furi imagined possible.

"Arm the cannons," Mary growled. "We're taking those bastards down."

Furi flipped the guards off the triggers again. "Chainguns up!" For a moment, she wondered if she knew any of the pilots. As if any Skyborn had been recruited into those elite ranks. Furi almost laughed at the absurdity of that idea.

The Skyborn were fodder for the monarchy. They might have been allowed to rise to the lower ranks on the warships, but they'd never be given their own ships. No matter how small.

She tracked the nearest striker as it wove through the sky, and when the cloud bank broke, she saw the swarm following the leader. There wasn't a need to aim carefully. They'd closed their formation too tight.

Furi squeezed the triggers, the chainguns spinning before they spat fire. Two strikers were consumed by fire a moment later, spiraling down into the sea like birds dying in midair. A third took a direct hit and dropped like a spear, crashing into one of Fel's destroyers before both ships burst into flame.

The formation of strikers scattered, and all sense of order fled in a heartbeat. The easy targets gone, Furi tried to lead some of the strays, eventually catching two as Mary took the Skysworn to its limits. Furi had once heard Jakon talk about a daredevil captain, but he never said where she was from or what ship she'd flown. The longer Mary cut through the skies, evading every striker and salvo that came for them, the more Furi suspected she knew exactly who Jakon had spoken of.

"Cover our back!" Mary shouted over the horn.

Furi swung the gun pod to the aft once more as the rhythmic fire of the forward cannons joined hers.

"Mary," Smith called out. "Mary, you are running low on rounds. Furi has two hundred left and the forward cannons less than that."

Mary cursed. "Tell me when we're down to fifty and we'll disengage."

"One minute of sustained fire. That will drain the forward cannons."

The Skysworn leveled out as another striker fell behind them to Furi's barrage.

"Mary?" Smith said. "Mary, what are you doing?"

"Furi, take aim at the hangars."

Furi started to ask what Mary meant until she looked over her shoulder and saw the carrier looming off the bow.

"Mary!" Furi shouted. "They have ballistae mounted on the carrier. We can't!" But even as she spoke, she swung the gun pod around and Mary dropped their altitude until they were nearly even with the deck. So even, in fact, it felt as if the gun pod itself might shear off when they reached the edge of the massive ship.

But Mary knew the Skysworn better than most captains knew their vessels, and when the forward cannons spun up, throwing round after round into the nearest hangar, Furi joined them.

It wasn't much at their current speed. They only had about fifteen seconds to deliver as much damage as they could before Mary pulled up in an evasive maneuver, skimming a ballista as Furi shot it to pieces.

The Skysworn looped around and dove beneath the carrier, vanishing into a cloud bank that Mary stayed inside until they exited on the far end, nearly to the beaches.

From above, Furi could just make out the Titan Mechs that were still fighting. Some were flat on the ground, and another was in pieces inside a crater in the sand, but two of the amphibious mechs fought on, while more of the bipedal monstrosities had joined them.

They couldn't keep Ballern away forever, but they'd protected the docks from the infantry. Furi looked back to the sea, and it crawled with more of the landing barges.

"Looks bad," Smith said.

"We still have the docks."

"For how long?"

Smith didn't finish his question before a squadron of brigs shot by overhead. Furi watched as they dove at the beach, and flak cannons rained shrapnel on the incoming barges. As the brigs pulled away, some of the barges drifted listlessly, and Furi had little doubt what had happened to all aboard those ships.

The brigs circled back, and while some engaged the small strikers, others limped away, damaged by harpoons.

Mary guided the Skysworn into the airspace around the docks.

"Smith, how many more rounds do we have?"

"On the docks? A handful. Enough for ten minutes of sustained fire, maybe."

"What about the workshop?"

"If we can get to it, a bit more. I believe there are ten belts assembled."

Mary hesitated. "Landing lines, then. We drop in, pull you out, and get back in the fight."

"We need to repair the armor on the hull first. One more hit from those harpoons could sink us."

"Make it fast."

The Skysworn drifted backward until it bumped up against the superstructure and came to a stop.

CHAPTER SIXTEEN

T HE NEXT CORNER brought them to the edge of the battlefield. Jacob looked out over the ash and fire and ruin. Belldorn's infantry positioned themselves behind the rubble of destroyed buildings, while Ballern's forces had done much the same. It appeared they'd fought to a stalemate not far from the entrance to the underground.

Above them soared three Dragonwings, one with a cloak snapping in the wind and polished bracers Jacob couldn't mistake for anyone else. He squeezed Alice's arm and pointed up at the trio.

"Drakkar?" Alice said. "It looks like they're landing. Hurry."

A bolt whistled past Jacob's head and shattered on the brick wall behind him. He ducked and ran as fast as he could to the slim shelter of the crumbling wall. Alice grabbed his arm and slowed as they reached a pocket of Belldorn soldiers.

"Ballern is inside the city to the north! Watch your backs!"

Alice's warning was repeated in a circle, and the last man raised the polished box of a transmitter to his mouth. Jacob heard the warning going out to the other infantry, and he only hoped it would reach them in time.

"This would have been easier if Lady Katherine had provided the frequencies for her units."

"Too much risk. She doesn't know us. She might trust Mary, but for all she knows, *we* are the spies inside the city."

The conversation died off as they ran to intercept the circling Dragonwings.

"Drakkar!" Jacob called out, but the Cave Guardian didn't hear him.

Alice raised her voice, reaching an octave Jacob never could as she screamed Drakkar's name.

This time the Cave Guardian looked over the side of his mount and signaled the others. The Dragonwings swooped low, alighting on rubble perches behind the mangled ruin of steel and what appeared to have once been a playground for the children of Belldorn.

"Alice!" Drakkar said. "What are you two doing here? I thought you would be with the Titan Mechs."

"We lost one last we saw. Ballern is inside the city. And Fel, Fel has ships on the water like you have never seen."

Drakkar looked to Rin. "Our options are fleeting, Dragonrider."

"What's Kat's plan?" Jacob asked, rubbing his chin. "If the Porcupines circle around, they can bomb those ships into oblivion."

"Mary and the others are docked," Drakkar said. "They encountered a new kind of airship over the Crystal Sea."

"Strikers," Samuel said. "Sound nasty. Why don't we regroup at the Skysworn?"

"It'll take us a while to get there," Jacob said.

Samuel laughed, a harsh, humorless thing. "No, it won't, kid. Hop on."

"With me, Alice, if you wish," Drakkar said.

"Well, I'm sure not riding with Samuel."

Drakkar smiled and offered his hand, helping to swing her up into the rear saddle. "You are very wise."

Alice mouthed the word "sorry" to Jacob as he made his way up to Samuel.

"It'll be just like riding around Ancora on Bessie," Samuel said, hoisting him up. "Only a hundred feet higher, and if you fall off, you die. So don't fall off."

"Fasten the harnesses at your waist," Rin called out. "It will keep you in the saddle even if you lose consciousness."

Jacob slid his legs into the loops and fastened the center line around his waist before pulling it tight. When he looked to Alice, she'd already done the same.

"Let's go," Rin said, and it was all the warning they had.

At first, Jacob wondered why Rin had warned them about losing consciousness, and then Samuel hammered out a brief rhythm on the plates mounted to the Dragonwing, and the world became a blur. He could barely keep his eyes open against the wind until he leaned closer to Samuel and looked down at the city instead of forward at their destination.

If it wasn't for the battle below and the dread in his chest for what was yet to come, it would have been one of the most amazing things he'd ever done. The glider packs were one thing, carrying him through the air and responding to his every whim, but the Dragonwing felt like riding on a bolt fired from a ballista.

He could not find the words to express the exhilaration or the gut-wrenching thought of what *would* happen if he fell off at that speed.

But as fast as the Dragonwing was in the air, it came to a stop almost as abruptly, smashing Jacob's face against Samuel's armored back, so that when he pulled away, a vaguely face-shaped pattern of sweat and oil was pressed into the polished metal.

Jacob leaned back and looked around, trying to understand how they could possibly be perched on the deck of the Skysworn already.

Samuel glanced over his shoulder and grinned. "Well, not quite like Bessie."

Jacob gave a shaky nod as he unbuckled his harness and slid off the back of the Dragonwing. Samuel followed after opening the clasps along his leggings. Jacob was still a little unsure of his footing when Alice crashed into him, crushing him in a hug.

"That was amazing! Can you believe that? I want to learn to ride. Jacob, don't you? Jacob?"

For a time, all he could muster up was a weak smile.

"Maybe it doesn't agree with your biomechanics?" Alice asked.

"Sudden stops and drops?" Smith asked as he climbed out of the hatch in the center of the deck. "No, it most certainly does not." He slapped Jacob on the back.

Samuel exchanged grips with Smith. "Good to see you again."

"Always good to see a friend in dark times, Samuel. Welcome aboard."

"Rin?" Furi said, climbing out of the hold behind Smith. "Rin!"

He opened his arms to her and didn't let go for some time.

"Rin, you'll be so jealous. I got to use the chainguns."

"In combat?"

"Yes, in combat. How do you think we lost so much armor?"

Rin's eyebrows crawled higher. "*Lost* armor?"

"We did," Mary said, walking off the docks and back onto the Skysworn. "Took a few shots from the strikers. Nothing Furi couldn't handle."

"Me?" Furi said with a laugh. "More like you and Smith. I didn't know an airship this big could move like that."

Mary smiled at the compliment before turning to the others. "What are you all doing here?"

"You didn't answer your transmitter," Samuel said.

"Yes, well, I may have been speaking with Kat or fleeing for our lives, so you'll have to excuse that."

"Have you had word from Eva?" Drakkar asked.

Mary nodded. "Yes. They've moved against Fel's ships on the Crystal

Sea. It's a mess, Drakkar. I'm not going to lie to you. The brigs can do tremendous damage to the seagoing vessels, but to dive on them exposes their gas chambers to attacks from above."

"A stalemate, then."

"For the moment. Until they lose one too many brigs."

"Does Lady Katherine have a plan?" Alice asked.

Mary blew out a breath. "Many."

"The Porcupines could destroy the forward lines," Jacob said.

"Too close to the city," Mary said. "Lady Katherine won't risk it unless it's a last resort."

"She has more than one last resort in mind," Rin said. "Lady Katherine has provided us the bait boxes for the Emerald Needles. I fear to unleash a swarm such as that."

Mary looked up from her hands and studied Rin. "You're smart to be worried, but we may not have another choice."

"It would help if we knew how they were communicating," Furi said. "If things haven't changed since my dad was in the fleet, then it should still be a series of beeps to give orders."

"Beeps?" Alice asked. "What do you mean?"

"The communicators they use. It isn't words, exactly, but beeps and changes in pitch."

"Did you ever use them on your ship?" Jacob asked.

"No, but the Nightingale wasn't coordinating with ships they couldn't see. We used flags. But communicators should be all over the carrier. Every hangar would have one." Furi tapped her chin. "The supply ships should have them too."

"So the beeps are like a code?" Alice asked.

Furi nodded. "Ballern doesn't have transmitters like you do in the east. At least not that I've ever seen. We just need to get a receiver and we could listen in. But more than that, we need a translator."

Jacob glanced between Furi and Alice. "You're a translator."

Furi laughed and shook her head. "No, no. It's a document that lists out a series of maneuvers. If we know what they're doing ahead of time, Lady Katherine could intercept them."

Jacob nodded. "We could try the beachhead, but I doubt there's much left. That fire was huge."

"Yes, it was," Samuel said, slapping Drakkar on the shoulder.

"Maybe we could find something in the wreckage? Either way, Ballern's rear line is too dense, and the way the ships are acting as armor in front of the carrier would funnel us together until we were easy targets."

Alice looked up when an airship's engines roared to life, sending the vessel to circle out to sea. "What about one of those?"

Jacob pursed his lips. "A clipper? It's possible. They're smaller than the Skysworn."

"With the new gliders?" Alice asked, but the roar of the engines continued above them.

"You mean jump off an airship?"

"Probably easier than the wall."

Jacob could still feel the trembling walls of Fel as they were brought low. Leaping off an airship didn't seem nearly as terrifying as that moment had.

"I think those clippers would be too noisy," Alice said. "Maybe the Dragonriders would help."

"You two are mad." Furi ran her fingers through her hair. "But I've known Rin since we were kids. He'll help."

Rin breathed out a low laugh. "You assume much, Furi. How do you know I haven't changed the reckless ways of my youth?"

In answer, Furi walked over to Rin's mount and patted the Dragonwing between its huge eyes. "Call it a hunch."

Rin's smile grew to a broad grin.

Crackling whispers rose from the cabin, and Mary hurried inside. "Say again?"

Jacob and Alice followed.

"Skysworn, avoid the beaches. Porcupines will engage in a blanket operation shortly."

Mary looked back at Jacob and Alice. "Lady Katherine, our losses will be substantial."

"I don't have any other options."

"What if you did?"

"If you have an idea, speak it now."

Mary took a deep breath. "We may have a way to intercept messages between the airships, and possibly Fel's vessels, as well."

"How?"

Mary repeated Furi's idea about seizing a communicator from a supply ship, or even the carrier itself.

"Stay away from that carrier, Skysworn. We've lost enough ships to it already. You have my blessing on one condition. The Dragonriders *must* agree to deploy the bait. This is not negotiable."

Jacob followed Mary's gaze back to the door where Rin, Furi, and Smith stood.

"It's up to you," Mary said.

Rin gave one sharp nod of his head. "I hope the lady will help us eliminate the Emerald Needles in the aftermath."

"Whatever you and Canopy need, Belldorn will offer it. But I cannot offer aid if we lose the city."

Rin looked down at Furi and closed his eyes. "Then it is agreed."

"Good. I expect a status update within the hour. Succeed or fail, we must keep the lines of communication open."

Furi opened the locker in the back of the cabin and pulled out her glider pack. "Then we better go."

"You're coming too?" Alice asked.

"You don't know what you're looking for. I can help."

Alice nodded. "Good. Let's go."

CHAPTER SEVENTEEN

A DRENALINE MIGHT HAVE signaled to Alice that she was ready to go, but it did not overrule her preference for caution and planning. She took more than a few magazines for the air cannon at her hip and several more clips for the bolt glove. Alice was also glad Smith had given her a pair of goggles. The wind on the back of the Dragonwings was severe.

If they were going to land on an enemy ship with no way off but the gliders, then she was going to be ready for anything. And *anything* had proven itself a formidable adversary more than once.

Alice followed Drakkar and Furi out onto the Skysworn's deck. Furi had been right about Rin. He hadn't so much as hesitated before agreeing to take them deep into Ballern's forces. No one said it, but Alice knew how big a risk they were taking. The thought of losing more people chilled her, but the thought of what could happen if they did nothing was a far darker prospect.

Drakkar offered his hand and hoisted Alice onto the Dragonwing's back. She adjusted her seat and then slid into the harness that would keep her from being thrown off. The Dragonwing's scales felt soft beneath her fingers, almost furry on the outside of the larger plates of chitin.

She twisted around in her seat to get a better view of Samuel and Jacob. The Spider Knight was still fastening the clasps on his leggings while Jacob secured his own harness. Alice reassured herself that even if they were spotted, with the speed of the Dragonwings, any ship would be hard-pressed to shoot them down.

Despite her worries of what was to come, Alice couldn't shake her memory of the ruins in the Deadlands. There was more to the Great Machines, of that she was sure, though she still didn't know what it could be. Why would the Children of the Dark Fire have stayed so loyal to their mechanical gods? Furi thought it might have been a ruse, simply an idol to help control their followers. And maybe she was right. There was power in symbols, a strength they'd seen in Fel and in what Mordair and his brother had wrought in Dauschen, Ancora, and now on Belldorn's shores.

Drakkar turned in his saddle. "Ready?"

Alice adjusted her goggles again before wrapping her hand in the thick rope across the saddle that served as something like a pommel. "Ready."

Drakkar grabbed the wide drumsticks from their mount and tapped out a quick rhythm as Rin and Furi took to the air. There was a brief pause as they hovered over the docks, and then it felt as though she was being pulled backward as the Dragonwing shot toward the horizon.

A glance to the side showed Jacob and Samuel close to them, with Jacob in the rear, crouched down behind the Spider Knight. Alice smiled at the sight and wondered if Jacob had forgotten he was wearing goggles this time.

The Titan Mechs Jacob and Smith had worked on were only in sight for a moment, but seeing them defend the outskirts of the docks gave Alice a sense of pride in what her friends had done. She hoped Jacob knew how much good his work might do, and that he wasn't saddened only by the carnage it might cause.

She supposed, in that way, Jacob would always be tied to Charles's legacy, a legacy that was far more complicated than she had first realized. But she'd read more of the journals Samuel had brought back, more of the deeds of a man she looked to as a grandfather, but she could not recognize him in many of those earlier words he'd written.

A bright flash caught her eye, and Alice watched as one of Fel's great destroyers on the water split in two, spilling sailors and fire alike across the sea. But the cost had been high, and a brig limped away in a cloud of black smoke. She lost sight of the exchange as the Dragonwing climbed higher.

The battle didn't seem real from that height, as the smallest of Ballern's strikers almost disappeared against the vast blue and crystalline greens of the sea.

The shadow of the carrier loomed in the distance. It looked like an easy target until they grew closer, and Alice could clearly see the many ballistae mounted along its perimeter. It was not only the ballistae that threatened the airspace around it. Several cannons to rival those of Belldorn pivoted in slow arcs as the Dragonriders passed by far to the north.

The Dragonwing changed direction, following the erratic pattern of Rin's mount, and shaking Alice's grip on the rope. Their flight evened out and slowed. Before she had time to prepare herself, Drakkar spoke.

"Alice, go, now."

She looked down, and far below them, drifting slowly to the east, waited a supply ship. Alice didn't stop to think, only freed her hand from the rope, and slid out of the harness. Even as she made ready to jump, she saw Furi fall first, a thin shadow against an infinite sea. She tapped Drakkar on the shoulder, and then slid off the Dragonwing, the air catching the flaps of her glider pack as if wanting to pull the entire assembly away. But Alice knew that was nothing compared to what would happen when she threw the lever.

She risked a glance back up at the Dragonwings and found Jacob falling beside her.

He held out three fingers, then two, before Furi, Alice, and Jacob pulled the levers to open their gliders.

The impact was far more violent than what Alice remembered from the wall. And impact was the only word she could think to call it as the wings caught the air, and the snap of inertia and resistance threatened to tear them from her back.

Once the gliders leveled off, it almost felt like they were motionless, suspended in air compared to the Dragonwings, surrounded by an ocean breeze that offered a calm she could not feel.

Furi pulled up, high enough she could talk to the others. "I'm still not sure on landing this!"

"It'll work," Jacob shouted back. "Just pull the lever back in when you're above the deck. But either roll or run, or you're going to get hurt."

They'd gone over the gliders with Furi, but to call their current predicament a trial by fire was a vast understatement. Furi needed to lead the way, as she was the only one who knew her way around Ballern's supply ships. But Alice worried Furi might pick an area to land that was good for what they needed to find, but impossible for the gliders.

Furi led them in a lazy circle as they grew closer to the deck. It wasn't long before they could make out more details, and Alice was happy to see the deck itself was empty of soldiers.

But instead of the wide-open center of the deck, Furi angled for a small strip of wood to the aft. It showed her inexperience with the gliders. Alice knew the walk was bigger than it looked, but considering the rest of the ship, she doubted Furi could stop in time. And almost on cue, Furi snapped her wings shut, the glide going into a short fall that led to her stumbling and crashing into a cabin door.

Alice cursed under her breath as she circled around again and saw a soldier standing over Furi with a sword drawn. A *sword,* of all things. Furi had her hands up, inching away from the man as he leaned forward.

Alice took aim with her wrist launcher, letting it spin up as she awkwardly tried to control the glider with one arm. She couldn't hope to hit the man in that kind of wind, but if she could hit the cabin …

Three bolts thunked into the wood, and the soldier looked up, confusion crossing his face as he tracked Alice. He never saw the thick blade Furi pulled from a sheath half-concealed in her boot. Never saw the flash of steel before it slammed into the base of his jaw.

He crumbled in a bloody heap as Alice aimed for the center of the deck, beneath the gas chambers. Her wings snapped closed at the last moment, and she sprinted into the fall, slipping to the side of the cabins before hurrying around the back.

Alice found Furi there, standing over the body, blood staining her hands and the blade she held.

Jacob joined them a moment later. "No hiding that. Come on. We have to find the communicator and get out of here."

Furi nodded before picking up the sword. At the center, the cross guard was adorned with a small, engraved flame with the shape of a pennant carved around it. She cut the sheath off the soldier's belt and clipped it to her own before sliding the sword home.

"Children of the Dark Fire," Alice whispered. "I know that symbol."

"Yes," Furi said. "In Ballern, they call it the Queen's Crest. It looks a little different now that we know more of the story behind it." She led the way into the cabin.

Jacob hesitated and then dragged the body inside too. It wasn't going to help with the pool of blood outside, but Alice wasn't sure if spreading the blood inside was a better idea. But there wasn't time to argue. Furi was already heading down a narrow set of stairs.

Alice followed, pausing at the dim lights that stretched the length of the ceiling. She ran a finger across them and frowned. "What is this?"

"Trapped gas," Jacob said. "Charles had something like it in Ancora, but not nearly that big. It also exploded, so don't touch it."

Alice yanked her hand away like it might be burned.

Furi opened the first door she came to and studied the room. Alice leaned in next to her and saw nothing out of the ordinary. Three beds sat unmade, stacked so close on top of one another it made the Skysworn look spacious. Lockers in the corner and an old photograph tucked into a bedframe were all the decoration in the bleak space.

"Barracks near the rear mean this is a crawler transport." Furi pulled the door closed.

"What does that mean?" Jacob asked. "Good news or bad news?"

"I don't know yet. It means the ship has a large crew, but if they've already deployed the crawlers, most of them will be gone."

"And if they haven't?" Jacob asked.

Furi grimaced. "If they haven't, we may need to run. Follow me."

She took off down the hall with renewed speed. Where before her steps had been tentative, as if she wasn't entirely sure where they were, now Alice had to jog to keep up. Outside of the main hall, shadows cloaked the corridors. They were an excellent place to hide, but it could also conceal things they should be hiding from.

Other than a few shallow alcoves with corkboards plastered with all manner of random things, the hallways were bare. The only thing that changed as they turned at another intersection was that the gray metal walls gave way to dark stained wood showing the wear and shadows of untold years.

Beyond, lit by the sun, waited a massive cargo hold, empty of all but a few soldiers in the far corner. Alice took note of the titanic gears and pistons propping up the second level of the hold, and she could only imagine what Jacob thought of it.

The gear towers in Fel had been imposing, but this was built into an *airship.* If Bollwerk did the same, they could carry twice as many troops.

Maybe more.

Furi tugged on her sleeve and pointed to a door just off the corridor. Alice twisted the lever to open it, and it squeaked like a knife on a plate. There wasn't a point in waiting after that. She shoved her way into the room and found a soldier drawing a crossbow.

"Knife!" Jacob shouted as he raised the air cannon, catching a second soldier whom she hadn't seen in an alcove. The report deafened the room, and Alice had little doubt the soldiers from the hold would be coming to see what had happened.

She didn't let it slow her aim as her wrist launcher spun up and lodged two bolts in the man's chest before he could fire his crossbow. His weapon clattered to the ground as he grabbed his chest, as if he could keep the blood from draining away.

Alice didn't wait for him to die. She cracked his skull with her bolt glove and let him fall to the floor, covering his crossbow. Alice looked away. She didn't need to see the blank eyes and shock, staring at nothing.

"This is it," Furi said, gesturing to an alcove with a wide metal console. "This is what we're here for."

Jacob stuck his head out the door before slamming it closed. "They're coming."

"Move," Alice said, elbowing past him. She drew a compound bomb from a pouch on her glider pack.

"Maybe we don't want to be on the ship when that goes off," Jacob started to say.

But Alice clicked the igniter, flipped the shell closed, and hurled the device down the corridor. She caught the eye of one of the soldiers while the others watched the metal ball roll past them. Alice slammed the door.

"Was it a dud?" Furi asked a moment before the entire world shook around them. The corridor channeled the blast, and the edges of the door flashed orange and red as fire scoured everything that had been standing outside.

"No," Alice said. "But if they didn't know we were here before …"

Furi huffed and looked down at the console, jamming her blade into the corner of a panel before prying it up. She pulled a length of wire out with it and a strange lever with what appeared to be coiled copper, springs, and a circular strike pad.

"The antenna is mounted outside. We'll never get it, but if we can wrap the wire around something that conducts the signal, it should work."

"Like the transmitter on the Skysworn?" Jacob asked.

Furi nodded. "Exactly."

The ship shook beneath their feet, and something loud crashed outside the door before the screech of rent metal followed. The corridor brightened, and Alice frowned as the floor started to bend away at the edge of the room.

She pointed at the widening gap. "I think we might have a problem."

CHAPTER EIGHTEEN

J ACOB THREW THE door open and reeled away from what waited on the other side. Pieces of the airship cascaded through the air below them, falling into the Crystal Sea.

The corridor was almost gone, with only a fragment of steel hanging onto the opposite wall.

"We can jump," Furi said, "take the gliders."

Jacob shook his head. "Not from here. You open the glider in that, and the debris will cut the wings to pieces. And if you're lucky enough not to hit any of the falling metal, pretty sure the impact would still kill you."

He glanced at the room behind them. No other way out. No passage, no hatch, no ladder, nothing. But one thing he was sure of, the longer they waited, the less likely they were going to survive.

"Come on. Keep your toes against the wall and fall forward until you can prop yourself up on the opposite wall. Follow me." He turned to Alice and took some measure of comfort in the calm on her face. However worried she was about the ship collapsing around them, she looked more determined than anything else.

"Wait! We need a translator." Furi rushed back to the alcove, reaching up to tear something off the wall and stuffing it into a pouch at her side.

Jacob grabbed the doorframe and swung out over the bottomless corridor, letting his heels slam into the outer wall. It didn't move under the impact. With the frame of the ship bending farther, he could see that the steel beneath their feet was part of a larger plate. The force of the blast had sheared away a great deal of the floor, but a sliver framed each side above the abyss.

He took a deep breath and let himself fall forward. The hall was narrow. Narrow enough he could touch either side with his arms outstretched, but his heart still hammered before his palms caught the far wall and he stared into the falling field of debris.

Jacob didn't look back, only moved one leg at a time where his heel and toes balanced on the remnants of the floor. One hand, one foot, next hand, and he continued that way, inching down what remained of the hall as the ship rattled all around them and started to list to one side.

He spared a look to Alice and Furi. Both had their palms on the opposite wall and were shuffling as quickly as he had. Every foot they covered gave them a less severe debris field. If they could just make it to the end, they could be off that ship with ease.

But even then, could the communicator survive the sea? Jacob cursed under his breath and carefully pressed the transmitter in his cuff.

"Skysworn, we have a problem."

"Go ahead," Mary's voice answered.

"Might have blown a hole in the target. Trying to get out now, but package won't survive the water."

"Smith, engines, now. Where are you? How do we find you?"

"Supply ship to the northwest of the dock. It'll be the one raining metal and fire and crashing."

Mary cursed. "What can we do, Jacob?"

"We just have to keep Furi out of the water. Get as close as you can."

"On our way."

A horrible screech echoed through the hall, and Jacob felt the wall slipping away beneath his fingers.

"Hurry!" Alice shouted.

And he did, as best he could, one foot, one hand, and another over and over as the wall grew farther away. And he knew Alice and Furi didn't have the same reach he did.

Jacob threw himself to the side, bouncing onto the surviving plates of the corridor before he spun to reach for Alice. She jumped past him, nearly to the ladder, when the wall finally gave way.

Furi slipped, her eyes going wide as gravity did the rest.

With only a second to spare, Jacob reached out to grab Furi's glider pack. But the angle was awkward, and it dragged him forward, showing him the long fall to the sea once more until Alice grabbed his pack and leveraged him back, leaning against Furi's inertia with all her weight.

"Don't drop me!" Furi cried out as the debris falling away became a dripping inferno and smoke began to fill the corridor.

Slowly, by inches, they dragged Furi into the corridor, and she rested her cheek on the cold steel floor.

"Come on," Alice said, giving them no further time to recover. "Up the ladder."

Jacob followed her, his breath ragged as he raced up the rungs, offering a hand to Furi as they reached the deck and the pool of blood they'd left behind. He ran to the rails at the stern of the ship, skidding into them as the entire vessel tilted further.

They had moments before the ship either exploded or fell from the sky. Moments before the Skysworn appeared in the distance, and Mary dove close to the sea. But she couldn't get closer, and Jacob knew it. Either the gliders would take them far enough, or they wouldn't, and the exercise would be a waste.

A boiler ruptured near the front of the ship. There was no mistaking the boom of a tank under too much pressure, or the arc of steam and shrapnel as it billowed into the sky above. The deck shifted violently beneath their feet.

"Now!" Alice said as she hopped onto the railing and dove.

Furi followed, and Jacob did the same as he regained his footing.

Alice kept her arms tight and sped toward the water before throwing her wings open and swooping up into the air. It was a maneuver they knew, but Furi couldn't possibly have known.

"Do what Alice did!" Jacob shouted over the roar of wind and the staccato of explosions above them. The first traces of burning debris fell around them as Jacob opened his wings, and Furi followed.

She didn't have the angle quite right and nearly flipped backward before getting her glider under control, but they were airborne, and in moments had crossed out of the debris field with nothing more than a few singed bits.

Alice angled toward the Skysworn as Mary adjusted her position, tilting the ship slightly toward them to give them an easier target. Alice folded her wings at the last possible second, crashing onto the deck and rolling to a stop before she hit the railing.

Jacob followed, stumbling on the high angle of the deck before spinning to watch Furi. He could see the fear on her face as she dove hard toward the deck, pulling up a little too hard at the last moment as she collapsed the wings and squeaking as she dropped some seven feet to the deck below.

The deck's angle probably saved her a broken bone as Mary shifted the bow back toward land, and they sped away from the supply ship as it finally broke in two, casting a tower of flame skyward before it crashed into the sea below.

Jacob flopped onto the deck and took a deep breath.

Alice rolled over to grin at him. "Sorry about that."

He laughed quietly and let his head fall back against a coil of rope.

The hatch opened next to Furi, and Smith poked his head out. "Anyone dead?"

"Not yet," Furi muttered, rubbing her elbow.

Alice pulled Jacob up to his feet before Smith did the same for Furi.

"Into the cabin, all of you." Smith herded them forward along the railing, past the coils of landing lines and lockers, before pulling the cabin door closed.

"Are you all okay?" Mary asked.

"Okay enough," Alice said. "A few bruises and burns here."

"Same," Furi said, and Jacob agreed with a nod.

"What happened on that ship?" Smith asked. "I have never seen a modern supply ship torn apart like that."

Jacob raised an eyebrow and turned to Alice, who gave Smith an awkward smile as she shook out her hair.

"I might have thrown one of the compound bombs into the hold."

Mary spun around in her chair and gawked at Alice. "That would have blown a hole straight through the hull."

"I'm aware of that," Alice said.

Smith choked back a small laugh.

"Pretty much tore the ship in half," Jacob said. "Unfortunately, we were still inside it."

"Well, yes, I didn't expect it to do that."

Furi blew out a breath as she shrugged her glider pack off her shoulders and unfastened the leg straps. "We're alive, they aren't, and we have what we went for. It was a good day."

Jacob could see the small scorch marks on the edge of one of Furi's wings that hadn't fully retracted yet. It had been close. Too close.

"You got it?" Mary asked.

Furi pulled the communicator out and passed it to Smith. He turned it over in his hands and frowned. "This looks ancient. This is what they use to communicate?"

Furi nodded and opened the pouch that had been strapped to her leg. "And this is the translator." She unrolled the parchment to show a document written in Mokuskrit, Standard, dots, and lines.

Smith's eyes widened. "That is Ohm's code. Targrove used to talk about the code. It was more common before the Deadlands War."

"I've never heard it called that," Furi said. "We just need the translator to read it. We couldn't get the antenna, but I think if you wire this into your transmitter, it should be able to receive."

Smith ran his fingers down the length of wire and nodded. "I believe I can weld this to a clamp. If we leave it attached, it would be able to transmit?"

"I don't know," Furi said. "Oh, but if it tried to send your voice instead of a simple code, I don't know what it would do. It could tell them something is wrong."

"Exactly. I will get to work on this."

With that, Smith made his way out of the cabin, headed to his workshop below decks.

Jacob and Alice slipped out of their glider packs, and Jacob went to work investigating the damage. None of them were burned through, which was a lucky thing, but his own pack looked the worst. He'd need to replace the wings as soon as he could. For now, patches would hold, but he wouldn't want to rely on that for too long. The extra stress from the stitching around any patch could tear a hole.

He glanced at Furi's scorched wings. It *had* been close.

CHAPTER NINETEEN

LATER THAT DAY, Gladys found herself at a small bar inside Fel, sitting beside George in a tall chair that was a bit too high for her. It made her feel like a kid, and that somewhat annoyed her. But the feeling was brief and fled soon after the royal guard struck up a conversation with the bartender.

"Not from Fel, are you?" the bartender asked.

George let a small smile slip. "No, my friend. We are certainly not."

"Did you come in with the fisherfolk? Or on one of them airships?"

George glanced at Gladys. "We came through the wall in a crawler from Bollwerk."

The bartender nodded and slid a mug to George. "I'll get something for your daughter. Looks a bit young for the drink."

Neither of them corrected his assumption. George sipped at his mug and choked.

The bartender grinned. "Strong yes, but it gets the job done."

"Sir, I believe *I* may be too young for this drink." But George didn't put the mug down. His proceeding sips were only somewhat more measured.

The exchange made the bartender laugh as he passed them a small bowl filled with strange-looking nuts and seeds.

"What are these?" Gladys asked.

"Elderwood berries from Ballern. Not really berries, mind you, but that's what they call them." He shrugged and picked up one of the long thin seeds beside it. "These are what you really want. One of my favorites. One of the king's favorites, too, I'll have you know." He paused. "Though I suppose you lot may not care about that. From the lands to the far east they are."

"Ancora?" Gladys asked, knowing that was the furthest city to the east on their continent.

"No, lass, much farther than that. Across the Silver Gulf itself. Beyond the whirlpools, they say."

Gladys had heard stories of the mighty currents far out into the Silver Gulf. Huge spirals of water that sometimes collided and sometimes generated enough force to pull the largest ships into their depths. The seas were treacherous, and she'd long been taught that fact had given rise to the age of airships.

But if that were truly the case, why did Fel still maintain a seagoing fleet? It was a question that had bothered her on more than one occasion.

"Do you trade with the lands beyond the gulf?"

"Me? No, I don't much trade with anyone, lass. I'm here to serve drink and tell stories when folks have none of their own to tell. But I'm afraid most of the stories in Fel of late are dark indeed."

George gave Gladys a meaningful look before turning a smile on the bartender. "I may have a story worth your time. One from the desert villages, and Midstream itself."

The bartender's eyes lit up. "Have you been? It was a beautiful place before the warlords came. I haven't been in twenty years or so, I suspect."

"You have heard tales of Rana? The great warlord of a lost village not far from Gareth Cave?"

The bartender blew out a breath. "Of course I have. Everyone here has heard the tale of Rana."

"But did you know it was an Ancoran who threw him down? Killed a warlord to save the Princess of Midstream, no less! I would have never thought her an Ancoran, so pale as she was with brilliant red hair."

The bartender's attention was locked on George now. This was indeed a story he hadn't heard, but Gladys thought his attention had been piqued by George's description of Alice.

"Pale as linen with hair of fire?" the bartender asked. "Like the stories about those across the Silver Gulf?"

George smiled. "Yes. And she was befriended by our princess, did you know? In many ways, that girl was saved by our princess as much as the princess was saved herself. I think those tales about the nations across the gulf may have been exaggerated. If you were to visit Belldorn, you would find more than a few not so different from those stories."

"That may be, sir, but the story of the princess and the Ancoran was not a tale I had heard! The fact the princess still lived would have been enough to bring a warmth to my heart. There's been goings on in Fel, bad things, I tell you, and I worried for your city. Good people there, and there's good people here. I know it can be hard to see, but it's true. I swear it on my bar."

Gladys reached out and took the bartender's hand, and the man froze when the cuff of her cloak rose to reveal the edge of a silver bracelet. Gladys pulled the sleeve higher to reveal it in full.

"You ... you're ..."

"She is," George whispered, casting a scowl at Gladys. "But I'd be most appreciative if you could save that tale until tomorrow."

"Of course, of course. Well, perhaps not tomorrow, but I'll promise to keep your secret until this evening." The bartender leaned in closer. "Does that make you a royal guard, sir? Now them I've heard tales about! Fighting all manner of desert creatures and piloting a machine that can crush armor."

George smiled and put his arm around Gladys. "Did you hear that, Princess? We royal guard are known as far north as Fel."

Gladys groaned. "I'm never going to hear the end of this."

"When this … war is done. When the fighting stops, I'd like to come see your city again."

The bartender didn't call Midstream a village, and that made Gladys proud in a way she hadn't expected. It had long been a village, but her family had raised it up to be more than that. An oasis in the Deadlands where there were few, and those often had walls to keep people out as much as shield their own.

But Midstream had better ways to keep the Tail Swords and Fire Lizards at bay. If Red Death had been a bigger threat in the desert, then perhaps Midstream would have had walls too. But as long as she could, Gladys would keep the city open to all travelers and traders alike because she knew, as her parents did, some who visited would never leave. They'd settle down and open stores of their own and build new homes until they too were part of the fabric that held the city together.

Gladys folded her hands, one on top of the other. "We would welcome you. Please visit when you can. And please be careful in Fel. Mordair may be gone, but Archibald has already found pockets of his loyalists who remained."

"You mean the Speaker? Pretty words that man has. But pretty words and no action invite revolutions. And I've seen enough of those in my life. Reckon he'll find more of those traitors sheltering in the city. And it's why *you* should be gone by tonight."

"We will," George said, sliding two large silver coins across the bar, engraved with the cityscape of Fel. "And I thank you for your honesty, friend. May the desert find you well."

"An honor." The bartender bowed ever so slightly to the pair of them.

✧　　✧　　✧

THEY WERE ALMOST to the exit when a cloaked figure appeared from a corner table, pulling back his hood to reveal a closely cropped beard and deep-set eyes.

Gladys didn't miss the shift in George's posture. Subtle, but putting him in a position to strike the man down without Gladys being in the path of his blade. As if she'd be worried about a single man.

"A word, wanderers," the man said. "I could not help but overhear that you are from Midstream."

George risked a glance at Gladys, and she didn't miss the hint of *I told you so* in that look.

"You leave them alone!" the barkeep shouted. "I let your kind drink here with one rule. You don't peddle your faith to my customers."

George held his hand up, and while the barkeep didn't look happy about it, he didn't interrupt the cloaked man again. "Is that what you wish to discuss with us?"

"Of course," the man said. "You live in the desert. In the shadow of the Great Machines. I've come from far to the west, past Ballern, to spread the word of their divinity."

George's posture relaxed a hair. "We've no interest in your tales, preacher."

"Preacher? I am no preacher, sir. The world is changing. *Has* been changing for many years under the power of the Great Machines."

George looked like he was about to interrupt again before Gladys put a hand on his wrist. She understood what this man was now, she'd seen the flame and sword on his belt and when his arm flourished to emphasize his words, a steel-plated flame tattoo peeked from his sleeve.

"They are the source of the Dark Fire. The giver and taker of life. All will be united under their banner, even you noble desert dwellers. Do you not know the slumbering god in the southern desert?"

"We do," Gladys said.

"Journey west and you will find Great Machines that are not so dormant. Find displays of their power, divine and purifying, giving life to the creatures we both love and fear. That is the only message I bring. Do with it as you will."

"Thank you for your kind words, sir," Gladys said. "Please be well in your travels."

"And be you blessed by the Dark Fire."

George ushered her to the door without another word.

"ARE WE LEAVING?" Gladys asked once they were back on the streets. She glanced back at the bar and the heavy wooden sign swaying in a strong breeze. It must have cost a fortune given how little wood was around the city, and the coat of arms was beautiful, showing a Tail Sword crossed with a dagger.

"Not yet," George said. "First, we tell Archibald what our friendly barkeep had to say, and then we talk about why *you* need to be more discreet in strange places."

Gladys rolled her eyes. "This city is broken, George. If I can brighten it some tiny bit by telling a bartender my name, I'm going to do it. And I hope he does come visit us after the war. And I hope he brings more of the people from Fel."

"You mean well, Princess. You always do. I only mean to keep you from trouble."

"You're not very good at that."

George sighed and led the way to the guards who would get them to Archibald.

CHAPTER TWENTY

DRAKKAR AND SAMUEL found them at the docks soon after Jacob had finished tying off the ship. They weren't the best knots, he knew, but it shouldn't let them drift away either.

Samuel undid the clasps on his leggings in a few quick sweeping motions before hopping down from his Dragonwing. "Jacob! You all made it back?"

Rin's Dragonwing landed beside Drakkar, and they soon joined the two Ancorans near the railing on the deck. "Have you learned anything?"

"Smith's testing some materials for an antenna. Well, not an antenna exactly, but a way to connect the communicator to a transmitter's antenna."

"Where's Furi?" Rin asked.

"In the cabin with Alice and Mary."

Rin left them on the deck as he made his way toward the bow and the door to the cabin.

"Let's check on Smith," Samuel said. "See if he's getting close or if we need a different plan."

Jacob nodded and walked over to the hatch, which he lifted with ease. He led the way down the ladder and took the short corridor into Smith's workshop by the engine room.

The tinker was hunched over a tangle of stripped wires while a small lantern sat close by, its brilliant blue flames licking at the air. He used a gloved hand to pull a length of metal from the fire before touching it to a narrow wire. When the two met, the wire melted, pooling on the stripped wires and the small metal lip underneath.

"Any luck?" Samuel asked.

"Your timing is impeccable." Smith leaned back and lifted the assembly, inspecting both sides of what Jacob could now see was a clamp with a spring in the middle. He looked at Jacob and the others.

"Samuel, Drakkar, glad to see you back."

"Rin is in the cabin too," Drakkar said. "He has proven a good guide, and an ally I welcome."

Smith turned the flames off on the small lantern before sliding the superheated metal back inside its gray housing and locking the assembly closed. "Jacob, I think this is as good as the clamp is going to get. Let's get up to the cabin."

Smith was first up the ladder, clutching the communicator to his chest as he ascended with one hand. If Jacob had tried that, he was pretty sure he'd either fall down or be incredibly slow. He put his hands on the cold steel of the ladder and followed Smith up and back to the cabin.

"See!" Furi said, gesturing to Smith as they all entered the cabin. "I told you we got it."

"That doesn't change the fact you could have been killed, Furi," Rin said. "I had no idea you meant to blow up the airship while you were still on it!"

"My fault," Alice said. "But it was that or face more of Ballern's soldiers."

Rin glanced at Alice, his mouth pulling into a tight line before returning his attention to Furi. "Regardless, you need to be more careful, Furi. We fight for all the Skyborn now. And there are few of us outside Ballern who know the truth of things."

But Furi didn't back down from Rin. Her brow furrowed as she stepped closer to the Dragonrider. "We aren't *on* the docks anymore,

Rin. You *left* us. Did you forget that? You never even told us you were alive. And how hard would it have been to send a letter?"

"Canopy forbid it, Furi. I couldn't—"

"Maybe you couldn't, or maybe you wouldn't, but I haven't forgotten for one second who the Skyborn are to me. They're my family, my friends, the people I trusted most in this world. And do you know what they did, Rin? They tried to kill me because, at some level, the Skyborn are still obedient soldiers. Just like I was. Just like you were. And they *have to* know the truth, or they'll be ruled by that cult for the rest of their lives."

Furi turned away from Rin, not giving the Dragonrider a chance to respond.

For a moment, it looked like he would anyway, but something in his shoulders gave way, and his body sagged a little as he sighed.

Furi studied Smith. "You did it?"

Smith stuttered, apparently as taken aback at Rin's verbal evisceration as the rest of them. "Ah, yes. I just need to connect it to the transmitter in Mary's console. It should only take a moment. Do you know the frequency it should be attuned to?"

"There isn't one," Rin said, clarifying once Smith raised a skeptical eyebrow. "I mean, there is, but no one knows it outside of the manufacturers. It's built into a unit inside the springs."

"Truly?" Smith said, eyeing the communicator with a newfound interest.

Rin nodded. "Ballern may not have as many tinkers living in the city, but their manufacturing district is formidable."

"I have seen parts of it," Smith said. "They are formidable, yes, but to see the true power of an organized factory, you must visit Bollwerk. And I say that as a student of Targrove. Belldorn is no slouch, but what Archibald has wrought in Bollwerk has rarely been seen outside of the

Deadlands War."

"Smith," Mary snapped. "Why don't you install that thing?"

Smith smiled at the captain of the Skysworn as she stood up and walked away from the console. He slipped into her seat and then undid a run of latches along the wall just below the horns.

Jacob stepped closer to watch what the tinker was doing. Once the panel was open, three wires waited inside. They were insulated, but Smith made quick work of stripping them, exposing the copper underneath. With that done, he slipped the clamp onto the first wire before closing a second on another.

There was no delay with what came next. The small hammer mounted on the springs of the communicator bobbed up and down, producing a subtle high-pitched squeak. Jacob couldn't imagine how any of that was communicating anything, but the sudden appearance of Furi and Rin at his side told him they understood far more than he did.

"That's it!" Furi said. She rushed back to her jump seat and grabbed a notebook before returning to Smith's side.

"That's it?" Jacob asked. "It's just beeping."

"I told you that was all it did," Furi said. "Now, let me listen."

"Take my seat." Smith stood up and gestured to the captain's chair.

Furi didn't argue. She sat down with a pen and notebook and started to draw a series of dots and lines, some higher than others, and some bent at an angle.

"She's changing the marks with the shift in pitch." Alice's voice startled Jacob out of his fascination with Furi's scribbles. He watched her again for a time, and only then did he hear the difference. It was subtle, so subtle it was easily missed. But some of the beeps started out with a single tone and then rose in pitch.

"How?" Jacob asked. He couldn't see anything on the device that would alter the tone, much less act as a horn or a speaker.

But in that short time, Smith had already figured it out. "It is a shift in frequency. Conducted through the striker, on the base of the communicator there."

He cursed and leaned across Furi, double-checking the connections inside the wall. Smith straightened and let out a long sigh. "If that was connected to the broadcast wires of the transmitter, I am afraid they could have noticed someone had intercepted a communicator."

"I doubt it," Rin said. "The communicators are notorious for having issues. It's not uncommon for a transmission to break down into unrecognizable squeals."

Before Rin finished speaking, Furi sat down her pen. "The message is starting to repeat." She stood and hurried to her jump seat, where she unrolled the translator and handed it to Alice.

One by one, Furi drew letters beneath each line, slash, and dot. When they failed to form a word, Furi started grouping the symbols together based on the patterns on the translator.

"Amateurs," Furi muttered. "They are supposed to space these out better."

"They may have been panicked," Rin said. "There have been losses on both sides this day."

Furi nodded and got back to sectioning off portions of the symbols until they formed words Jacob recognized. She continued like that while the others watched in relative silence. It wasn't until Furi reached the bottom of the page that she looked up from her notebook and locked eyes with Mary.

"Get me to Lady Katherine, now."

CHAPTER TWENTY-ONE

JACOB READ FURI'S notes over Alice's shoulder for what had to be the tenth time. It didn't make sense to him, as a handful of standard characters were switched out for Mokuskrit, but Furi's explanation was disturbing enough.

The parts he *could* read still told the same story, only with key names and places translated into another language. The Children of the Dark Fire had their hands in more of Ballern than they'd realized, and that was a sobering thought considering what they *did* know.

"Do you have a way to reach Jakon?" Furi asked.

"Do we have to?" Mary muttered before she sighed. "Yes, I have a frequency he should be on."

"Please. I need to talk to him. He's one of the very few people I trust who know both sides of this war."

Mary nodded and spun the larger dial on the transmitter before slowly turning a second to lock in the frequency. "Ray, come in. This is the Skysworn, over."

No one answered.

"If he's down at the market, he may not have access to a transmitter."

"Still selling soup?" Mary asked.

"Of course," Furi said. "And it's still some of the best I've ever had." She glanced up at Smith. "Next to The Copper Spoon, anyway, but don't tell him I said that."

Smith grinned.

"Skysworn, message received. Something new to sell? Somewhat irresponsible in these times of war, I'd say."

"Irresponsible?" Mary said, her voice climbing nearly an octave. "You have some gall."

Furi hopped out of her seat and ran over to the transmitter. "It's Furi. Have you spoken to Kura? Do you know if she's safe?"

"Don't use your name, girl. You never know who's listening."

"*We're* listening," Furi snapped. "We got a communicator off a supply ship. Apparently, the carrier is being refueled by transports coming from the forest. But that doesn't make any sense. Do you know what it could be?"

Jakon hesitated. "I might. These are interesting times, Furi. Most interesting times indeed. I spoke with your teacher just this morning, before I met Mordair."

Silence hung in the air before Mary said, "You *what?*"

"A dock rat brought him to my shop. Rest assured, I did not seek him out. I'll never scrape the stink off his coin."

Furi mashed the button for the transmitter. "Fine, but what about Kura?"

"Yes, your teacher. You know, some *unscrupulous* folks trade with the forest villages, yes? Well, it appears the monarchy has been refining fuel for their fleet at a Great Machine."

"The Great Machine at the edge of the Gray Woods. That's what they meant by the forest."

"Likely so, yes."

"Then if we brought down their Great Machine, we could cripple their entire fleet."

Jakon outright laughed. "Maybe, but you could not possibly bring down a machine the size of a city, Skyborn. Perhaps Belldorn could, but the lady is in no position to move across the seas. Not without sacrificing her own people."

"There is a way that could be changed," Drakkar said, drawing the attention of everyone in the room.

But it was Rin who looked defeated as he spoke. "The bait boxes."

"Yes. So long as the supply line exists between Ballern's fleet and their resources, we will not defeat them, Dragonrider."

Rin closed his eyes for a moment and then nodded. "So be it. And may history be kind to us for what must be done."

"Rust it all, Skysworn. What are they talking about?"

Furi leaned closer to the transmitter. "A way to free Belldorn's fleet."

"I would appreciate a word of warning before you attack Ballern. Need to keep The Ray tip-top, you know."

"We'll contact you," Mary said. "The time to run may be at an end."

"The time to run is never at an end, Skysworn. That's how we stay in the air."

The transmitter grew silent as Jakon disconnected.

Mary turned the dial on the transmitter and hit the button. Jacob didn't doubt who she was contacting, and when Lady Katherine's voice came back, he knew he was right.

"Mary, what is it?"

"We need to talk. In person, and as soon as you can. Are you still on the bridge?"

"Yes, but we're docking now. Come to my ship."

"No, Kat, I need you here. You have too many people on the bridge, and we need privacy."

Kat paused for a time. "Very well. Where are you?"

"Meet us at the Skysworn. Alone if you can."

"My guards won't agree to that. They'll be stationed on the dock."

"That's fine, so long as we have privacy. Is Eva still deployed?"

"Her brig should be on the docks too. They were recalled after the strikers found a vulnerability. Our tinkers are working on them now. I'll see you soon."

Mary shifted the transmitter's dial again. "Eva, come to the Skysworn immediately. We have news."

"On my way," was Eva's only response.

Jacob put his arm around Alice. For a time, silence reigned in the Skysworn's cabin. Jacob knew the lull in the battle would soon be broken as Ballern and Belldorn regrouped.

✧   ✧   ✧

LADY KATHERINE ARRIVED with Eva, and as Kat promised, her guards remained on the docks, well out of earshot of the conversation on the Skysworn. Jacob had never seen Kat look quite so tired. Heavy circles framed her eyes, but she still moved with quick gestures and confidence that commanded any room she stood in. And the cabin of the Skysworn was no different.

Kat held Furi's notebook in her hand, reading through the transcription several times. "Your Mokuskrit is beautiful, Furi."

"Thank you. I haven't met many people in Belldorn who can read Mokuskrit."

Kat smiled. "A few of us do. For a long time, it was required in our schools. I should like to introduce that again, I think." She took a deep breath and looked around at the gathered people. "So, these are who you trust above my own guard, Mary?"

Samuel crossed his arms at what had been close to an insult.

Rin stiffened when Kat's gaze fell upon him.

"With my life," Mary said without hesitation, wrapping her hand in Eva's.

Kat inclined her head. "I ask that you do not act on this." When protests started to rise, she amended with, "Not yet. We know almost nothing of the Great Machines. To attack with abandon would be to throw our lives and resources away. We need knowledge before we act."

"We don't know that much about them," Furi said.

"Then I ask, child, where can you learn of them?"

Furi frowned, started to speak, and then froze. "The ruins in the Deadlands!"

"Yes. Return there, and when you have at least a plan to infiltrate one of the Great Machines, and the battle for Belldorn is done, we will strike. But I cannot abandon my city. It pains me even to see the Skysworn leave for a short time."

"One day," Mary said. "We can make it there and back in one day."

"Let us hope that is enough."

"We may be able to help with that," Drakkar said.

"Oh?"

The Cave Guardian gestured to Rin. "The Dragonrider has agreed to move forward with the Emerald Needles. Samuel and I will ride with him."

"Tatsu will join us," Rin said. "I'm sure of it. Four of us can cover much of the fleet in a matter of minutes if we aren't boarding them."

"I think we've had enough of boarding the enemy ships," Kat said with a meaningful glance to Alice and Jacob.

Jacob offered an awkward smile in response.

"Go then, with my blessing. Make for the remains of the Great Machine while we defend the city. The battle will be won with help from the Dragonriders. And perhaps we can still save more lives than we would have."

Lady Katherine turned to leave before glancing back. "Eva, please oversee the repairs on the brigs. I'm promoting you to commander, as the position has recently opened."

"Thanks, Kat."

She nodded and left the Skysworn.

"Recently opened?" Mary asked.

Eva rubbed at her cheek. "He blew up."

Mary grimaced. "Well, that's horrible."

"Tomorrow, then," Eva said. "Tell me when you're on your way back. I'll give you an update on where it's safe and where it isn't."

Mary wrapped Eva up in a hug before they parted ways.

"I need to tell Canopy what's happening," Rin said. "Samuel, Drakkar, you are welcome to join me, or you can wait here at the stables."

"We'll wait here," Drakkar said. "I am in need of rest, and I can tell by Samuel's lack of complaining he feels much the same."

At first, it looked like the Spider Knight was going to argue, but then he just shrugged.

✧   ✧   ✧

THE DISTANT FIGHTING had grown silent as evening fell. After the losses of the day, Ballern was apparently no more anxious to fight in the dark than Belldorn was. A late dinner brought them to a different restaurant. While Jacob wouldn't exactly have called The Copper Spoon fancy, Potters Nibbles wouldn't have been out of place in the Lowlands or the tiny restaurants set up along the docks in Cave.

And that didn't quite explain how small the room was. Jacob could barely slide by between the wall and the stools as he made his way to the back. There were only eight seats in total, and Smith took the last of them, closest to the door, to give himself a little extra space. But even at opposite ends of the counter, Jacob could easily hear the tinker.

Across the bar were wide strips of metal with a sign by each that warned against touching them. Jacob knew why when the barkeeper turned the knob and one of those plates rose a fraction of an inch away from the wood. A quiet hiss sounded before an igniter clicked and a small burst of flame licked at the sides of the metal, also revealing the metal lining the wood itself.

"Smith, Mary, what will you be having today?"

"Privacy," Smith said.

"Still conducting business in the middle of this battle?"

Smith smiled and shook his head. "Not so much that. We have spies in the city, you know?"

The barkeeper laughed. "Other than yourselves?"

Mary scowled at the man. "Just because we've sold information to you in the past doesn't mean we're spies."

The barkeeper held his hands up in surrender. "I meant no disrespect. Only pointing out the irony of a spy concerned about other spies."

"I don't think that's an irony at all," Mary said. "We know better than most what lurks in the back alleys of Belldorn."

"You trust him?" Furi asked.

"Of course they do," the barkeeper said.

"Of course we do," Mary echoed his words. "Craig has been a staunch ally and a good connection for our trade. Unless someone else offers more coin, of course."

Craig flashed a predator's grin, turning to Alice and Jacob. "What would you folks like this evening?"

Smith leaned forward, crossing his arms on the bar top. "I would recommend the fish."

Jacob looked up at the board hanging at the center of the far wall. A chalk menu had been written out, detailing a few variations of fish and several dishes that centered around a Tail Sword.

"How is the Tail Sword?" Jacob asked.

"Crunchy," Smith said. "And usually burnt."

Jacob pursed his lips. "I think I'll try the fried fish."

Craig smiled and turned to Alice and Furi. "And for the ladies?"

"Fried fish," they said in unison before exchanging a smile.

Craig didn't ask Mary what she wanted. Only poured a clear liquid into a short glass and passed it to her. "I assume you won't go against tradition?"

Mary picked up the glass as he poured another. She held it out when he was done, and Craig cracked his own glass against hers.

"To better years."

Mary nodded. "Better years." In one swallow, they downed their glasses, and Craig cringed at whatever had been inside it. Mary didn't so much as flinch.

"I'd challenge you to a game, but I learned my lesson long ago."

A sly smile slipped across Mary's lips. "I'm surprised you remember learning that lesson."

"Yes, well, it *is* a bit fuzzy in parts." Craig took both of the short glasses and dropped them into a soapy sink. "What brings your group here so late?" His focus shifted to the narrow counter below an array of bottles, where he pulled a long iridescent fish from a trough of ice.

"Traveling deep into the Deadlands in the morning," Smith said. "A task for the lady."

"Ah, say no more. That's the kind of task I'd rather not know of."

Mary grunted. "I know what you mean. But you're going to hear something of it tonight, as we leave early, and there is still planning to be done."

Craig nodded. "Fair enough, Captain. You have my word of silence."

"And I accept."

Alice glanced between Craig and Mary. "Is this some kind of pirate thing?"

Craig flashed her a smile. "That is not a word we use lightly around these parts. It would be best if you kept that to yourself."

Smith blew out a long breath. "As if the entire city does not know who you serve in this bar."

Craig ran a thin blade down the stomach of the fish, and faster than

Jacob could follow, the bones and innards ripped away and splashed down into a trash can. A few more strokes of the blade removed the bulk of the scales and a cleaver made quick work of breaking it down to rectangular segments.

The barkeeper's skill was an intimidating thing. Jacob wondered if the man had as much experience using blades for other things, knowing that at some level, he knew the pirates of Belldorn.

Craig pulled a wide lever, and something behind Smith clunked before the door slid closed, hiding the street.

"Thank you," Mary said.

Craig nodded, focused on a large mixing bowl where he whisked yellow batter together. With that done, he placed a wide-bottomed bowl on each of the hot plates, filling a portion of it with some sort of oil.

"We're leaving early in the morning," Mary said, refocusing her attention on the others around the bar. "My only plan at the moment is to go back in the same way as before. And make our way to the control room. Do any of you have objections?"

Furi grimaced. "It's such a huge structure. Are you sure retracing our steps is the best thing to do? Targrove told us about the other entrance, and we could check there for something new."

"What about the manual in the control room?" Mary asked. "What if you missed something in there?"

Furi nodded slowly. "It's possible. We weren't looking for a way to shut something down last time we were there."

"You said there were a lot of stairs?" Jacob asked.

Alice let out a stuttering laugh. "I wasn't exaggerating when I told you how high that place was. Easily taller than the Highlands walls."

"Then we use the gliders. Get to the control room, find what we need, and use the gliders to reach another part of the structure."

Smith leaned back on his stool. "Jacob, that may entail more risk than you realize. There are Shadowwings and beetles, and other things we may not even know about yet."

"What do you think's going to happen when we get to Ballern? I'm guessing we'll see a lot of things we haven't seen before."

"I can help with that," Furi said.

Craig turned and glanced at Furi. "You're one of the Skyborn, aren't you?"

"I am." The lack of hesitation in Furi's answer surprised Jacob. But maybe the trust Mary had shown Craig warranted a bit more comfort in Potters Nibbles.

Craig gave her one sharp nod. "Good people, the Skyborn."

"There's another problem," Alice said. "Even if we take the gliders, the control panel is at too low a level. We'll have to go back up the stairs, anyway."

Mary poured a glass of water from a tin pitcher. "It could still be faster than taking the Skysworn across the structure. One advantage to using the gliders would be avoiding the unknown."

"What do you mean?" Smith asked with a frown.

"We could drop them off at the second entrance, and it may be nearly as fast, but that entrance is far to the west. They'll nearly need to cross a city's worth of darkness. And we have no idea what's waiting there."

Smith rubbed at his chin. "I had not considered that. It is a risk, either way."

"I can look the gliders over tonight," Jacob said. "I think Furi's may need to be replaced, but the others can be patched easily enough."

Smith nodded. "There are a few at Theodosia's workshop. I will bring some for myself and Mary, as well as a replacement for Furi."

Alice shook her head. "I don't know if that's the best. Like you said, we'll be going into the unknown. We might need you to come rescue us if things get bad."

"I'm afraid if things get bad, we won't be able to get to you in time. Whoever goes into that place on the gliders is going to be on their own."

Smith leaned forward. "Maybe not. There may be another way. I will consider it."

"Well, consider what?" Mary asked.

"I will let you know when I have worked through the idea."

Mary stopped just short of rolling her eyes. "If I'm dead by the time you work through it, I'm going to be annoyed."

Small clouds of steam rose while the oil bubbled and popped in the small wells. Craig stepped to each of the heated plates, dropping in four sections of battered squares.

"Should be done in just a minute. You can leave them in a bit longer if you like them crunchier."

"Leave them in longer," Mary said.

Jacob did and waited until the crust that had formed along the outside changed from a pale tan to a rich brown. He snatched the pieces out with chopsticks and piled them onto a plate between him and Alice. Mary split hers with Furi while Smith kept four to himself.

Jacob wasn't sure what to make of the thick square of fried fish, but after it cooled, he bit into it.

"Wow," Furi said.

"Right?" Alice broke off another piece. "It's crunchy and rich and … Craig, these are amazing."

"You should be selling these on the docks at Ballern!" Furi said.

"Or Cave," Jacob added, chewing on a bite of the salty fish. Of course, he would have preferred to be at home in Ancora, where Craig could have set up a stall in the Lowlands, but those times were gone for now. Maybe one day.

Craig wiped his hands off after cleaning up the bar where some of the oil had splattered into a mess. "It's no soup from The Copper Spoon," he said with a glance at Smith, "but I do pride myself on that batter. Family secret."

"And whose family did you steal that from?" Mary asked.

Craig placed a hand over his heart. "You wound me, Captain."

They stayed in the small bar for a time, listening to Craig's stories about some of the more famous patrons he'd had over the years. He swore Targrove had once visited Potters Nibbles, but no one believed him, as Targrove had died the year before.

No one responded to that story, and Jacob was fairly certain Craig was too sharp to have missed that.

It wasn't until they were leaving that Craig mentioned it. "I always knew that old man was still alive."

Mary laughed as they made their way back onto the streets of Belldorn.

CHAPTER TWENTY-TWO

Samuel fitted the Dragonwing's saddle the next morning. It was still before sunrise, and he doubted he would have been awake if Drakkar hadn't been more reliable than an alarm clock. Perhaps more disheartening was the fact Tatsu had already been working for an hour.

"An hour?" Samuel said with a groan.

Tatsu laughed from the next stall over. "Yes, Spider Knight. It is hard to sleep after a night flight. Surely you have felt that rush of adrenaline, riding on the Dragonwings? I feel it every time I take to the skies with Buzzer."

He had, but he certainly hadn't felt it in the middle of the night. That, frankly, sounded terrifying. It was bad enough riding Bessie in the dark, though at least he could trust the Jumper not to fly directly into a mountain.

"Has Rin returned?" Drakkar asked.

"He left shortly after I did, once the council disbanded. It should not be long before he arrives."

Samuel supposed they could move forward without Rin if they had to because the Dragonrider had left the bait boxes locked away in the stables. Tatsu had already taken them out of the lockers, distributing them to Samuel and Drakkar.

Even as Samuel thought about it, he double-checked to make sure the full load was secured in the leather satchel on the Dragonwing's back. A quick glance showed him the organized bolts and reinforced how misleading a name like "bait boxes" was. The transmitter itself, a long slender thing nestled in the shaft of the bolt, might have been square, but it still seemed odd to call the entire assembly a box.

Samuel closed the satchel and checked the straps on his backup crossbow. One would be anchored to his back, while the other was tied to the saddle itself. It was unlikely a crossbow would fail, but considering speed was of the utmost importance, they were taking no chances. Drakkar, Tatsu, and Rin would all have a backup weapon.

With the buckles of the saddle secured and a small trough of Sweet-Flies devoured, Samuel's Dragonwing was ready to fly.

"All set here!" He called out.

Two shadows appeared outside Samuel's stable. Tatsu stepped into a sliver of light cast down between the towers of Belldorn and into the clearing.

"The sun will soon rise in earnest. If Rin has not returned shortly, this mission will become ours and ours alone."

"Patience," Drakkar said. "Dawn still provides some cover, but the sun provides protection as well. Fly Dragonwings as if you were piloting an airship against enemy forces. Keep the sun at your back, and it will blind those who would strike you down."

Samuel eyed the Cave Guardian. Drakkar was peaceful and incredibly patient about a great many things, but his knowledge of combat rivaled that of the most experienced of the Spider Knights. Not for the first time, Samuel wondered about the training regimen in Cave.

Tatsu's gaze rose above them and a smile lifted his lips. "I do not believe that will become an issue."

A moment later, Samuel heard the buzz, the incredibly fast movement of a Dragonwing, turning the air around them into a strong breeze as Rin's mount settled onto the stables.

"Ready?"

Samuel nodded. "Do you have your bolts?"

"No. Tatsu?"

Tatsu tossed a leather satchel up to Rin before handing him an extra crossbow for his saddle. Rin glanced inside, nodded, and then fastened both satchel and crossbow to his saddle.

"Time grows short. The battle will renew at any moment, and I have no desire to fire these bait boxes if those ships grow any closer to the city proper. Come. We make for the mountains, and once the Emerald Needles are released, we visit a horror on Ballern's people that will never be washed from our hands."

With that, Rin took to the air once more.

Samuel looked to Tatsu. "That is a very strange rallying cry."

Tatsu grinned. "It is better than his usual."

"And what is his usual rallying cry?" Samuel asked.

"Don't die."

Drakkar chuckled under his breath as he made his way back to his Dragonwing's stall. "I feel as though Rin and Charles may have had much in common."

Samuel smiled at the thought as he mounted his own Dragonwing, connecting the clasps to his leggings and anchoring himself to the saddle as best he could before signaling to the beast to take flight. It was only a minute before they joined Rin in the air and followed him to the east toward the lightening mountains.

In minutes they reached the gap in the mountain that acted as both a shelter for Belldorn's soldiers and containment for a swarm of Emerald Needles. Rin stopped his Dragonwing short and hovered outside a guard tower concealed in the tree line. He signaled the soldiers below by pointing forward and up with both hands and then spreading his arms wide, the sign Lady Katherine had given him.

It was then Samuel noticed the rise of a distant buzz, a higher pitch than the Dragonwings. Only with some horror, he came to realize it was not so distant at all. As the mountain slid open, he could see the housing that caged the Emerald Needles. So fine a mesh shouldn't have been able to hold creatures like those, the brilliant green bodies and fast-moving wings a mass of clicks and whirs.

Samuel knew the stories of Emerald Needles. He knew what most people feared. They'd been known to use living creatures as a nursery for their young, like a parasite taking over its host. But there was a far more immediate danger with Emerald Needles. They bore stingers that could run a fully armored soldier through with little effort, and their forward legs were more like scythes than limbs—a horrible trait they shared with Tree Killers.

And it was with that thought Samuel realized why those soldiers below were taking shelter in a thick bunker. Rin raised his voice and Samuel could barely hear the strained words over the buzz of the Dragonwings and Emerald Needles.

"As soon as the mesh drops, we fly! And we do not stop!"

That was all the warning they had before the uppermost section of mesh folded down. Samuel had a split second to realize that it wasn't a fabric mesh, but flexible steel, before Rin shot past him. He hammered on the plates of his Dragonwing, spinning around to follow the Dragonrider beside Drakkar and Tatsu.

Rin raised a crossbow just high enough to be visible to Samuel and the others. He meant to fire at these speeds? The accuracy would be terrible. But that was part of why Rin didn't want the bait boxes closer to the city, Samuel realized. They had to do this while the ships were out at sea or far to the north, or those Emerald Needles would swarm Belldorn itself.

Samuel took a few panicked breaths as he took the crossbow off his back, staying low to the saddle so he didn't lose his grip on the weapon in the wind. He understood now why Tatsu had insisted they use the less traditional crossbows, more a bolt thrower than a true crossbow. They could hold a clip of five bolts before they had to be reloaded, and the bolt couldn't be blown off the internal housing.

The Spider Knight spun the inset crank on the side of the stock as fast as he could. The angle made the crank awkward, but the springs jumped in his hands with a heavy click. They were almost past the edge of the city now, and a glance back showed him a swelling storm of Emerald Needles glistening in the breaking sunlight.

Rin veered to the west, cutting across the southern border of what had become a no man's land. Ash and twisted metal, fallen buildings and broken bodies littered the ground. But even the feast for the Carrion Worms below could not distract the Emerald Needles. The brilliant green carapaces pursued the Dragonriders with a terrifying relentlessness.

At first, Samuel thought Rin would hit the airship docks Ballern had constructed, but instead, he angled out to sea, into the slow-moving supply lines drifting between the distant carrier and the docks farther south. Wind pulled at Samuel's goggles and armor like a greedy claw, trying to rip them away as the Dragonwings sped over the Crystal Sea. He could just make out Drakkar's cloak, snapping in a wild dance where it wasn't pinned to his body by bracers.

With his mount's wings buzzing to either side of him, Samuel struggled to find somewhere to aim that wouldn't risk hitting the Dragonwing. It wasn't until Rin pivoted in his seat and aimed his crossbow to the rear of the saddle that Samuel understood.

The Spider Knight did the same, aiming just before the wings behind him where the saddle met the armored plates of the long-tapered tail. The first airship passed below them, and Samuel loosed a bolt. He thought he'd missed, waited too long to fire at the speeds they were traveling, but the bolt found the bow, and the horde descended.

It was not a slow death for the sailors on that ship. One moment they were watching the skies, and the next, the Emerald Needles had scattered them across the sea in pieces. The carnage might have been distant by the time it was over, but Samuel's stomach heaved, nonetheless.

He twisted the crank on the crossbow until a bolt clicked into place. The next target was a group of slow-moving strikers, escorting a supply ship. Samuel's bolt sailed wide, missing the tiny airship he'd been aiming for, but Drakkar and Tatsu hit their marks.

The first striker fired, cutting into the line of Emerald Needles that roared across the sea, but nothing could have stopped them. Scythe-like limbs opened the ship like a can until the creatures could reach the pilots, and the ships started to fall from the sky.

Something exploded in the sky not far from the Dragonriders, and a quick turn in his saddle showed Samuel the cannons of a supply ship taking aim at them. Their group scattered, giving the cannons four targets instead of one, and then closed on the supply ship itself.

Samuel stuck a bolt in the gas chamber, reloaded, and put his second shot into the deck by the forward cabin. The supply ships were far larger than anything they'd hit with bait boxes so far, and Rin didn't hesitate to put two more bolts in the aft deck as they circled once and then fled down the line of ships.

Even that short delay, a single circle, left them close enough that Samuel could hear the screams as the cloud of Emerald Needles descended. A piercing cry as a sailor was run through by a two-foot stinger before the Emerald Needles rent bodies asunder.

A glance backward showed Samuel the frenzy from the Emerald Needles as they attacked the bolt with such violence that the chamber itself ruptured. A burst of air threw the Emerald Needles into the sky before they reoriented and attacked again.

The scene repeated itself again and again. The Dragonriders fired a bolt into an unsuspecting ship, and the Emerald Needles killed everything on board. What few survived were left on an ailing vessel as it drifted aimlessly or crashed into the water below.

If there was one thing Samuel knew for certain as they continued down the line of Ballern ships, Lady Katherine was beyond ruthless. Not since the Fall had he seen that kind of violence visited on a people. And though it might have been his allies who gave the orders, it was still his hand putting bolts into those ships.

As merciless as the first few attacks felt, the resistance grew stronger. More ships exited the carrier as they moved closer, firing into the bulk of the Emerald Needles. Every shot struck down more of the creatures, but no matter how many fell in a spiral of glistening chitin, more came.

The Emerald Needles took down a second supply ship before the Dragonriders angled for a destroyer. It was the last vessel between them and the carrier. But the thunder from the cannons ripped through the cluster of Emerald Needles. Still, they reformed, chasing down activated boxes.

Samuel let one of his empty clips fall into the sea below. He hurried to load another, spinning the crank to prime the bolt thrower. The destroyers were heavily armored ships. It would take time for the Emerald Needles to bring one down, and apparently Rin had the same idea.

The Dragonrider fired a series of bolts into the base of the cannons. Samuel followed Tatsu and Buzzer to the peaks of the gas chambers, areas where the armor was not so thick, and unloaded multiple rounds. Should one bait box be destroyed, the frenzy would continue until the Emerald Needles had found the rest.

Samuel circled around the destroyer, passing close to Drakkar as the Cave Guardian reloaded. Rin signaled Tatsu, a complicated gesture Samuel didn't recognize. A moment later, Rin slowed to flank Samuel, yelling over the buzz of wings.

"Carrier! Now!"

Samuel nodded and signaled his Dragonwing to follow Rin once more. He glanced back at the destroyer as it fired frantically at the swarm. As many of the brilliant green carapaces that might have been killed, there were enough to turn the destroyer into a seething mass of Needles and scythes. Even as he watched, the second gas chamber ruptured, and the destroyer listed to the side.

The Spider Knight leaned close to the saddle of the Dragonwing as the beast suddenly rose. It wasn't that Samuel didn't trust the clasps on his legging to hold him in place, but he was still unnerved by the feeling of falling backward. And a Dragonwing didn't have that reassuring hump to lean against like Bessie did. It was another world, fighting in the skies.

The storms came as they reached the carrier. A torrential downpour opened above them while the sun still shone in the distance. But it was the sun that Rin was aiming for, Samuel realized as they flew past the carrier, only to circle back and dive toward the deck.

But what could they hope to do against such a monstrosity? The possibility of the Emerald Needles bringing down a vessel that large felt unlikely at best, and a fool's way to die at worst. But Rin angled toward the deck, skimming the surface as his Dragonwing flitted between docked airships, and then fired a volley of bolts into those left upon the carrier.

Samuel cursed at himself that he hadn't realized Rin's plan earlier. Every airship on top of that carrier was vulnerable to the Emerald Needles. He picked off every striker he could, trying to ignore the fact he and the Dragonriders were rushing toward the swarm that had finished devouring a destroyer only minutes before.

Rin and Tatsu made a sharp turn, heading back to the west as Rin signaled to the north. Drakkar and Samuel turned north, continuing to ship after ship on the carrier as a claxon boomed across the decks. What had been a nearly empty platform a short time before started to pulse with a flood of soldiers. The first shot almost took him in the shoulder, but his Dragonwing avoided it and dodged another volley.

Samuel took the lead, skirting by a hangar, and in a ruthless moment of his own, fired two bolts deep into the shadows of the hangar. Drakkar followed suit, echoing his shots and taking the lead on the next hangar. They repeated that to the far corner of the carrier and looped back to follow Rin and Tatsu as they passed by overhead.

But as they soared to the Crystal Sea, Samuel fired two last bolts into the gas chambers at the carrier's edge. It might not be enough to sink it, but the repairs would certainly devour the enemy's resources. And sometimes that was the only advantage you needed.

One clip remained in his saddlebags. One more clip he loaded into the bolt thrower as they sped away from the carrier. Rin dove at a flanking destroyer, peppering it with bolts before speeding away. Tatsu and Drakkar followed, while Samuel emptied his final shots into the bow.

Their path took them across the northern edge of the city, where a line of Titan Mechs now defended the beaches. They were an imposing sight, but Samuel worried those machines would not be able to stand another full assault from Ballern.

A backward glance showed him Ballern would be tied up for some time, and their losses would not be insignificant. Even Fel's ships on the water had turned their attention to the swarms of Emerald Needles.

Rin led the group to the stables where the Dragonwings crashed down, their wings stopping almost immediately in a display of exhaustion Samuel had rarely seen from them.

Drakkar dismounted and walked into Samuel's stall moments later, clicking the transmitter in his cloak. "Eva, the bait boxes are away. The supply line from the docks to the carrier is disrupted."

"Understood," Eva said, her voice crackling over the transmitter. And Samuel heard the order she gave to the crew of her ship. "Take the docks."

CHAPTER TWENTY-THREE

J ACOB, ALICE, AND Furi all listened with rapt attention as Mary spoke to Drakkar. They'd been in the air since just before sunrise, and were only now hearing about the results of the mission. What relieved Jacob the most was that all four of them had survived.

"Did you catch all of that, Smith?" Mary asked once she disconnected from Drakkar.

"Yes, it sounds good, for the most part. And they are already moving to take the docks?"

"Yes."

"Taking the docks should prove easier with a disruption in the supply lines. But it will be temporary, Mary. I think you know that."

The dim light of the desert slowly turned bright as the sun crawled higher. A few Fire Lizards roamed the wastes, but most of what sped by below them was sand and scrub brush.

The second group of peaks that belonged to the Dragonwing Mountains appeared on the southern horizon for a short time. Not so grand as those closer to Belldorn, most not high enough to have snowcapped peaks, but they were still enough to make Jacob think of home.

"Have you heard anything from Ancora?" Jacob asked.

"Smith, what did Ambrose say when you spoke to him this morning?"

Jacob's eyebrows rose as he exchanged an excited glance with Alice. "You talked to Ambrose?"

"I did," Smith said. "Had some trouble with two of the bolt cannons Archibald delivered. I helped talk Ambrose through filing down the plates without damaging the springs."

"How are they doing?" Alice asked. "How far have they made it on the wall?"

"They started on the south wall just yesterday. The western wall is done, other than the towers, of course."

"They're going to add towers?" Jacob asked, thinking about the grand guard towers that dotted the Highlands walls.

"It makes sense," Alice said. "I don't think anyone can argue that the wooden walls aren't good enough anymore."

Jacob nodded.

"I can't believe anyone ever argued for wooden walls," Furi muttered. "I mean, if Red Death can climb wood easier than stone, that should have been the end of the conversation."

"Furi, think of it like the docks," Smith said. "You can live on them, and the Skyborn can even thrive there, but are you more likely to survive the winters compared to those in the monarchy? How much more likely are you to starve?"

Furi sagged back in her seat. "At least we don't have Red Death trying to kill us on the docks."

"Well, I cannot argue that."

"Smith," Alice said, "how have they gotten so much done on the wall?"

"Archibald. Bollwerk sent two of the Mech arms to Ancora, and one complete Titan Mech. Told them it was a gift from Jacob, he did." Smith laughed at that.

"Surprised he didn't take the credit for it," Mary said.

But the banter between Mary and Smith faded as a terrible knot untied itself in Jacob's chest. A dread he'd been carrying since he left

Ancora again, that Archibald might abandon his word and leave Ancora on its own.

He wiped at his eyes as Alice reached over and squeezed his leg.

"Skeleton to the north," Mary said. "You can just make out the shadow."

Furi stood and made her way up to Mary. The captain handed her a small scope, and Furi held it to her eye.

Jacob couldn't help but smile when a small gasp escaped Furi's lips.

"I've never seen anything like that. It's like the entire city was just abandoned."

"It's a lot bigger than it looks," Alice said. "More dangerous than it looks too." She gave Jacob a meaningful glance.

Furi turned to the cabin's interior. "What do you mean?"

Jacob knocked on his Biomech leg with his knuckles. "Tree Killers. And a lot of them."

"Right." Furi looked out the window one more time before handing the scope to Mary and heading to her jump seat. "I forgot that happened to you there."

Alice went back to her notebooks, combing through a mixture of loose pages stuffed between those still bound in Furi's handwriting.

Jacob turned his attention to one of Charles's more recent journals. It wasn't dated, but Jacob remembered some of the projects sitting on the old tinker's workbench. He had little doubt it was from just before he'd started pestering Charles some years before.

Sometimes he almost lost sight of the friend he knew when he read Charles's older journals. They were from a different time, a different conflict, and Jacob didn't like the fact that he could sometimes relate more to those old writings than to the man he knew.

So it was good to explore those more recent writings, where the most disturbing things Jacob found between those pages involved some of

Charles's tastes in food. *Who eats crispy Mantis brains?* Otherwise, the drawings and schematics were filled with things that might have helped Ancora, from city lights that would be easier to maintain to an automaton meant to help with the most delicate Biomech surgeries.

And it was that page holding Jacob's attention. Not only because of his own leg, but because of the Biomechs he had known and met in their travels. Perhaps automaton was not the correct word. But it was a machine that could perform a designated task at the mere switch of a lever. Not like the automated men some of the old tinkers told stories of at the Wild Horse, but the similarities drew connections in Jacob's mind.

He wasn't sure how long he spent combing through Charles's old notes, but it was Mary's voice that broke his concentration.

"Smith, we're at the ruins. If you're going with them, you best get ready."

"I do not have the grapples completed. Go without me. We can assist if the need arises, but Alice and Furi know the way."

"Are you coming with us?" Alice asked Mary.

The Skysworn's captain shook her head. "I'm staying at the helm. If you need a quick exit, I'll get there as fast as I can."

Alice nodded.

The conversation continued, but Jacob lost track of it when he saw the ruins of the Great Machine in the desert waste. Alice and Furi and the others had described it to him, but its sheer scope was hard to put into words. It was as if a ceiling had been built over an entire city and then buried in the sands.

Even then, looking at it with his own eyes, the scale was difficult to comprehend. Small shadows scurried across the top of the dunes, and it wasn't until they got closer that Jacob realized they were huge Fire Lizards. Once he understood that, it became clear that the strips of vegetation near the rivers were not merely grass.

Far more grew along the waters, and the narrow beaches gave way to dense scrublands before returning to sand at the foot of the Great Machine.

And it was there in the south that Mary circled the Skysworn. She turned in her chair. "You still remember the way in?"

Alice nodded.

"And how to get back to the control room?"

"I do," Furi said. "I'll never forget."

Jacob could understand why. She'd spent her entire life hearing about the Great Machines in Ballern, and lived on the docks with the Skyborn, where the Children of the Dark Fire spread their stories about mechanical gods that gave the world life. How could anyone forget stepping inside of a god for the first time?

Smith's voice popped up over the horn. "Be sure you each have a pair of wheels and an extra Burner. We may not have seen any major threats on our last visit, but you need to be prepared. Cutters can be unpredictable."

Jacob always had extra Burners and Bangers. They'd saved him more than once, which had turned the small orbs into essential equipment for him. He grabbed his glider pack, and the others did the same.

Outside the cabin, Alice handed a pair of wheels to Jacob and Furi before taking her own. She gave each of them a few Burners, and Jacob dropped the extras into a pouch at his side.

Alice pushed the railing open and let the landing lines unspool to the sand far below. Furi went first, answering Jacob's unspoken question of whether or not she was comfortable with the wheels. The Skyborn sped down the lines as if she was born to them.

"Go," Mary said as she joined them on the deck. "I'll raise the lines behind you."

Jacob and Alice both hooked their wheels onto a line and jumped.

Alice went a few seconds ahead of Jacob, racing down the parallel line as he swung out a little too far, and the inertia pulled him back underneath the Skysworn before his descent steadied.

The wind ruffled his hair around the goggles on his forehead. Alice had already detached her wheels by the time his feet slammed into the sand, harder than he had intended. The impact sent a bolt of pain through his capped leg. He shook off the sting as he pocketed his wheels.

"You okay?" Alice asked.

"Yeah, just hit a little harder than I'd planned."

Alice grinned. "One day, you'll learn. Don't try to catch me."

✧　✧　✧

JACOB FOLLOWED FURI and Alice down a narrow path that led to the base of the towering ruins. Or at least he thought it had been the base, until they stepped inside, and the expanse of what lurked beneath the sands opened before them.

Alice squeezed his hand as they stood on the grated walkway. "It doesn't get any less impressive the second time."

Furi led the way, her gaze looking up into the shadows and dim light above them. It was an odd mixture of glowworms and reflections of the sun in the distance. But what lurked below was far more unsettling. It was too dark to make out specific shapes, but the sun caught on chitin as creatures moved that had no discernible form.

Enormous wings drifted by overhead, the lazy flap of the shadow sending a shower of dust to rain around them. Jacob stared, caught by the swirls and patterns that looked like a predator's eyes on the back of the creature as it dove below them and looped back into the air once more.

"Shadowwings," he whispered. "I've never seen one before."

"They're all over the forests near Ballern," Furi said. "Not like this one, though. This one is beautiful."

"It is," Alice said.

They watched the graceful beast for a time until it swooped into darkness and settled in rafters they could barely make out.

Furi led them across the walkways and traversed stairs that took them to more walkways before they finally came to a doorway. Walking in the relative darkness of that place unnerved Jacob, but Alice and Furi didn't seem bothered by it, and maybe it was because they already knew what waited to either side of them.

But beyond that doorway, all thoughts of what lurked in the shadows fled Jacob's mind. In the light of Alice's lantern, it was easy to see it had once been a control center of some kind. An array of consoles sat below a wall filled with switches and gauges with purposes he could only guess at.

A sprawling curved window in the far wall showed dirt and sand clogging part of the facility, buried in tons of earth that had collapsed in ages past. Jacob knew it had to be ancient because there was no sign of the collapse on the surface.

"Here, this is the manual we found." Furi tapped on a console where the dust had been disturbed and the crumbling binding of an old manual sat open.

Alice pointed to the doorway at the back of the room. "And that's where we found the little booklet Furi translated for us. There wasn't much left."

"Maybe so," Jacob said, "but it gave us enough. Between that and what Charles burned in the Skeleton, we have some idea of what happened to the Deadlands. Or at least the Burning Forest."

Furi grimaced. "I still have a lot of questions that we don't have answers to. If the Great Machines served their purpose, why do they still function? Why are they still poisoning the air?"

"I don't think the creators ever meant to poison the air," Alice said. "How long do you think they had to test something like this? If the air itself was killing everything around them? I don't know if they even would've considered what could happen centuries later if the machines continued running."

"It was another age," Jacob said. "Our records of the Deadlands War are incomplete, and that wasn't that long ago. I don't know if we'll ever have a complete story about the people who built the Great Machines."

"The Children of the Dark Fire might. They have stories of their own."

Alice shook her head. "How can we trust anything they say? They're a cult that would bend and exaggerate any truth to fit their needs."

"I know," Furi said. "But it could give us ideas. Other places to look. There have to be stories that have survived in the remote forest villages and even the desert, where generations have lived together in relative peace."

"Maybe. But could they possibly know what happened?"

Jacob turned the page on the manual, surprised to find so much of it in the common tongue. After the booklet Furi had translated, with its large sections of Mokuskrit, he expected the manual to be almost as illegible to his eyes.

It was the bottom of an index near the last surviving pages of the book that caught his eye. He read it out loud, bringing Alice and Furi to silence at the words.

"Maintenance procedures require boilers to be cooled. Commands may only be executed from District Two."

Jacob frowned at the phrase that followed. "Furi, I can't read this. Can you?"

Furi stepped closer and leaned over the manual. "It says 'reference'." She gently tapped her finger on the next series of symbols. "This means 'manual'."

The number after the Mokuskrit symbol for manual was written in the common tongue, and Jacob said it out loud. "Two."

"Another manual?" Alice asked. "We've hardly found any paper or parchment that survived here."

Furi nodded. "One of the few things that did survive is whatever this manual is made out of. It's stiffer than paper, and it's far more intact than that booklet was. There could be other manuals that survived."

But there was more to the string of characters, part of which Jacob could read. "Manual Two. District Two."

Jacob looked back to the doorway in the long path they'd taken to get to the control center. "If this is District One …"

"Then where is District Two?" Furi asked.

"Follow me," Alice said. She hurried toward the back wall, pushing a sliding door a little wider, revealing a schematic engraved in metal and punctuated by countless lifeless lights. "This is the map."

Jacob frowned. "It is?" He paused and stared at the long-decayed bodies on the floor, flanked by the hollow carcasses of what looked like tiny Carrion Worms.

Alice followed his gaze. "Drakkar said one of them was a Founder from Cave. But look, we need to focus."

Jacob shook his head and returned his attention to the wall. "It's a schematic, but—"

"*Exactly,*" Alice said. "A schematic of a Great Machine. Look, it's not exact, only high level, but if you had to guess where we are based on what you've seen, maybe you can guess where District Two would be?"

"In any layout, District One and Two are going to be close," Jacob said, frowning at the wall. He didn't recognize all the symbols. A few he did, but the longer he looked at them, the less sense they made. "It's like one of Charles's schematics here. This is the symbol for an air pump. The circle with a hollow triangle? But just beside it is a closed loop that looks like something for a hydraulic system. But you can't … can't …"

"Jacob?" Alice said as he fell silent.

But the schematic resolved in his mind. It wasn't a diagram of one system inside the Great Machine. It was a diagram of every system that had been employed in the massive facility, overlaid in a single, tangled schematic.

"This is everything. The entire facility. All in one map. I think where the symbols overlay, where you have air and hydraulics mixed in bizarre fashions? Those are for different levels of the Great Machine. I need a light."

Fury fished a lantern out of her pack and struck the igniter, handing it to Jacob.

He leaned close to the wall, shining it directly into the dead indicator lights. "That's it. Look at these. They're color coded. Green, blue, red, and more."

"Here," Furi said, tapping the corner of the schematic. "These are the Mokuskrit words for colors. And by each one, you have common numbers."

"Floors," Alice said.

Furi nodded. "It has to be."

"But where do we go?" Jacob asked.

"We know how to sabotage a boiler," Alice said. "Where do we find boilers?"

Jacob grinned and turned back to the schematic. He tapped a strange symbol that looked like an open jug. One of many set in a line. "Here."

Alice squinted at the small light when Jacob held up the lantern. "Red."

"First floor," Furi said.

"District Two," Jacob said. "If they numbered this like I think they have … these fans marked here were above us when we came in, and if we're in District One …"

"Then the boilers should be District Two." Alice leaned forward and grabbed the sides of his face before kissing him. "Let's get down there and get out of here."

"Please," Furi said, shivering. "This place is creepy. I'm taking the manual because I don't want to come back here again."

Alice clicked the transmitter in her collar. "Skysworn, we found reference to another district. Looks like it might be where the boilers are to the north, so we're going to investigate."

"Understood," Mary said. "Use caution. Walkways may not be as stable deeper into the facility."

✧   ✧   ✧

MARY COULDN'T HAVE been more right. They made their way to the bottom walkway, but it had long since collapsed onto the floor below. And that darkness churned with busy Cutters hauling long-dead tree roots and other prey in and out of their nest.

"We can't walk through a nest," Alice said.

"No. No, we can't." Jacob sighed and looked up. One walkway stretched forward far above them. "We have to go back up."

Furi groaned, but she led the way to the spiral stairs. It reminded Jacob of taking the stone tower stairs in the Highlands, only these were metal and rang out with every footfall. They passed two levels before reaching the top, and every one of them paused to take several deep breaths.

"This place needs a lift," Furi muttered.

"It probably has several," Alice said. "Buried in the sand somewhere. Let's just hope we don't see anyone else while we're here."

Furi grunted and led the way over the highest walkway. It was two full sections above where they'd entered, and Jacob could make out the glowworms on the ceiling now. A drop from that height onto the myriad of platforms below and he wouldn't have to worry about finding the boilers. Not a reassuring thought as the walkway creaked beneath their feet.

From their vantage point, the sounds of Cutters far below were only a whisper. On one hand, Jacob thought it might be better for them to spread out, but on the other hand, he didn't want Furi or Alice more than an arm's length away. If they had to run, he wanted the group as close together as possible.

It seemed as if they had been walking for a good ten minutes before they reached the next pylon, a massive pillar sunk into the earth far below. Furi led them around the wide curve of the walkway to what should be their last stretch before entering District Two.

But the Skyborn came to a sudden stop and cursed.

Jacob wasn't sure why until he and Alice stepped to either side of Furi. The path they needed had collapsed long ago, taking the second level of walkway with it.

"Should we go to the bottom?" Alice asked.

Furi squinted into the darkness. "I can't be positive, but I think the lowest walkway is gone too."

Jacob looked around them, trying to trace the surviving walkways in the dim light. The second level was still intact closer to one of the smaller pylons. They needed to be on the ground level, but they didn't want to be there until they were far past the nest.

"I think we can make it to the broken walkway."

Alice raised an eyebrow as she turned to Jacob. "That is a long way."

Jacob nodded. "We'll have to dive, then pull up. Like we did from that supply ship. If we don't, we won't have the distance."

"It's risky," Furi said. "If you don't jump out far enough, you're going to land on the platform right below us."

Jacob tightened the harness of his glider pack. "That's why we're going to run right off the end of this thing. Be ready to open your pack if the walkway collapses under your feet."

"We need to get over there, and I'm not walking across the ground," Alice said. "Furi, are you comfortable with this?"

"Comfortable is a strong word, but I understand what Jacob means. Let's go."

"I'll go first," Jacob said. "If I make it, follow my path."

Jacob took a deep breath to center himself. The walkway was only six feet wide. That made it narrower than the alley he had once skirted through in Bollwerk on the glider. And far narrower than the pass he and Alice had taken at Fel. Alice had more practice with the glider than Furi, and while that concerned him, he had confidence in the Skyborn.

But six feet was a small target.

He blew out a slow breath and sprinted at the broken edge of the walkway, the jagged and twisted steel taunting him as his boots left the ground.

But something happened he did not expect to see when he threw the lever on the glider, and the wings caught the dead air inside the Great Machine. Two shadows swooped down to either side of him, their brilliant wings a beacon in the darkness as they followed his path, graceful movement in a panicked moment.

Jacob focused on his target, ignoring the grace of the Shadowwings as best he could as his arc took him nearly as high as the walkway he'd leaped from before he adjusted the wings and angled down toward the broken walkway on the second floor. As narrow as six feet was when he was standing on it, the minuscule target felt far more imposing when he was in the air.

The Shadowwings broke away from him, returning to the darkness above as his boots crashed down on the walkway, vibrating with the cables that held it aloft.

Furi went next. In the moment it took for Jacob to collapse the wings and turn around, Furi leaped from the tower. He cringed at the delay in her glider, worried she needed to open the wings faster, but when they snapped taut and she twisted back on them, she swooped into the air in a towering arc. It would be plenty to get her to the far platform.

Alice screamed. "Furi!"

Jacob saw nothing, and then he saw the shadow, its neck ringed with fiery red fur. He shouted a curse as he drew the air cannon from the clip at his side, working the pump to prime it, but he had no shot. If he aimed at the Dragonhawk, he could hit Alice, who had now followed Furi into the air.

But the buzz of wings grew louder, and more than one pitch-black shadow ringed in fire filled the air. Jacob swung the barrel of the air cannon to his right and fired. A second Dragonhawk spiraled into the shadows below, and Jacob hoped the Cutters would feast on the creature before it could climb back up to him.

Another shot cut through the red ring of fur when a Dragonhawk swooped at Furi, just missing her thanks to the glider's sudden swing to the side. Its head tumbled away before the body followed.

But the third closed on Furi with a vengeance, crashing into the leather wings and thrusting with a stinger long enough to be a short sword. Jacob couldn't see what happened, only that the Dragonhawk suddenly let go and turned on Alice.

Only then did Jacob see Alice and her wrist launcher hurling bolts at the Dragonhawk. And when the creature made the mistake of turning around, a volley of bolts took it through the eye and sent it reeling into the abyss.

"Furi!" Jacob shouted as the bent-winged glider started to drift off course.

She twisted as best she could, but she was going to miss the platform. Jacob raced to the railing and silently hoped it would hold as Furi drifted down in slow motion. He reached out his hand, and hers slammed into it. The impact threatened to pull him over the edge as she crashed into the side of the walkway.

Alice was there a moment later, her wings still collapsing as she threw herself forward, grabbing Furi under the shoulders as they both hauled her up.

Furi shook there on the floor, and the tears didn't stop.

Alice pawed at Furi's glider and back, looking for wounds, but Jacob didn't see anything severe. A few cuts and scrapes might have been from the impact with the Dragonhawk, or even the walkway, but the hole left by the stinger had torn through her wing and stuck in the pouch at her side.

"You're okay," Alice said, wrapping Furi up in her arms. "You're okay."

"I thought it had me," Furi choked out. "It *did* have me."

"Alice shot it," Jacob said, sparing a glance for the collapsed hole in the nearby roof. "Let's get out of here."

Furi nodded against Alice's shoulder and took a shaky breath. They both stood up before the group hurried down the path, taking the stairs down to the first level, where relief flooded Jacob. The walkway into District Two was still intact.

✧   ✧   ✧

If Jacob hadn't known how far they'd walked and glided inside the facility, he might have thought the control room for District Two was the same as District One, with a few obvious differences.

All three of them stood at the window and stared at the shadowy room on the other side. This one wasn't filled with dirt and sand, but it crawled with darkness. Alice's lantern barely cut through the edge of it, but the light was enough to see the enormous vats, furnaces, and boilers that waited beyond.

Some of the pipework had corroded and collapsed, but it was a sight to behold. As large as the corridor that connected the districts had been, this room looked nearly as wide. It wasn't something the schematics portrayed, and it certainly wasn't something Jacob had expected to see.

"Do you think they're all like this?" Furi asked. "The Great Machines near Ballern?"

"Could be," Jacob said. "I guess we won't know until we visit."

"Might just be easier to join the cult." Alice let out a humorless laugh.

Furi grinned at her. "Wait, go back. With your lantern, go back."

Alice moved it across the boilers again until Furi waved her hand.

"There. Look, that's a warning."

She was right, of that Jacob had no doubt. The symbol of a fire with a line drawn through it was something he'd seen in nearly every city he'd visited.

Jacob frowned when he noticed what was next to the warning. "They have furnaces right next to those tanks."

Alice swung the lantern across the room they were in. "Come on. Let's see if we can find another manual or anything that will help us sabotage something the size of a city."

But that thought alone was enough to give Jacob pause. Whoever built this facility to withstand the centuries, to even hold up to the weight of its own structure, had to have built a failsafe into the system. And likely several of them, at that.

Of course, the ruin around them showed that the Great Machines could be brought to an end. Even if this one had fallen to disrepair and time, they had to have vulnerabilities. And if those boilers and furnaces sat at the core of the pipeworks, well, they were exactly the kind of things Jacob knew how to break.

They spread out across the control room, lighting additional lanterns and attaching reflectors that cast the entire space in an eerie orange glow.

From one end to the other, they didn't leave a single drawer unopened or cabinet unchecked.

By the time they circled back to where they'd begun, one thing had become obvious.

"There's nothing here," Furi said.

Alice pursed her lips and turned to the rear wall. "This room is almost exactly like the other control room. What if they have more of those concealed doors?"

Furi gestured to the wall where the handle had been in District One. It was flat, polished, and showed no signs of an indentation, much less a door.

Jacob looked into the roomful of boilers beyond. "What if it's on the other wall? Between the windows?"

Alice stepped closer. There was a small gap between each of the large, curved windows. "It's wide enough to fit a door, but there isn't anything on the other side. We can see into that room."

"Look," Jacob said, pointing to his left. At the far end of the bank of windows, just inside the room with the boilers, sat a lighter shadow. The shadow of something that stretched out like a square before giving way to darkness.

Alice walked around the edge of the windows, following the long curve until she stopped at the farthest wall. Jacob and Furi followed.

"Sometimes I hate it when you're right." She grinned and reached into a dim break in the paneling that could have been another shadow. It clicked and pulled forward before sliding into the wall. Stale air rolled out to greet them.

Beyond was another schematic. A wall of dead lights and symbols that, while similar to the District One schematic, included far more details for the boilers that lay outside.

"The smaller tanks are hazardous. Look at this." Jacob ran his fingers along the schematic. "That's what we need to look for in the Great Machines. If those close to Ballern are anything like this one, it all connects back to the boiler room. Destroy that, and the Great Machines will fall."

"What's that smell?" Furi asked.

"It might be the gas," Jacob said. "Whatever's left in here that's flammable."

Furi wrinkled her nose. "Smells like oily steel wool caught fire. Have you ever smelled that?"

Jacob nodded.

"Here!" Alice said, picking up a manual from one of the two desks inside. She flipped through the first few pages and froze. "There's a map in here. An *actual* map. Not just a schematic." She winced as she unfolded it, and the page snapped off. "Let's take this with us. We can redraw it on the Skysworn. It's too fragile to be quick with it."

"Good. Let's go," Furi hissed. "I don't want to see any more Dragonhawks."

Furi's words reminded Jacob her glider was damaged. It might be able to fly, but it wasn't a risk they could take. They'd either have to go back along the ground or …

He clicked his transmitter. "Skysworn. One glider is damaged. We need another way out." For a brief moment, Jacob wished he'd had Charles's grappling cannon they'd used beneath Dauschen. But he shook the memory away as the events that followed crawled back into his mind.

"Where are you?" Mary asked.

"South of the big hole in the ceiling, if you can see that."

Mary relayed that information to Smith as the others listened over the transmitter. "Jacob, you three need to stay away from the walkways. Smith has some insane plan, and I'm not entirely sure the roof won't collapse."

"We'll stay in the control room."

But even as Jacob said the words, all three of them made their way back to the entrance. It wasn't long before a shadow crossed the gap in the roof, and a horrible clang sounded above them, echoing along the hollow expanse of the ruins.

"What are they *doing?*" Furi asked.

Pinpoints of light pierced the darker parts of roof above, and with the shriek of twisted metal, lifted away to reveal the Skysworn.

"What in all the hells," Alice muttered.

"Smith," Jacob said with a grin. "That's what he meant by a grapple."

The Skysworn drifted forward, and Jacob didn't have to guess when the plate released. It clanged above as if the entire building was a tuning fork. The ship came back, and the claw descended once more. But this time, its grip failed, and the metal fell as it curled back, breaking free of its anchors as it crashed to the ground far below.

Something buzzed and clicked in the shadows, the sound growing louder in the stunned silence.

"Are you all okay?" Mary hissed over the transmitter.

"Fine," Jacob answered. "Suspect the Dragonhawks on the ground won't be happy, though."

"Or alive," Alice muttered.

Furi let out a wholly inappropriate giggle.

"Dropping lines now," Mary said. "Don't climb them until they're stable. Last thing I need is one of you smeared across the roof."

"Let's go," Alice said, extinguishing her lantern before hurrying back onto the walkway. They didn't go slow this time, instead almost sprinting through the dim light until they reached the stairs. By the time they made it around the spiral to the second floor, all three of them were breathless.

But the sight waiting for them there was a welcomed one indeed.

"Furi, you first," Alice said. And it was the best option. If anything happened after Furi was gone, at least Jacob and Alice had gliders.

Relief flowed through Jacob as Furi reached the Skysworn far above, and Alice followed. He clipped his own wheels onto the line and lit the Burner. Cutters shuffled below, but he didn't look down as the wheels sped him toward the light. He'd either reach the Skysworn before something found him, or he wouldn't.

Breaking out from the shadows, he realized how low the Skysworn had been hovering in order to be sure the landing lines could reach them. If Mary hadn't been as skilled a captain as she was, they might have had a much more difficult time escaping the ruins.

Smith was there to pull him onto the deck, and Jacob had rarely felt such a relief to have his feet off the ground. The older tinker slapped him on the back and started reeling in the lines.

"Time to go!" Smith shouted toward the cabin when the last line finished spooling, and he closed the railing.

CHAPTER TWENTY-FOUR

"I F WE DON'T cut off their supplies, this war will continue indefinite-ly." Lady Katherine eyed the group on the bridge of Eva's brig. Rin, Tatsu, Drakkar, Samuel, and of course Eva. It was an odd thing, relying on relative strangers. But Mary and Eva had long been her closest confidantes, perhaps to an extent they themselves did not realize.

Rin squeezed his hand into a fist. "What are you asking?"

"I need you to help us. We need to get a small group of soldiers inside the enemy strongholds and take down their supply depots."

"They feed civilians with that food too, My Lady. The deaths you cause will not only be soldiers and fighters."

Rin wasn't wrong, but Lady Katherine wondered if that would truly stop someone who had defected from Ballern. But a failure to act, that could be far worse for Belldorn and her allies.

"The cost of war is a higher price than I wish to pay, but it will be visited on my own people if I do not act. Help me free the people of Ballern and bring an end to their tyranny."

Rin didn't answer for a time, exchanging a glance with Tatsu. "The people of Ballern believe *you* to be the tyrant, Lady Katherine. I don't think you will like what you find across the Crystal Sea."

"I have been called worse than a tyrant, Rin. And in war, I fear such words lose much of the definition they are meant to convey. We are all tyrants when faced with death."

"We deployed those horrors at your command," Tatsu said, standing up straighter. "I watched soldiers die horribly by your hand today."

"Would you have preferred them on the tip of your spear?" Lady Katherine asked.

Tatsu remained silent.

"Ask the Ancorans what these people have brought upon their enemies. Samuel was there at the Fall. Furi's friends, Alice and Jacob, saw the worst this world has to offer. And still, they fight to save its people."

No one responded. "You have my gratitude for what you did today. I hope you can find peace with it, as it will keep Canopy protected for some time."

"Canopy can protect itself," Tatsu snapped. "We don't need—"

"Tatsu," Rin said, making a sweeping gesture to the other Dragonrider. "Tatsu, that's enough. If Ballern came for us in force, there's nothing we could do to stop them. We've talked about this a thousand times. Canopy would fall without Belldorn."

Lady Katherine leaned across the table at the center of the bridge and released her hold on the transmitter. "Did you hear all of that, Skysworn?"

"Yes, we heard it." Mary blew out a breath. "We have a map, Kat. A map of a Great Machine. Maybe just as important as shutting down Ballern's refinery is the idea of proving the Great Machines are only machines. Machines that aren't gods."

"I thought you said you heard our conversation, Skysworn."

Mary's silence told Kat how angry she was, but this wasn't open to negotiation. "We have to go to Ballern and do this."

"Skysworn, no. Not yet. Not alone. We need to establish an alliance with the Skyborn. *That* has to be your priority. *Our* priority. The bait boxes worked. Ballern's air support has been crippled, and this battle will end on the ground, in our very streets."

Mary's voice cut in and out for a moment. "The Titan Mechs can handle ground forces. You don't need us in a ground battle."

"That's why I want you and your passengers to return to Ballern."

"I'll stay," Samuel said. "I'll fight with you so the Skysworn can go."

"As will I," Tatsu said, keeping his eyes on the transmitter. "If it gives us a chance to prove the Children of the Dark Fire are a sickness unto themselves, I will stay at your side."

"Rin?" Lady Katherine asked.

Rin nodded. "You have the support of the Dragonriders. We fight with Belldorn. But if this alliance turns out to be a ruse, your ties with Canopy will break. And I fear what that would mean for both our peoples."

"It will not break," Lady Katherine said. "Skysworn. Return to the docks and take what supplies you need. You should depart for Ballern by evening. To wait until morning will bring Ballern's reinforcements into your path."

"Understood," Mary said with no hint of disagreement.

Lady Katherine didn't show the gratefulness she felt. There were times when she needed to be as ruthless as those who would strike at her people. She only hoped those who would follow her into battle would one day understand the bitterness of necessity.

CHAPTER TWENTY-FIVE

WHILE THE RETURN to the docks had left them precious little time to resupply and get Furi's glider pack swapped out, Jacob was grateful for the small restaurants and bars along the docks. The idea of eating nothing but seeds and dried Pill-Bug for the next day was far from appealing.

But the other thing such a long journey gave them was time, time for Alice and Furi to copy down the layouts from various districts of the Great Machines. And time for Mary to cool down after that conversation with Lady Katherine.

Apparently, Alice had much the same thought as she picked up her soup from the bar. "I thought Mary was going to explode."

Furi snorted a laugh into her cup of soup.

"Do not be surprised if Mary throws you overboard if she catches you saying that."

Jacob startled upright at Smith's booming voice just behind him on the dock. "Smith, didn't see you there."

"I can tell by the soup on your vest."

Jacob glanced down and grimaced.

The other three burst into laughter before Smith patted Jacob on the shoulder.

"Finish your meal and get back to the Skysworn. Mary means to follow through with her promise to Kat, and that means we are leaving within the hour."

Furi watched him leave before she spoke again. "I'm worried about Tatsu. He sounded mad in that conference."

"I think we've all felt that way," Alice said. "It's a bad situation, but someone has to make a decision. Otherwise, we're just waiting for Ballern to attack again."

Jacob nodded. "And that would probably get more people killed than Kat's plan."

"Would it, though?" Furi asked. "Even if Lady Katherine's plan works, more Skyborn will be in danger."

Alice reached out and squeezed Furi's arm. "I would rather know what I'm fighting for than die for a lie."

Furi mulled that over as she sipped her soup. "I would too. The Children of the Dark Fire have to be stopped. And that means Ballern must be stopped. But I can't help but be sorry for those people who just want to live their lives in peace."

"Trapped on the docks for the rest of their lives?" Jacob asked.

"It's still home, Jacob. I've been happy there. Not always, but sometimes it's a good place."

"I'm sorry. I didn't mean to say it wasn't. It's just … I can't imagine living on a dock."

Furi smiled. "I can't imagine living behind a wooden wall, thinking I'm safe."

"Touché," Jacob muttered.

Alice laughed and patted both of them on the back. "Let's go. We have a lot to unpack, and I want to study the map."

✧   ✧   ✧

THEY HADN'T MADE it ten feet off the docks before Mary started arguing with Smith.

"Look, all I'm saying is that giant grapple has to weigh as much as filling half the cargo hold. We'll be slower."

"Mary, no. Stop worrying about it. It is inconsequential. We do not have a payload, so it is not an issue. Even if it was, the thrusters can handle it."

"If we have to refuel more often, it's going to slow us down. I'd be less concerned if we weren't crossing the sea again."

"We can siphon seawater into the secondary boilers, should it become an issue. Which it will not."

Mary grumbled something unintelligible and then closed the horn.

Jacob and Alice exchanged a grin before she went back to copying another section of the map onto a large stretch of folded parchment. It was slowly taking shape, and the only real loss had been the small pieces that had crumbled in the folds. Everything else had been clear outside of a handful of writing and smudges from some long-dead worker.

Furi leaned away from her notes and took a deep breath. "I kind of wish I could've seen the Emerald Needles. Can you imagine?"

Alice nodded. "I don't really need to imagine it. Jacob and I saw the same thing when Ancora fell. It may have been Red Death, and all of their black chitin and red skulls, but it's not hard to imagine what the Emerald Needles would have done."

"How bad was it?"

Alice glanced at Jacob before turning her attention back to Furi. As recent as the Fall had been, it wasn't often Jacob heard Alice talk about it at length. But Furi's question had come at the right time, as they worked on the map, with hours over the sea before them.

Not all parts of the story were bad. Alice recounting the dance at Festival and the game of Cork where they'd won more strawberries than they possibly could have eaten themselves were his favorite parts. But the story turned dark soon enough, and Jacob's own memories added to the horror of Alice's descriptions.

Furi's pen slowed as Alice detailed what had happened to the Lowlands. And she told of a great battle at the northern square between the Spider Knights and the Red Death that moved like water poured over a hill. Jacob hadn't seen that happen with his own eyes, only the aftermath as he and Charles had raced back through the ruined city on the steambike.

For a time, the cabin remained quiet after Alice's story, with only the occasional click as Mary adjusted levers and checked gauges on the thrusters. It was Furi who finally broke the silence.

"I had no idea. I knew it was bad. I just didn't realize …"

Alice gave a small nod. "It went on for days. I can't imagine what it was like for the people trapped out in the Lowlands. So many who never escaped."

"We had battles in Ballern," Furi said. "More than once, I've seen the villages march on the city, but always from a distance. I was too young to fight the last time they came, but we could see them from the docks. It was awful, but what you described was much worse."

"Even the best battles are awful," Mary said. "You'll learn that as you get older, if you haven't already."

Jacob was fairly sure Furi knew. She'd been on the Nightingale when it was shot down, seen the invasion in Ballern, and who knew the stories she had from the battles that came before.

✧   ✧   ✧

SHORTLY AFTER MARY announced they had an hour of flight left, the map was finally done. Alice carefully gathered the broken scraps of the folded paper and tucked them back into the manual. Then she unfolded the fresh parchment she and Furi had been working on.

Each opening fold revealed more of the layout of the Great Machine. And if they were lucky—Jacob felt anything but lucky—the Great Machine in Ballern might look similar.

"Clip it to the wall," Mary said.

Alice and Furi made their way over to the wall beside the cabin's door. A series of thick magnets held various maps and permits from all across Belldorn and Ballern. But a few of the magnets were empty, and it was those Alice wrenched away from the wall before letting them smack back into place on top of the map.

Furi did the same, adding a smaller magnet to the bottom to keep the parchment secured. That done, they both stepped back and stood beside Jacob, studying the sprawling structure of the Great Machine.

"It feels like we should be doing this first," Furi said. "Are you sure the Lady of Belldorn is right?"

Mary shrugged. "I don't think we'll know until it's done. It may be the right call, or it may end in disaster. What if there's more to the Children of the Dark Fire than we know? What if the Great Machine sits behind a strong defense? We don't know, and if I know Kat, she's trying to mitigate the risk. Before we land, mark the entrances you can identify on the map. Smith and I will work on a strategy."

"Are we going to go against Lady Katherine's word?" Alice asked.

"Not yet. If we can present a solid strategy that still meets her priorities, I think she'll come around. I'll need Eva to help pressure her, and she has lots of experience helping me with that."

"So we aren't even going to fly over the Great Machine?" Jacob asked.

Mary turned slowly in her seat. "For now, we stick with Kat's plan."

"Tell them why," a muffled voice said over the horn.

Mary flipped the cap so Smith's voice was clearer. "You tell them."

Smith let out a low laugh. "It is more important to establish an alliance with the Skyborn. And there is no better contact than Furi."

"What about Rin? Or Tatsu?"

"How long have they been gone?" Smith asked. "I know the Skyborn stories about the brainwashing in Belldorn. For Rin or Tatsu to reappear now, they would be labeled spies, and may not survive the day."

"And me?"

"You, you can be a brave escapee from the tyrants of Belldorn if it looks as though someone means to turn against you. A story of heroism will buy you more leeway. Exaggerate it if you must."

"I just need to find Kura. Kura is deeper into the resistance than I ever realized."

"You will need warriors too," Smith said. "You have spoken of your teacher, and she may have influence and power with the Skyborn, but there will be a time for action more than words."

"Kura will help," Furi said, and the confidence in those words gave Jacob a small measure of hope.

CHAPTER TWENTY-SIX

J ACOB SHIVERED WHEN his boots hit the metal lattice of Ballern's docks. He rubbed his arms as a chill ran through them.

"Something wrong?" Alice asked.

Jacob shook his head. "No, I'm fine. I was just thinking. Mordair is here. Somewhere inside the city."

"I know." Alice took a deep breath and started down the long arm of the dock.

Furi hurried to catch up, taking an extra moment to grab a satchel for her thigh. They had left the glider packs on the Skysworn. The newer models might have been smaller and easier to carry, but they still stood out. And if there was anything they didn't want to do, it was stand out.

"We can take the lifts this time," Furi said. "There aren't any guards this late at night."

Jacob yawned and nodded.

"Good," Alice said. "I have no interest in climbing up those broken ladders again. And certainly not without a glider on."

Furi grinned. "You did great."

"If by great you mean I didn't die."

Jacob watched every step for a time, and in the darkness, it was hard to imagine that the lights far below were actually the city of Ballern. Alice had climbed the outer reaches of the docks in daylight, and the idea of dangling out over that fall was unsettling at best.

"Are we going back to that same warehouse?" Alice asked.

Furi nodded. "Even if Kura isn't there, she will be soon. She gets in early to prepare the classroom. Always has."

"Early," Jacob muttered. "This isn't early. This is late."

"You'll have to forgive him." Alice gave him an apologetic look. "It's far past his bedtime."

Furi burst into laughter and turned right where the walkways intersected.

A number of the docks stood empty, and Jacob wondered how much of that was due to the battle at Belldorn. Part of him thought they should be back there, still doing what they could on the ground. But the attack with the Emerald Needles had gone well, and Jacob shuddered at the thought of what must have happened to those ships and soldiers.

"This way." They passed a number of small tents and bars that had been drawn closed against the chilly night. The walkway Furi turned down next led them to an octagonal tower. Nothing stirred on the docks, and the squeak of the latticed doorway sounded like a scream in the night.

The three of them piled into the lift, with enough room left over for ten more people. Jacob had seen at least one more lift set into another face of the tower, and if each face held a lift, the capacity was far more than he would have expected.

"How many lifts are there?" Alice asked.

"Four," Furi said. "Two for people and two for freight. The freight lifts take up most of the tower."

As loud as the door had been, when Furi pulled the lever for a different floor, the lift whispered along its cables. Only the distant hum of a motor sounded in the dark.

Jacob heard voices as they passed level after level of the docks, and more lights started showing intermittently between the latticework. He didn't understand why that was until the lift finally stopped and Furi slid the door open.

Directly in front of them was the shadowy form of a dark gray warship.

"Fel," Jacob hissed.

It had been one thing to know Mordair's forces were in the city, but it was another to see the brilliant red flag and the mosaic of a Tail Sword hanging from the ramps of a warship. As empty as the lower levels had been, these docks were well guarded.

"This way," Furi whispered.

They exited to the right, leaving the imposing silhouette of the warship behind them. The wide walkway narrowed at the next intersection, flanked by shops and a handful of restaurants where one of the chefs was already preparing for the breakfast crowds. They passed a pair of Fel's guards, but the two soldiers were distracted by an argument with each other, though Jacob couldn't make out the words.

The walkway narrowed again, and Jacob's relatively sure footing gave way to a brief panic as the metal shook beneath every footfall. He kept one hand on the railing and stayed behind Furi and Alice, as there wasn't room for three people side by side. Jacob had little doubt they were getting close to the area Furi had called the Bones.

Furi glanced back toward the soldiers and the docked warship as they made their way farther out onto the walkway. A cold breeze cut through them as they passed behind a large metal building.

"Almost there," Alice said. "It's the next building over, isn't it?"

"It is."

While Jacob was thankful for Furi's answer, he was more thankful when the latticed walkway gave way to metal plating that didn't allow him to see down to the dark city below. He might have been confident at that height with a glider strapped to his back, but it was far different knowing that an awkward misstep could be the end of him.

As they rounded the warehouse, out of sight of the warship, an entirely different view welcomed Jacob. Dim streetlights flickered in the dark of night, casting shadows across homes with roofs that came to graceful peaks. It was a jarring contrast between the warehouses and those homes, made all the more odd by the distant shadow of the warship.

Furi stopped at the next building and twisted a doorknob, bringing them into a towering warehouse that could have fit a destroyer inside. Or could have if it wasn't packed with so many crates and barrels that looked as though they might fall at any moment.

"The light's on," Furi said. "She's here."

A woman stood in an alcove deeper into the building, chalk squeaking across a cracked blackboard as they approached. Furi paused and watched, not announcing their arrival for a time, instead waiting for the woman with the salt and pepper braid to turn around.

"Furi!" Kura said, a broad smile crossing her face. "And Alice, wasn't it?"

Alice nodded.

"Welcome, welcome. And who is your friend?"

Furi fidgeted. "Kura, this is Jacob. He's from Ancora, like Alice. They're both Steamborn."

Kura blinked. "Steamborn, you say? Why bring them here?"

"Because Ballern is attacking Belldorn, and Fel is at our walls."

Kura walked back behind her desk and sat down, gesturing for the trio to do the same. "My dear, Fel is inside our walls. The docks on the sea are overrun with their destroyers, and our airship docks are soiled by those gray stains and bloody banners."

Furi leaned forward as she sat down. "Kura, do you know anyone in the resistance? Skyborn who might be willing to fight with us?"

"Fight?" Kura asked, raising an eyebrow. "Child, who do you mean to fight?"

"Against the queen, Mordair, everyone who is an enemy of the Sky-born."

Kura smiled and shook her head. "You cannot fight everyone, Furi."

"I can try."

Kura paused, glancing at Jacob and Alice before returning her attention to Furi. "You're serious?"

"I wouldn't be here if I wasn't. Rin and Tatsu and even Beck are in Belldorn. Beck might still be in prison. I don't know. But Rin and Tatsu are on the front lines. They might fight for Canopy, but it makes them an ally of Belldorn."

Kura sighed and ran her fingers over her hair. "You kids are going to get me killed. Or the stress is going to kill me. Either way, you're going to get me killed."

"You'll help?" Furi asked.

Kura looked up at the blackboard. "I will teach. The same as I taught you, and Rin, when you were both so small. But Furi, there is a difference between outright warfare and the education and skills I tried to instill in all the Skyborn. You must wait for the right time, or you will lead them into ruin, for the smallest chance of victory."

Furi's back stiffened. "You've lived on the docks longer than I have. You've seen the changes. The Children of the Dark Fire have their hands in more than the monarchy. And it's only a matter of time before they come for all the Skyborn."

"They fight with us in Belldorn," Alice said. "Skyborn, and those of us from Ancora who are known as the Steamborn. It was an insult from the Highlanders, but it's become something more now."

"There is power in a name." Kura looked down at her hands as she laced her fingers together. "And there is power in a bond. You will not be dissuaded?"

"Never," Furi said. "You always told me I should find my purpose. I did."

Kura whispered something under her breath that Jacob could barely hear. "Never have I wished Jakon was more wrong."

"Jakon?" Furi asked. "What does he have to do with this?"

Kura chuckled. "I know what he gave you. The question is, do you know *why* he gave it to you?"

Jacob's mind raced. He knew Jakon had given Furi and Alice a palace schedule and a legend to translate it. But he couldn't see what that had to do with their current conversation. A way to track down the queen, or to avoid detection if they infiltrated the palace, but what more than that?

"The queen is at odds with the Children of the Dark Fire," Kura said. Her words were met with stunned silence from the others. "You do not repeat this outside of these walls. There are few who know, and it would not be hard to trace these words back to Jakon, or me. And you know how that would end."

Furi blinked. "If she … if she wasn't loyal to the Children of the Dark Fire, they'd kill her."

"Yes. And to protect herself, she would have to kill me, or Jakon, or both. So you understand the need for secrecy."

"Why would you say this in front of us?" Alice asked. "You don't know us."

Kura smiled. "I could list on one hand the number of people Furi has trusted in her life and have fingers left to spare. And yet here you sit, Steamborn from Ancora, risen from the ashes of war to stand at her side. And what price might that cost you? Children who have seen the worst the world has to offer? People from your world do not see the Skyborn as allies. That might cost you everything, and yet here you stand."

Alice stared at Kura, wide-eyed.

"That, child, that is why I speak openly to you. And why I tell you all is not as it seems in Ballern. There is more division than you know, and the arrival of Mordair has strained the monarchy. Their ships are far to the south, transporting supplies in the west, while Fel's own warships take their docks.

"Mordair is no fool. Neither is the queen. The outcome in Belldorn will dictate much inside the walls of Ballern."

The truth of what Kura was saying hit Jacob like a punch in the gut. "You mean the queen is helping the resistance?"

The savage smile that crawled across Kura's face chilled him to the bone. "Oh yes, and that is why you must seek her out. That is why Jakon gave you that parchment. Who in Ballern would suspect a group of Skyborn to be a threat? At worst, you would be ejected from the palace. Perhaps imprisoned for a short time. But it is common for the Skyborn to visit the lower levels."

Furi stared at Kura. "What do you know about the Great Machines? I intercepted a communicator and ..."

"*Intercepted* a communicator?" Kura asked, her brow wrinkling.

"Fine, we broke into a supply ship and stole it before sinking it in the Crystal Sea, but—"

Kura burst into laughter. She held her hand out as if to ask for mercy and then said, "Continue, please, you've made my day."

Furi glanced at Alice and Jacob. "Well, their supply lines take them back to the Great Machines. Apparently, some of the fuel for the warships is refined there."

Kura's humor vanished in the blink of an eye. "You're certain you translated that correctly?"

"Absolutely. You taught us to years ago." Furi looked away for a moment before returning her eyes to Kura. "You taught me everything I needed to know. Except how to build an antenna, and Smith took care of that."

"That is interesting. I was hoping they may have said more over the communicator."

"About what?" Furi asked.

"About where they are acquiring their explosives. Jakon identified a few sources, imports from Fel and black market trades with Belldorn. But none of that has been in a quantity large enough to arm a fleet."

Jacob frowned at that. "They don't produce it inside the city?"

Kura shook her head. "Not in any place we've found."

Alice rubbed her cheek and leaned back in her chair. "The Great Machines certainly have the space for additional factories. It's possible they are manufacturing explosives there too."

"I don't think that's something we can know until we have eyes and ears inside their facilities."

"And we don't?" Furi asked.

"No," Kura said. "What few have tried have been discovered, or so we assume. They were not heard from again."

Jacob glanced between Kura and Alice. "What if they are using the waste from the Great Machines? What if they aren't burying it like the one in the Deadlands?"

"Trapping the gases in the runoff?" Alice asked. "It could explain their cannons when they don't have the benefit of Theodosia and the others. Maybe."

Jacob blew out a frustrated breath. "This is why we should be going to the Great Machines. The queen might be an ally to the resistance, but we might have a chance to cripple them."

"No." Kura said the word with absolute authority. "You cannot go to that place as it is now. Even if it looked like you had grown up on the docks, the Children of the Dark Fire are merciless. You will need the help of the villages to navigate the woods and the creatures that surround the Great Machine, and the easiest way to gain their trust will be at the behest of the queen. So, I tell you again, that is who you must seek."

Kura reached out and took Furi's hand. "I can see your hesitation. But I can see the bond you have formed with the Ancorans too. You have grown, Furi. But there is more you must do. For the sake of everyone on the docks, and most especially the Skyborn. We are a family stronger than blood."

"And we will leave no one behind," Furi whispered.

"No one. You have the schedule. Find the queen, tell her the forest is in danger, and she will know you are an ally."

"What about the Skyborn?" Furi asked. "How many of them know the queen is an ally?"

"Very few. But they know Fel is a threat, and they have not taken kindly to the soldiers on our docks. As poorly as the Children of the Dark Fire and their ilk have treated our kind, they have tolerated us for the services we bring to the docks. Fel will not be so benevolent."

Jacob thought benevolent was an odd word to describe the Children of the Dark Fire. They knew the history of what that cult had done, and who they had killed, and it was a list of misdeeds and misdirection. They had long worked to remove the truth of things from the knowledge of the Skyborn, and while they might not have succeeded in full, the damage had been done. Jacob worried that the loyalty between those who lived on the docks might not hold if their monarchy crumbled.

But perhaps he was thinking more of the people from the Lowlands. Because while the Skyborn might have faced threats to their very history, something else had happened to the Steamborn. For so long they had been looked down on by the Highlands, it had become a truth most Steamborn accepted—that they were something less, valuable only for what skill they had, and nothing more.

"Maybe that's the goal of the Children of the Dark Fire in Ballern," Jacob said. "To crush the spirit of the Skyborn slowly but so thoroughly there wouldn't be an uprising. No conflict as their entire history fades away."

A chill ran down Jacob's spine as Kura nodded. He shook off the feeling as Furi stood to embrace Kura.

"Wait until dawn to visit the palace. You may raise suspicions if you arrive in the dark."

"Let's go back to the Skysworn and rest," Alice said. "We can sleep for a couple hours, and that's better than nothing."

"How can you sleep?" Furi asked. "Everything we need in Ballern hinges on finding the queen. That's not going to be easy."

Alice yawned. "I think I can manage."

"Alice is right," Kura said. "Get what rest you can. Hard days lie ahead, and you will need your strength."

With that, they left the warehouse and started back to the lift. The smallest hint of light traced the edge of the far horizon. Dawn would come soon, and then they would go hunting for the Queen of Ballern.

CHAPTER TWENTY-SEVEN

Sleep didn't come easy back on the Skysworn. Jacob was somewhat surprised to find Mary and Smith already slumbering when they climbed down to the berth. Furi took an empty top bunk and Jacob the one below it.

"Scoot," Alice said, plopping down on the bed beside him.

Jacob grinned and raised the blanket. Alice rolled underneath it and sighed as he wrapped it around her, taking in the scent of her hair as they settled into the pillow. The bunks weren't really made for two people, but Jacob didn't care. Being close to Alice was worth having the cold steel at his back.

Alice's breathing changed after a time, and the steady rise and fall of her chest was like a quiet lullaby, slowly chasing away the darker thoughts in Jacob's mind until sleep finally took him.

✧　✧　✧

"Jacob! Alice!"

Jacob startled awake, almost catching an elbow in the face from an equally startled Alice.

Mary stood above them, holding a lantern out. "Furi tried to wake you up, but she was a bit too delicate, I think. Time to go."

Jacob yawned and stretched as Alice threw the covers off and rolled out of bed. She gave Mary a dour look that only made the Skysworn captain's smile bigger.

Alice grabbed a small leather pack when Furi held it out.

"These will pass for something the Skyborn would wear. And here's a hairband for you. The Skyborn wear bronze jewelry a lot. And put on denim if you have it. Jacob, you could put a leather apron on too. They'll think you're a Skyborn tinker from the lower docks, and you actually *are* a tinker, so it's a good disguise."

Jacob blinked at Furi. "How are you … *so awake.*"

"Smith gave me a small cup of coffee this morning, very small, and apparently very concentrated? I don't know. It has me awake."

Smith walked into the berth with two cups, not much bigger than the glasses most bars used for their finer drinks.

Alice took one with a nod, inhaling the steam before thanking Smith.

Jacob did the same, frowning at the pitch-black beverage. It smelled good, but Smith's idea of coffee was closer to fudge than liquid. And without the sweetness. Jacob took a tentative sip and raised an eyebrow at the mild bitter notes. "This isn't terrible."

"See, Mary?" Smith said. "One day, I'll be a retired barista in Pirate's Cove."

"It's excellent," Alice said, blowing on the small cup before taking another sip.

"I agree," Furi said. "And energizing!"

Mary blew out a breath, and Jacob didn't miss the slight eye roll. "He's never going to stop making that sludge now."

Smith cast a grin and a wink at them when Mary turned to leave.

"Let's get down to the city," Furi said. "I can't wait for you to see it in the daylight. It's far less unsettling than the docks at night. I promise."

Jacob gulped down the last bit of Smith's concoction and could have sworn his body was starting to vibrate. He grabbed a leather apron off the far wall before trading out the contents of his own pack with the pack Furi had given him. That done, he slipped it over his shoulders and took a deep breath.

"Ready?" Alice asked as she adjusted the hair band behind her ears. The bronze looked aged, and the contrast against Alice's red hair and pale skin was stunning.

"You look great."

Alice froze for a moment before smiling. "Thank you."

"Let's go," Furi said. "The sooner we leave, the more time we'll have in the markets before the palace opens."

They followed Furi onto the deck of the Skysworn before heading to the docks. The sun was just breaking over the horizon now, which meant they'd soon be able to visit the palace. Jacob shivered at a slight chill in the brisk air as he followed Furi and Alice onto Ballern's docks.

✧   ✧   ✧

FOR ALL THE imposing shadows seen in the middle of the night, the docks by day were a different beast altogether. Even out on the Bones, far in the distance, Jacob could see people milling back and forth. And the farther they got from the Skysworn, and the closer they came to the lifts, the crowds grew ever denser.

Where the night before they'd only seen a handful of shopkeepers preparing for the next day, every street and intersection on the docks now moved like a hive of Cutters. It was a rare thing to see those kinds of crowds in Ancora. Festival, and the occasional fair, were really the only times the streets were so choked with people.

"Welcome to Ballern," Furi said with a wide grin.

As tempted as Jacob was to stop at every stall and restaurant to see what they were selling and building and cooking, Alice and Furi kept him focused. It wasn't long before they arrived at the octagonal towers of the main lifts. Where before they walked on without a delay, that morning involved some fifteen minutes of waiting before they could finally squeeze into one of the smaller lifts together.

Between the latticework, Jacob caught a better view of the city of

Ballern below, a shining beacon of pale stone and silver spires reaching into the sky.

"I forgot how clean it looks," Alice said as the lift crossed into the same airspace as the towers. Her comment got a few strange glances from the other passengers.

"It's the stone," Furi said. "Repels most dirt and doesn't like mold much either. Except some of the older buildings. Like there." She pointed into the distance at a squat square facility with dark gray columns that hadn't aged evenly.

The lift slowed, and the latticework opened. They had to fight against the rush of people trying to get on and those trying to exit. Jacob grumbled about how much easier it would be if people just waited for the lift to empty.

Furi led them away from the docks and cut into a dim alley. It was a narrow thing that reminded Jacob more of Ancora than anywhere else they'd been in Ballern or Belldorn. But even there, where a small amount of litter had collected, the streets were immaculate compared to the Lowlands.

It hurt his heart to realize how neglected the Lowlands truly were. And he might never have realized it if he hadn't ventured out into the world. If the Butcher hadn't brought the Fall. He'd help rebuild the Lowlands better than they were before. The new wall would be the first step, but there was more to be done.

He shook off the thoughts as they crossed out of the alley and came to a less-populated street. Furi led them down to another alley, which in turn opened in front of a towering arched gateway. Beyond, framed by the pale stone of the wall, sat rows upon rows of tents and tables, dwarfed only by the massive steel warships docked in the distance.

"Come on," Furi said. "Let's get some food. The back alley here is best. At least, when Jakon isn't here, it's best."

"There's so much more space inside the walls," Alice said. "Why don't the vendors set up inside?"

Furi shook her head. "They aren't allowed outside of celebrations and parades. They can set up here, or on the airship docks. There isn't anywhere else, really."

As remarkable as some of the stalls had been in the air, the lower docks were just as enticing. Jacob paused at a vendor table, looking over an array of hammers that would have put Smith's best tools to shame. They also had a series of miniature tools, like clamps and pliers that looked small enough to fit inside the narrowest of consoles.

"Jacob!" Alice said.

He looked up, finding Furi and Alice a few booths down. He hurried to catch up, just hearing the beginning of Furi's conversation with the chef.

"Lee, it's good to see you."

"I'd heard a rumor some of the Skyborn on the Nightingale had survived." Lee leaned closer and smiled. "Best not to show your face around anyone in Fleet who might recognize you."

"I know," Furi whispered in reply. "But right now, I'm hungry."

Lee's smile widened. "And I suppose Jakon isn't set up today?"

Jacob didn't miss Furi's momentary fidget.

"Jakon has the best soup, but you have the best breakfast."

"That I do. The usual? And what about your friends?"

Furi nodded. "Three orders."

Lee and Furi bantered for a while as the chef cracked several oblong eggs and whipped them with an odd-shaped beater on a crank. He poured the mixture into three rectangular trays on a griddle before turning back to the group.

"Just a couple minutes. Where have you been?"

Part of Jacob was worried about the openness of the conversation. He supposed, with the chaos and noise all around them, it was unlikely anyone would be listening in. And even if they were, they might not realize what they were hearing.

"On a ship, and far to the south. I saw Rin."

Lee's eyes widened just a hair. "Truly? Just how far south have you been?"

Furi flashed a sly smile. "Beyond the city, and into the forest."

"Is it true what they say about the prisons?"

"What who says?" Furi asked. "I'm free and alive, which should tell you what you need to know."

Lee nodded as he started covering the eggs in cheese and rolling them up. "It tells me much. I'm glad to see you well. Have you spoken to Kura? I'm sure she would be interested to hear that Rin is alive."

"I did. We probably won't be here long, Lee."

"Then I'm glad I got to see you. Let me get your food." Lee took the rolled eggs and slipped them into what looked like a crunchy shell. He handed one to each of them and held out his hand to stop Furi when she reached for the coin at her waist. "Keep yourself safe. That is payment enough."

"Thanks, Lee."

Jacob bit into the rolled eggs, the shell crunching before he found the spongy interior and the creamy cheese. It was saltier than he expected, and the cheese had a pungent bite, but the combined effect was delicious. "This is amazing!"

Alice nodded in agreement and Lee smiled at them both.

He leaned over the small counter of his booth and whispered conspiratorially. "Now you only need to convince Furi that my soup is better than Jakon's too."

Furi laughed as she said her goodbyes, and the group continued down the row of vendors. They were nearly to the end of the back row, in clear view of the wider paths filled with shuffling crowds, when Jacob found a small stall filled with toys and gadgets.

One in particular caught his eye, a copper Pilly that could move on its own before rolling into a ball. "May I?"

"Of course!" the vendor said. "Half off today. Only five silvers."

"Five silvers," Furi said. "I could eat for a week on five silvers."

"Maybe at Lee's stall," the vendor said with a grin.

But his answer told Jacob the man had been watching them. Furi didn't seem concerned by that, which also told Jacob he was probably a regular vendor. Jacob's experiences in the Lowlands gave him another insight. The man thought he was a mark. Targeting outsiders was an easy way to make some coin, or steal it.

Jacob turned the Pilly over and frowned. He'd expected fine clockwork, or even the gears of a watch transplanted into the copper body. Instead, it was filled with tiny hoses and a miniature console that could have been a model of a Titan Mech's innards.

He slipped a magnifier out of his leather apron and looked closer, moving the switch on the Pilly's back, which triggered a series of minuscule pistons as the spring pushed back against them. It was a simple enough design, but the precision was astounding.

"I can trade if you don't have the silver," the vendor said.

"Trade for what?" Jacob asked.

"That chisel you have?"

He glanced down at the apron and found a pale handle poking out of one of the many pockets. He slid the tool out, not realizing he'd been carrying it. It was a newer ironwood chisel. Not worth much at all.

"I collect those ironwood handles," the vendor said. "An even trade if you like."

"That's fair. Thank you." Jacob handed the chisel over with a nod.

"A good day to you, lad. Enjoy the market."

Jacob fiddled with the Pilly as they started down the next aisle.

"What in the world do you need that for?" Alice asked.

Jacob slipped his magnifier back into a pocket before holding it out to Alice. "Look at it! It has hydraulics built in. This small. I don't understand how it hasn't dried up or leaked or—"

"Okay, okay, I understand now. New gadgets."

"Better than that. *Ideas* for new gadgets!"

Furi hesitated, looking up at the looming ships from Fel. "It's odd seeing those here."

"Soldiers close by," Alice whispered.

Jacob caught sight of a group farther down the row, their stark gray uniforms only broken by the red flag of Fel on the breast pockets, and the black sword engraved on their belt buckles.

"Time to leave," Furi said.

Jacob gave one last glance up at the warships and the billowing flags, more like tapestries at that size, that loomed over the docks of Ballern. He didn't suppress the shiver that came when he remembered the Butcher had come from Fel, and Mordair was somewhere in Ballern.

Back inside the wall, the sun had risen higher, and the light now bounced through the alleys and streets alike. They were two streets into the city when Furi grabbed Alice's arm and dragged her toward a storefront. "Come on. It's time you learned some *real* history." But the emphasis Furi put on the word "real" made Jacob think they were about to find anything but inside that store.

Jacob and Alice froze when they stepped inside. It wasn't merely a bookstore, but a floor to ceiling spiraling hoard of books. Some looked as if they'd been printed that morning, while others closer to the clerk at a glass counter looked older than the tomes in the basement of the Crown Library.

Furi nodded to the clerk as she led the way up one of two sets of iron stairs, each framed with the falling pages of a book that had been carved in metal. She stopped at a short aisle beneath a placard that simply said *History*.

"They don't mind if you come here to read. They don't ask many questions, either. I don't think the owner likes the monarchy much. Story goes they had to burn a lot of their inventory two decades ago."

"Not just a story," the clerk called up from below them. "It was quite true."

Furi grinned.

"Can I help you kids find anything today?"

"Just looking for a few books on the Great Machines," Furi said.

"Ah, yes. Because the Skyborn adore the Great Machines," the clerk muttered.

"It's for research!"

"Third shelf, back against the wall. As out of sight as we could get it."

"Thank you."

The clerk grunted and went back to reading.

Jacob followed Alice and Furi to the back of the short bookcase. By the wall, on the top shelf, exactly where the clerk had directed them, were several titles that gave away what waited inside.

```
The Lost Machines. A Desert Tragedy.
War! The Triumph of the Great Machines Against
    Heathen Aggressors.
Lost Souls. The Binding of the Fire After the Death of
    a Lady.
The Great Machines and the Salvation of Karn.
The Undying Threat. Peace in an Age of Loss.
A True History of the Gray Woods.
```

"None of them have an author listed," Alice said, picking up two of the tomes. She hesitated and then hefted another one onto her stack.

"What are you doing?" Furi asked.

"Did you see these prices? I'm buying them."

"With what?"

"I brought money from … well, you know."

Alice made her way down the stairs, followed by a perplexed-looking Furi.

The clerk eyed the books and sighed. "Are you sure you want to buy these? We have a much more interesting selection in the back."

"These will be perfect, thank you."

"Good kindling, I suppose. Try not to let them corrupt your mind. These are about as factual as the bedtime stories I tell my kids."

"You're awfully open about that," Jacob said. "I thought everyone here had to respect the monarchy's rules."

" 'The monarchy?' " The clerk turned his attention back to Furi. "Kid, where did you find these two?"

"Down by the docks. I think they may have come in with Fel. Thought I'd show them the best bookstore in the city."

The clerk chuckled. "I'll take your money, but you need to lie better." He took a couple coins from Alice and then passed the change back. "Be careful out there. And have this one as a complimentary sale." He dropped a fourth book onto Alice's stack, and Jacob eyed the cover.

    Remembering the Mountainfolk. My Time in the Gray
    Mountains. Alexis Brands.

"Thank you!" Alice said, stuffing the stack of four tomes into her backpack as they turned to leave. She glanced at Furi as they stepped back onto the streets of Ballern. "You know him?"

"Not really. He's there every now and then. I probably shouldn't have shown my face in there, but I couldn't resist. I know how much you liked the Crown Library."

Alice smiled and looked back at the old bookshop. "It's a beautiful store. Maybe one day they'll be able to sell more than what the monarchy deems fit."

"Maybe." Furi's smile didn't reach her eyes. "Let's get into the palace."

CHAPTER TWENTY-EIGHT

"**M**Y QUEEN," MORDAIR said, nodding to the lithe form that appeared in the doorway. He offered a reserved bow before straightening his back. A single guard stood at the queen's side. "You sent for me?"

"Yes, Mordair. I have received word of the battle in Belldorn. There is much of your guidance that has proved incorrect. The beach to the west was indeed fortified. Titan Mechs, engines of war not seen since they were rumored to stalk the deserts some fifty years hence, guard the city."

"Yes, but I understand the airships dealt with them well enough."

"For a time. Until the Lady of Belldorn unleashed a swarm of Emerald Needles."

Mordair didn't allow his expression to change. Control of a swarm was a rare ability. There were only a handful who understood it, and Newton and Atlier both had not been close enough to the Lady of Belldorn to reveal something so dangerous.

"Do you know who has technology such as that?"

"Technology, My Queen?" he asked, raising an eyebrow.

"Do not play coy, Mordair. I know who orchestrated the Fall of Ancora. I know what your brother wrought on that city. We lost spies of our own in that tragedy."

"Ancora was an enemy of Fel and Ballern alike."

"A distant enemy at worst. A potential ally at best."

"You would ally yourself with the filth who harbor war criminals?

They let Charles von Atlier live inside their walls for decades."

The queen's eyes narrowed. "They harbored your brother within their walls, Mordair. That was their greatest sin. The Butcher of Gareth Cave. A travesty of a man. You will not find my city such easy prey."

Mordair didn't rise to the bait, only rested his hand on the breathing mask clipped to his belt.

"Take your fleet south to Belldorn. We will coordinate our attack on the city there. Our … *differences* … can be settled after the battle."

"Differences?" Mordair said, a thread of rage leaking into his words. "You would speak to me of differences as you beg me to send my soldiers to their deaths. What fool am I?"

The queen took a step back as Mordair's voice raised, and her guard stepped forward, hand on the hilt of his sword.

"Patrice! Assassins!"

The Red Hand moved unseen from behind the queen and her guard. Blood sprayed from the guard's neck as he crumbled to the ground in a satisfying fountain of gurgling blood. Mordair stepped forward as he lifted the breathing mask from his belt and slid it over his face.

"My dear, dear, queen. It was such a tragedy to hear of your assassination."

"Guar—"

Her cry was cut short as Mordair lashed out with the blade hidden in his palm, a short, curved hook whose anchor could have been mistaken for a simple ring. A deep enough wound that her scream turned into a hiss. She stared at him, stumbled two steps toward the door, and collapsed.

"Leave," Mordair whispered.

The Red Hand slid the guard's dagger out of its sheath, slamming it into the queen's back twice before dropping it beside his hand.

With the stage set, Mordair took a deep breath and drew a long gash across his forehead, a superficial wound that would turn his face into a gory mess. He returned the breathing mask to the clip at his waist and let out a quiet laugh as he made his way to the locked door, now being hammered on by the guards outside.

Mordair swung it open, hiding the smile when he recognized two spies in the queen's guard. "The queen has been assassinated! Betrayed by her own guard! He could not have acted alone. Find the traitors!"

Chaos flowed from Mordair's words, and within minutes the bells rang out. He already knew what would happen. They'd find terrified citizens and believe their silence to be that of a conspirator. The citizens of Ballern would die at the hand of their protectors, and the line of Mordairs would return to power at last.

His brother had been a fool, pining for Ancora. He never understood what they could truly have. Their homeland, reclaimed from the usurpers who dared steal it from their ancestors. Mordair looked down at the corpse of the queen. It was time for a new empire to rise.

He could feel the blood as it dripped across his smile.

CHAPTER TWENTY-NINE

J ACOB STUDIED A large plaque set at the base of a golden statue. The words were repeated in Mokuskrit and the common tongue, but he didn't read much past the fact it was a representation of the Lady of Ballern, who was assassinated around the time of the Deadlands War. Instead, his attention was on the guards, hidden behind quick glances and a façade of awe as he took in the room's opulence.

Alice studied the map over Furi's shoulder. They were all huddled by the tall golden statue on the first floor, and from what Jacob could barely hear, Furi said the throne room was directly ahead of them. But if the schedule she held was correct, the queen wouldn't be in the throne room for at least another hour.

Their opportunity came like clockwork when a series of chimes resounded through the room and the guards walked down the hall. The schedule Jakon had provided had been accurate so far, and the moment the guards vanished, the trio rushed forward and slipped into a narrow hall to the west of the throne room's towering doors.

As stunning and almost sickening as the entry hall had been, the narrow path they found themselves in now was bare, unlit, and clearly meant only for servants and assistants to the queen. This was not a place for guests' eyes, with its unadorned stone and few doorways.

Furi led them to the end and turned left. They could hear the armored boots of a guard clicking against the stone floor nearby. They hurried up a wide spiral staircase, moving as quietly as they could as they raced to the third floor.

There was only a gap of one minute between the changing of the guards. One minute wasn't enough for an enemy force to slip through undetected, but for a small group with both the queen's schedule and a map through the tower, it could be enough.

They were halfway down the hall when they heard the calamity. The sounds of soldiers hammering on wood and the screams to open the door. They froze there, between a curtained window and an ornate table that sat across the hall.

"Come on," Alice hissed. She grabbed Jacob and Furi by the arm, crumpling the map against his wrist as she dragged them both into another narrow hallway. The light reached the edge where they stood, but the first guard to race by didn't glance at them, and the shouts grew louder.

For a terrible moment, Jacob thought they'd been found. Someone had noticed three infiltrators inside the palace where they shouldn't be. But he couldn't figure out how because they'd stuck to the map and the schedule.

It was then that the bells rang out and Furi stiffened. "No …"

Jacob started to ask what she'd heard that he hadn't. But he heard the shouts echo through the hall and the frantic sprinting of the royal guards.

"The queen is dead!" A guard cried out.

"Did someone find out she was sympathetic to the resistance?" Furi whispered.

Jacob didn't need to hear more to know. "Mordair." He had no doubt what happened. Mordair was running two schemes for every one they discovered, just like his brother had. The removal of the queen would allow the King of Fel to sow the same kind of terror and dissent that lived in his own city.

Jacob squeezed his hands into fists. "We need to get out of here."

Alice folded the schedule and slid it into a pocket on her vest before pulling her cloak tighter. "Back the way we came. The longer we wait, the more guards we'll have to contend with."

"What are you doing?" Furi hissed as Alice slid her hand into a bolt glove.

"We might not have a choice. Be ready for anything."

"The map, show me the map again."

Alice pulled it out and handed it to Furi.

"Here. This passage. It's at the end of the hall and to the left. Should give us access to one of the minarets and we can take it down to the first floor."

"It's guarded," Alice said, tapping the small oval that indicated as much.

"What part of the palace isn't going to be well guarded right now?"

Alice rubbed at her forehead. "No, you're right. Okay. We make for the back passage."

Jacob suddenly wished very much that he had his air cannon with him. The blades hidden in his apron felt wholly inadequate. He wasn't skilled with a knife, like Gladys, but whatever came, he needed to be ready.

Furi took a deep breath. After the next pair of guards sprinted past, she whispered, "Now!"

They followed the pair at a distance, keeping close to the wall so that even their shadows were as small as possible. The guards never looked back after they reached the next intersection, and as Jacob and the others sped by, he understood why.

An ornate door stood bowed and chipped, and on the ground he could just make out bloody boot prints across the polished tiles. But what chilled him to the bone was the man standing behind the line of guards, and the spiked mask hanging at his waist.

"Go!" Jacob hissed.

They scampered around the corner in front of a rich tapestry that showed the entirety of the lands around Ballern. There was so much more to the woods and mountains beyond than Jacob had ever imagined, but he didn't have time to study them now.

Another narrow servant hall took them to the back of the tower, and a single stone pathway stretched out to the minaret that flanked the palace, briefly casting them in sunlight before they reached an iron-banded door.

"Was that … was that Mordair?" Alice asked as the heavy door thunked closed behind them.

"Yes," Jacob hissed. "Mordair killed the queen, or one of his assassins did. What do we do now?"

"It doesn't matter," Furi said.

"Of course it does!" Alice snapped in a hushed whisper.

"No, no, I mean right now. We have to get away from the palace."

Jacob's back stiffened. "Or they'll blame us."

Furi gave one sharp nod and led the way down the narrow stone steps, each capped with a textured metal slat to offer more traction.

What would happen if they were caught and blamed for the death of the queen? Jacob shivered at the idea. They'd take more than his hands; of that, he was sure. And the thought of Alice and Furi suffering the same fate … He pushed the spiraling thoughts aside and focused on the stairs.

Bells sounded from the towers above, soon joined by others, a dissonant cacophony warped further by the acoustics of the minaret. It was a twisted noise, and one that had to be echoing from one end of the city to the other.

Every so often, they encountered a step where the textured metal wasn't secured as well as it could have been. Each footfall on those stairs was a thunder that crawled up and down the minaret, and at the speed they were moving, it repeated three times like clockwork.

Jacob's heart pounded in his ears as they reached the bottom. Just outside was where the guards had been marked on the map, and he didn't miss Alice's tightening of her bolt glove before Furi opened the gate and ran outside into a panicked mob.

If there were guards, they were nowhere to be seen. The cries and shouts of the people drowned out everything else. Jacob stayed behind Alice as she followed Furi's mad dash through the courtyards. Finely trimmed hedges and carefully maintained flowerbeds were trampled as surely as the grass beneath a Walker.

Chaos ruled Ballern in that moment as blood-red pennants unfurled from the sides of the palace. Jacob didn't have to know what they meant. He heard the cries of the citizens.

"The queen is dead!"

"Where is the guard?"

"Find the assassins!"

If not for Furi, they would have been lost in the crush. If not for Furi, they might have been caught by the guards before they cleared the palace grounds. But instead, the Skyborn darted through narrow arches at the edge of the garden before sprinting to the end of the alley.

Their pace slowed from there, blending into the crowds on the street as they surged and waned like a giant formless beast. But Furi always dragged them to the west when they hit one of the alleys. Jacob wasn't sure why until he saw it around another bend.

The towers that would take them to the docks, the Skysworn, and a chance to escape.

None of them spoke as they waited in the crush of people for the lift. Few were journeying up, but each lift spilled a dozen Ballern citizens and Fel soldiers onto the streets. Finally, they stepped inside the metal cage, and Furi threw two levers to the side. A shiver ran through her, one that

Jacob had no difficulty in seeing.

"Are you okay?"

Tears had carved a path down her face as she turned to face Jacob and Alice. "She would have helped us, wouldn't she? All this time … I thought, I thought she was one of *them*. But she would have been one of us."

"It's too late for that now," Alice said. "We need to get back to the Skysworn. Mary and Smith will know what to do."

"How could they possibly know?" Furi whispered.

"Pirates," Jacob said with a sad smile.

Furi took a shaky breath and nodded. "Mordair. I never would have thought he would do something so brash in the daylight."

"A lot of dead people didn't think he would either," Alice said. "It's a hard lesson we learned with the Butcher. And it appears his brother is not so different."

"I think he *is* different, Alice." Jacob stared through the lift's lattice at the red banners falling from the towers as if the city itself was bleeding. "I'm afraid he is terribly different."

They remained silent for the rest of the ascent, listening as the bells sounded both an alarm and a mourning cry for their lost queen. Mordair had come to Ballern, and the price would be dire.

✧　✧　✧

JACOB WATCHED AS Furi stood on the docks not far from the Skysworn. He understood why she couldn't look away. There was nothing left but ghosts on those docks now. Almost the entirety of them must have fled to the lifts, judging by the crowds who had been waiting to take their place.

"Let's go," Alice said, pulling on Furi's sleeve.

They made their way over the short plank and onto the deck of the Skysworn. Jacob didn't wait to see if Mary was in the cabin or if Smith was onboard. He retracted the plank before locking the railing closed. It would be harder for anyone to board them without it.

But when they opened the cabin door, they found a worried looking pair waiting inside.

"You're okay!" Mary hopped out of her chair and rushed over to the trio, hugging each of them in turn. "The queen was assassinated."

"We know," Alice said. "We were in the palace when it happened."

Smith cursed. "Did anyone see you?"

"Probably," Jacob said. "But Mordair was in the room where the queen died. I think it was him."

"Did you see the floor?" Furi asked. "Boot prints made of blood. No one steps in blood on purpose, and they were full of prints."

"We should leave now," Smith said. "It could raise suspicions, but from the look of the streets, no one is going to be organized for some time."

Mary nodded. "Untie us. I'm contacting Archibald. He needs to know what's happened."

"You think he'll come to Ballern?" Furi asked, and the hope in her voice was like a dagger in Jacob's chest.

"No, Furi. But I may be able to convince him to send more ships to Belldorn. If Mordair cut off the head of Ballern, he's not going to be quick to reinforce their ships to the south."

Jacob watched Mary's cold calculations with a kind of detached awe. Because she was right. The assassination could disrupt their supplies, and what ships remained in Ballern certainly wouldn't be deployed south with the queen's death.

"They won't retreat from Belldorn, will they?" Alice asked.

Mary shook her head. "Can't you see what's going to happen? Her death will be blamed on Belldorn, and every last soldier loyal to Ballern will fight to the death."

"No, they won't," Furi said. "The Skyborn won't. They'll surrender when they can. Some of them think it's their only way out. That's who we need Kura to help reach."

Mary rubbed her forehead. "It's a gamble. Get in your jump seats. We're leaving as soon as Smith gets belowdecks."

By the time they'd stashed their packs and fastened their harnesses, Smith's voice sounded over the horn. "Boilers are prepped. Ready to depart."

"Buckle up," Mary said. "I'm going to hit the thrusters the moment we reach altitude over the Crystal Sea."

"Understood."

But in the meantime, Mary used the transmitter to contact their closest allies.

CHAPTER THIRTY

ARCHIBALD CROSSED HIS arms and listened to the captain of Warship One. The idea of leaving Fel so soon did not sit well with him, but the alliance with Lady Katherine had to stand if he hoped to establish a lasting peace from one end of the Deadlands to the other.

And for that alliance to stand, Belldorn had to survive. But the news from Mary and the others fleeing Ballern had been dire. Though dire was not nearly a severe enough word to encompass Archibald's fears about the situation. And they *were* fears.

"How long can we maintain the engines at full thrust?" Archibald asked, interrupting the captain's explanation of why it would take them so long to reach Belldorn.

"In theory, sir? Five hours."

"Enough to bring us deep into the Bay of Sorrow," Archibald said.

"Yes, Speaker, but our fuel will be spent. We will be a floating target once the boilers run cold."

"No." Archibald uncrossed his arms and looked out toward the Red Woods. "Send word to the supply ships. They are to meet us in Belldorn with solid fuel from Bollwerk. Bleed the factories dry if you must. This battle will determine the fate of tens of thousands."

"Yes, sir." The captain inclined his head and started shouting orders.

It would be a grave risk to send both warships to Belldorn, but this might be their last chance to crush Ballern. Mordair had miscalculated. He should have melded their fleets before striking Belldorn. Archibald had thrived for decades by recognizing an opportunity when it arose. And crushing Ballern's fleet would be no different.

A victory would still leave them with the looming conflict at Ballern itself. But now, instead of an experienced fleet that knew the terrain all around, they would face Fel's fleet. Ruthless and cunning, yes, but inexperience in the Gray Mountains would cost them.

"Take the Titan Mechs from Midstream."

Archibald turned to look at the child who had spoken, the Princess of Midstream. "Gladys, I will not leave Midstream wholly undefended."

"It won't be. We still have hundreds of traps from the last shipment, and the cranes can fight well enough."

Archibald rubbed his chin, glancing at George, who had said nothing from his post beside Gladys. "A supply ship could bring them to Belldorn, but there are still pockets of Fel's forces in the Deadlands. I feel as if I have taken too much by redirecting this warship."

"Then at least put Theodosia and her assistant on standby," Gladys said. "If the worst happens, they can send a supply ship themselves."

Archibald nodded. "It will be done."

"You both risk much," George said. "If this is Mordair's plan to expose a path into Bollwerk, you could lose more than you think."

"All of his ocean liners and destroyers are gone, George." Archibald turned back to the table at the center of the bridge. "He may have soldiers fighting for him in the Deadlands still, but I doubt those who are deployed realize they have been abandoned."

"How can you be sure?" Gladys asked.

"He's done it before. A very long time ago. And Mordair has sacrificed a great many allies to solidify his rule. What better example than executing a staunch ally who has been proven a traitor?"

Gladys hesitated. "He executed allies who weren't traitors?"

"Some were, certainly. But others were simply a threat to his power, and it cost us more than one spy to discover that. He saw potential obstacles, and therefore removed them. Hung them from the walls."

Gladys shivered.

Hours vanished as they studied the maps and discussed options for the supply ships with Theodosia and Targrove. Before long, they had a loose plan. Only one ship would remain behind in Midstream, while two of the Titan Mechs would be shipped to Belldorn with a cache of solid fuel.

Shortly after disconnecting, Archibald saw it. A mass of forces inside the Red Woods near the hidden base. But instead of waterlogged crawlers and soldiers retreating from the collapsed tunnels, they were venturing into them.

"No," Archibald whispered. "No."

"What is it?" Gladys asked.

"Why would they be entering those tunnels if they didn't have a way out?"

Gladys looked up at the Speaker, and he could see the shock on her face. "You think there are tunnels that didn't flood."

"Or those weren't the only tunnels."

CHAPTER THIRTY-ONE

"D RAKKAR, CAN YOU hear me?" Lady Katherine's voice crackled over the Cave Guardian's transmitter.

"Yes, My Lady."

"There is a second wave of airships, and they are supported by more of Fel's ocean fleet. Deploy the remaining bait boxes at will. The Queen of Ballern has been assassinated."

"What?" Drakkar snapped.

"We need to buy Archibald time to arrive with his warship."

Drakkar frowned at the command, but if the queen's death had been blamed on Belldorn, or indeed if Belldorn *had* killed the queen, dark times were coming. "Do you have more Emerald Needles we are unaware of? Another nest?"

"No, and the bait may not be as effective because of it. But the Emerald Needles will still be feeding. They will heed the call."

"Understood."

Drakkar looked to Rin. "You have more of the bolts?"

Rin grimaced and walked to the lockers set into the stables. "Yes. In case a second volley was needed." He passed two clips of bolts each to Tatsu, Drakkar, and Samuel.

"Eight shots," Samuel said. "That's not nearly enough.

"It is enough to cause chaos," Tatsu said. "And to slow the enemy as we wait for our allies."

"They aren't all enemies on those ships, Tatsu," Rin said. "We're killing Skyborn and loyalists alike."

"Such is war. Mourn for the lost when the day is done. For now, we fight."

A deafening buzz sounded above them as the sun itself darkened, and a spiral cloud of Dragonwings circled the stables. An azure blue mount flitted across the stables before coming to a stop at the perch above them.

Drakkar smiled up at Allie, the councilor from Canopy, and the brilliant silver fist of the Steamsworn emblazoned on her breastplate.

"Cave Guardian. We have received news from Ballern, and we have come to fight."

The air vibrated around them, sending Drakkar's cloak to ripple in the wind. "And we welcome you, Madame Councilor. It is an honor to fight at your side."

"Let us hope it is an honor we both survive." She eyed the bolts in Rin's hands. "These are the devices you spoke of?"

Rin inclined his head.

"You will need more. You will need the lure of the devils themselves."

Drakkar studied Allie. "What do you mean?"

"There are scouts in the mountains, and those who are not our own. Fel's soldiers gather in the north, but we cannot locate their source."

"How many?" Rin asked.

"A dozen of Fel's scouts, no more."

"Then we should strike them down now."

Allie shook her head. "Wait until our own scouts report. They will keep an eye on the woods while we fight in the skies."

Samuel raised a finger. "Umm, what did you mean by the lure of the devils themselves?"

Allie smiled, and it was a terrifying thing to behold in the shadows of her helmet. She reached into a satchel at her side and tossed a small box to Samuel.

Drakkar could see it only had one button. But it wasn't the first time he'd seen a device like it. "Where did you get that?"

"A gift, from the citizens of Fire Island. Their curiosity at the Fall of Ancora has borne fruit."

"Targrove," Samuel hissed as he turned the device over in his hands.

"What was that?"

"Nothing," the Spider Knight muttered.

"Do not fear what happened in your city, Samuel. It will not call to the Red Death as it did in Ancora. This will call to the Scythe Beetles of the mountain caves. Use them sparingly."

Samuel had seen the relentless charge of a Scythe Beetle. As terrifying as a horde of Red Death could be, their greatest strength laid in sheer numbers. A Scythe Beetle could destroy a crawler in a single charge. Samuel gave one sharp nod.

"Now, soldiers of Canopy, Ancora, and Cave, I implore you. Fly with us."

✧   ✧   ✧

DRAKKAR HAD HOPED for more rest after their last strike. But it was not to be. News of the death of the queen in Ballern was the last thing to break the stalemate of their decision. They had to return to the field of battle once more, and having Allie at their side could swing the scales in their favor.

Or so Drakkar hoped. He kept the bolt launcher primed as they soared past the city skyline. The pace less frenetic now that the Emerald Needles were not pursuing them as fast as they could. The looming violence to come darkened his mind as much as it weighed on his heart.

But it was in that darkness he remembered how welcoming the shadows of Cave could be. How in the blackest corners of the underground, light and life found their way in. Be it from Fireworms or the ingenuity of the people, light would always shine in the darkness.

It was a reassuring thought in a moment of chaos as the Dragonriders' front lines reached the edge of the sea, and the full scope of the battle unraveled before them.

Ballern's vessels all trailed thin red flags that dripped down their bows and fluttered beneath their hulls. A declaration of mourning, and a promise of vengeance. He had never seen the red flags fly before, and only knew the legends of what had happened in the Deadlands War. And legends they were, for it seemed much of the truth had died with those who lived through it.

A low note sounded from above him that rose into a shriek. He caught sight of Allie, the curled horn of some long-dead creature pressed to her lips. And the call echoed down the line of Dragonriders. Their casual pace turned into a scattering cloud of Dragonwings, all moving at different speeds, at different targets, and the confusion across the Ballern ships was clear to see as the battle paused while they tried to target the Dragonwings.

But targeting a creature that could move fast enough that the rider had to be fastened into the saddle was a difficult thing indeed. Of course, it also made aiming difficult as Drakkar cursed at the sudden jaunt of his mount, zipping to the side as a ballista bolt sailed past.

Samuel dove ahead of him, the polished armor of the Spider Knight's pauldrons flashing in the sun. He fired one bolt into the deck of the destroyer, close to a ballista, and then dove below, passing out of sight beneath the long airship.

Drakkar went higher, following Allie as she made for the strikers now deploying from the distant carrier. The bait boxes wouldn't do as much good on a ship that could outrun the Emerald Needles when they weren't in a swarm.

Apparently Allie realized the same as she signaled for Drakkar to back away. He did, catching sight of a trio of bolts as she launched them into a striker. Two caught the cockpit, and the third missed. From there, he didn't see what happened, as his attention turned to the length of red cloth hanging above him not a quarter mile away.

Drakkar adjusted his grip on the crossbow and signaled the Dragonwing to rise. The creature's sudden change in direction felt as if it might pull the goggles from his face. But in moments, he was above the deck of a supply ship. He fired, and the bolt pierced the deck just below one of the mounts for the gas chamber.

Not taking chances, he fired a second bolt into the cabin, piercing the windscreen as soldiers scrambled behind the broken glass.

The Dragonwing lurched to the side without prompting, and Drakkar wasn't sure why until he saw the single emerald-green carapace slam through the windscreen with no thought of self-preservation. Its scythe-like limbs cut the captain into two wholly separate pieces as anyone else in that cabin was trampled to death.

Drakkar watched the scene unfold, horrified at what his hand had brought upon those sailors. But he pushed the emotion away as the Emerald Needle threw itself against the back wall of the cabin. In moments it had broken through, its shell oozing fluid that meant the beetle had been injured, and badly. It didn't stop its irregular, frenzied march to the second bolt, where it dug into the wood of the ship itself until the bolt finally snapped beneath its fury.

The Emerald Needle stopped then, but the damage was done. The surviving bit of the support for the airship fractured under its own weight, and the deck swung toward the sea as the gas chamber nosed toward the sky, metal screeching before the entire assembly ruptured.

Drakkar fled on his Dragonwing as the furnaces spilled over, and a billowing fire consumed the decks before the entirety of the supply ship plunged into the Crystal Sea, the red banner turning to ash as it followed the ship to the water.

A detached part of Drakkar's mind wondered how such a vulnerability could be left unguarded on a supply ship. But then, most of the forces those ships might encounter wouldn't be launching an Emerald Needle into its support structure. It might have been armored on three sides, but a Dragonwing could outmaneuver any airship.

With a grim sense of satisfaction at the wreckage below, Drakkar fled deeper into the battle, where the Dragonwings and strikers exchanged fire that left dead from both sides floating in the seas below.

CHAPTER THIRTY-TWO

Alice looked over at Jacob's notebook, a detailed schematic already taking shape of the small toy he'd purchased at the market. Part of her wondered how he was able to concentrate on that with everything going on around them. She supposed she had some idea of how as she returned to reading one of the books she'd bought in Ballern.

"Furi, were these really what they taught you in school?"

Furi looked up from her notebooks as Alice turned the book to face her, scanning the page before laughing. "Yes, it was. Before Kura took over on the docks, at least. All the desert people from Midstream to Bollwerk and beyond were cannibals. That's how they substituted their meals on such sparse lands, didn't you know?"

Alice looked back at the excerpt and grimaced. "Who would believe this … trash? And it's not just that they're cannibals, but they have farms to raise people? That's insanity, Furi."

"Wait until you get to the part about Ancora."

Alice's brow furrowed as she flipped back to the table of contents before finding references to Ancora. She settled in to read, trying not to notice as Furi glanced up at her every minute or so to gauge her reaction.

    It has been well documented that the savageness of
    Ancorans toward outsiders is surpassed only by their
    treatment of their own kind. The ruling caste is penned
    in much like livestock behind formidable walls of stone,
    taking to hurling inferior citizens from the walls in
    times of celebration.

Alice frowned and read the proceeding passage out loud. "Many contests are held in the winter months to see which children can survive the cold the longest. Those who are not disfigured and therefore abandoned by their families will one day have a chance to live above the squalor." Alice blew out a short breath. "This is disgusting, Furi. Are all of these books full of ridiculous lies like this?"

"And worse," Furi said. "Some of it is much worse. I doubt the store we were in would have sold those books to you. The shopkeeper is well known for defying the Children of the Dark Fire and letting Skyborn read 'inappropriate texts.' "

Alice skimmed several more passages. "It seems we're cannibals too. Good thing we escaped that." She rolled her eyes. "They mention Festival here, but we don't have winter celebrations in Ancora, for the most part. Unless you count staying inside by a fire and studying, which I certainly do."

"You don't throw your friends off the wall to see who can make a larger splat?" Furi asked in a jarringly regal tone.

Mary chuckled at that before turning away from the windscreen. "Save one of those books for me. I'm dying to hear what they say about Pirate's Cove."

"Oh, I can already tell you that," Furi said. "Pirate's Cove doesn't have any real people. It's a poison land filled with nothing but ghosts and death."

"What?" Smith barked over the horn. "How can any of that be in a *textbook?*"

Furi took a deep breath. "Because everything the Children of the Dark Fire do, everything they've done, has been to turn their own gods into the only gods. It's … you have to understand. When I was living it for so many years, it was our truth. An absolute truth that was just accepted. And if you grow up hearing that repeated over and over and taught to you, there's no reason for you to question it."

"Until you travel with the fleet," Mary said. "And see the world outside your own."

Furi hesitated. "Even then, we're isolated on the airships. If it wasn't for Kura, I don't know if I ever would have believed we'd been lied to."

"Maybe once you were in prison," Alice said in far too cheery a tone.

Furi laughed at that and cast Alice a smile. "Maybe then. I'll see if Kura can add that to the Skyborn curriculum. *Get shot down and thrown in prison. Befriend enemy for extra credit.*"

"It could work," Alice said with a laugh.

Their good humor fell away as they closed on Belldorn. It wouldn't be long before they were back on the front, and possibly in more danger than they'd been in on the ground in Ballern.

✧　✧　✧

ALICE LISTENED TO the transmitter as Kat spoke. Each bit of information she relayed seemed worse than the last. The battle of the Crystal Sea had grown worse, but the Dragonwings of Canopy had joined them. Alice wasn't sure how important that was, but the shock on Mary's face told her it was more significant than she'd realized.

As soon as Kat disconnected, Mary reached out to Eva. "Brig Three, this is Skysworn, come in."

Eva's answer came fast. "Skysworn, this is Brig Three."

"Where are you?" Mary asked.

"Near the peninsula. We have word of scouts in the mountains from Canopy, and the lady wishes to keep a close watch. Bollwerk is coming."

"What do you mean?" Mary asked.

"The Dragonwings deployed to buy Archibald time to arrive. They have a handful of bait boxes left, but it may not be enough."

Mary adjusted the course of the Skysworn. "We'll come in behind Ballern's lines. Do what we can."

Eva hesitated. "Be careful. The strikers are formidable."

"We know." Mary disconnected, and Alice didn't miss the slight sag in the captain's shoulders. "Smith, how do you want to do this?"

"Put Jacob on the chainguns. We go in above them. I believe Alice can handle what comes after that."

Mary turned to look at the trio in the jump seats.

"What about me?" Furi asked.

"You'll be on the deck with me," Alice said. "On the other side of those bombs, for a change." She reached out and squeezed Jacob's hand. "Be careful."

"I will. You too. And don't forget to clip onto the safety lines."

Alice slowly raised an eyebrow.

"Not … not that you would!" Jacob stammered. "I mean, I just want, I just want you to be safe. And you could wear your glider and it would probably be safe, but—"

"Jacob," Mary said.

Jacob looked up at the captain, wide-eyed.

"She's trying to get inside your head." Mary shook her head for a moment before bursting out with an honest laugh.

Alice hid her own smile and squeezed his hand again before leaning over to kiss him.

They went back to their books and maps then, filling the time with some fleeting sense of normalcy. In the past weeks, Alice had learned that was one of the best things they could do. Focusing on smaller tasks kept her thoughts from going to the darkest possibilities. And while reading the insane, fabricated history from Ballern might not have been the *most* relaxing thing she could think of, it did at least distract her for a time.

✧   ✧   ✧

"I THINK THAT part is true," Furi said, pointing to a passage on the page Alice was reading.

Alice took a closer look, reading about the Children of the Dark Fire having to conquer the monsters that once roamed the Great Machines. "Do you think they were as big as what we have now?"

Furi shrugged. "Don't know. I guess it's possible. But that was in the old textbooks Kura had too. Before the monarchy updated them to these stories."

"If it's just Cutters like the Deadlands, I'd be okay with that."

"Unless we have to walk through their nest," Alice said. "Pretty sure none of us would be okay with that."

Jacob frowned at the idea. "That would be bad."

"From the description, I think they're Armored Walkers," Furi said.

"What's an Armored Walker?" Jacob asked.

"We learned about this in Miss Penny's class," Alice said. "Don't you remember? They're too flat and wide to actually ride on. And their chitin is so thick it's said airship armor used to be crafted from it."

"That sounds familiar."

"I'm amazed you remember anything that doesn't involve gears and pistons," Alice muttered.

Jacob grinned.

Mary leaned forward in her seat. "Crew, we have hostile airships off the bow. I think we found our targets."

Alice focused on the view outside the windscreen and shivered. The blue sky looked poisoned, streaks of smoke near the horizon while dark shadows drifted all around. And beyond it, only a ghost itself, was the distant skyline of Belldorn.

CHAPTER THIRTY-THREE

FOR ALL THE bizarre stories and obvious lies inside those texts from Ballern, Alice found grains of truth hidden within. And perhaps that was what horrified her the most. How better to manipulate an entire people than to pin so many lies together with a handful of truths?

That wasn't the only thought going through her mind as she watched the battle over the Crystal Sea and gave Furi a brief introduction to the launchers for the bombs. Furi's physical strength gave her an easier time than Alice leveraging the cannons into place and locking them into a firing position.

Alice double-checked both of their clips on the safety lines. They'd taken the glider packs with them because she'd rather have the option, if it came to it. But she couldn't shake the sight of Furi with those cannons, dropping a compound bomb into the groove before taking aim and launching it in a low arc.

Furi caught Alice watching. "It's better on this side." As if accenting the thought, the bomb detonated below them, and one section of her target's gas chamber failed spectacularly, sending fabric and debris into the air as the ship lurched to one side.

The rhythmic hammering of the chainguns sounded from below, but Alice knew so long as that terrible noise stayed in the air, Jacob was alive.

"Are you okay?" Alice asked.

Furi nodded. "I know not everyone on those ships is a bad person, Alice. It's just … that part is hard. They're just following orders like they've been trained to."

"They're still responsible for what they do."

"I know …" Furi's voice trailed off as she primed the cannon again. "It's just, they don't even realize they're wrong, you know?"

"That doesn't mean they won't kill you."

Furi nodded and took aim. This time they were over a destroyer, and as Alice tracked the gentle arc of the compound bomb, her heart hammered in her chest. She clicked the transmitter in her cuff and shouted, "Go!"

Alice wrapped her arms around Furi and pinned her to the deck as the Skysworn tilted to the side and sped away from the destroyer below. They were far too close to it, but every moment that passed gave them a chance to escape.

Furi started to ask a question before the compound bomb detonated. But the initial blast was followed by something far more severe, and the sky soured, growing orange and black and peppered with falling debris, some of it pinging off the deck around them. The Skysworn leveled out, and Alice scrambled to the railing.

Far below them, and trailing a red banner, one of the cannons and its explosives had blown a hole from the deck through the destroyer's hull.

It was only then Alice realized the chainguns had stopped. "Jacob!" she shouted into the transmitter. "Check on Jacob."

Her heart pounded in her chest until the hatch on the deck clanged open, the vibration calling her attention back to Smith. He offered a thumbs-up before pulling the hatch closed.

"Nice shot."

Furi gave her an uneven smile.

Alice blew out a shaky breath and waited for the next ship to come into their sights.

✧　✧　✧

JACOB HAD A hard time catching his breath. That could have been the end of him, and he knew it. He looked down at the ripples in the sea below where the bank of cannons had exploded off the destroyer and spiraled into the water. Even the smoke still trailed after the wreckage in a lazy, looping twist.

He took several deep breaths, trying to calm his nerves when the hatch above slid open and Smith's face appeared.

"Are you injured?"

Jacob shook his head. "I'm good. That was too close."

"The girls are too good a shot, I think you mean."

Jacob let out a nervous laugh and tried to let his anxiety settle as it tingled down his arms and into his fingers. Smith disappeared, but he left the hatch above open. Jacob was glad for it. It felt like it would be easier to escape the gun pod.

He didn't have long to calm himself before the slow arcs of the compound bombs started up again, peppering a supply ship and tearing through a gas chamber. Shrapnel pinged against the thick glass as Jacob hung suspended over the water. It was almost more unsettling than being over land, but he wouldn't let his friends down either way.

With a twist of the controls, the gun pod swung to his right. A small adjustment in elevation, and the chainguns roared to life once more, vibrating his hands enough that he knew they'd be numb in a matter of minutes.

A hail of fire sliced through a red banner on the supply ship as he traced a line of shots up to the bow and cut down the crew who had taken it upon themselves to return fire at Alice and Furi. He knew how limited their sight would be, sheltering at the edge of the deck on the Skysworn, but Jacob could lower their risk.

And that was what he told himself as men and women died at the end of his barrels.

Mary made a violent turn, and Jacob wasn't sure why until the Skysworn evened out, and he caught sight of the small vessels giving them pursuit. The strikers might not be an imminent threat to the Porcupines, who now lit the sky on fire with their cannons, but they could take on supply ships and smaller with alarming proficiency.

"Jacob," Mary's voice was clear over the transmitter, so close to the cabin. "Take down those strikers. I'll clear the way forward."

Jacob clicked his transmitter and answered. "Get Alice and Furi inside."

"Smith, you heard him."

Heavy bootsteps sounded above him in the hold. Mary's flight pattern grew more even, and Jacob had little doubt it was in an effort to let Alice and Furi cross the deck.

But an even flight meant an easier target, and the strikers didn't miss their chance. A bolt crashed into the gun pod, and more went higher. Jacob knew they'd been hit, but he had no way of seeing how bad the damage was.

It didn't matter. An easier target for them was also an easier target for him. The chainguns spun up, and Jacob clamped the trigger locks in place. With that done, he adjusted his angle of fire and swept the barrels across the air just above the strikers.

For a second, it looked as if they might have survived, only a few sparks to show for his efforts before the bulk of the volley reached the strikers and tore them to pieces.

The first broke up, sending fragments into the sea before the second detonated as if a bomb had been set off inside it. And depending on what that ship had been carrying, that might have been the truth of it. Jacob unlocked the triggers and let the barrels spin to a stop, but the rhythmic bursts of fire still sounded, though more distant.

He looked over his shoulder to find two chainguns off the bow, churning the air with fire as fast as the barrels could spin. The cabin of the destroyer fore of them never had a chance. Glass and wood exploded away from every impact as metal bent and caved against the onslaught.

The Skysworn veered around the wreckage, and Jacob took aim at the ballista below, shattering its arms and the bolt loaded against its drawn rope. The sudden release of tension, in a manner the machine wasn't built for, snapped off the surviving arm.

Mary guided the ship deeper into the conflict until Jacob saw them. The Dragonriders and the Emerald Needles that followed in their wake, buzzing from ship to ship as they tore into cabins and gas chambers and sailors alike.

The Skysworn's guns fell silent as they watched, the damage they'd done to the rear lines forcing the ships to wheel around into the Dragonriders' path. They couldn't have planned it better if they tried.

"Hold tight," Mary said. "We're getting out of here. Before a Dragonrider tags us by mistake."

It was only then Jacob realized there wasn't a single airship from Belldorn at the core of the assault. They were all closer to the city, firing on the formations that had already been struck by the Dragonriders, or those ships they had yet to reach.

The Skysworn angled its nose up, and the sudden increase in thrust pushed Jacob against his harness, giving him a sickening view of the carnage and debris now floating on the sea between Fel's destroyers.

There was much to be done.

CHAPTER THIRTY-FOUR

"Y OU HAVE TO get us to the city center," Jacob said after Mary disconnected from Eva. She'd seen some of Ballern's ground troops deeper in the city, and they all knew what that meant. "We can't let them get established. You have to!"

Mary blew out a breath, "No, I don't."

"You heard Eva," Alice said. "They moved more soldiers under the city. We need to guard the exits so any of them that survive the traps don't get out and into the city."

"I'm with Alice," Furi said. "Drop us off and then do what you have to."

"Kids are right," Smith said over the horn. "Drop them near Theodosia's shop. They can resupply and get to the tunnel by the Crown Library quickly."

Mary cursed under her breath. "Fine, but I don't have to like this. You're safer on board." But she still turned the Skysworn to the southeast, heading for the workshop.

Many of the streets didn't look much different from when they'd left, but Jacob could just make out some of the skirmishes on some of the side streets. They couldn't be sure how many of Ballern and Fel's forces had made it into Belldorn already, but they had to cut off their entry points.

It wasn't long before Jacob found himself standing in front of the workshop, looking up as Smith retracted the landing lines. If the reports were correct—and judging by what they'd seen, he didn't have reason to doubt it—they didn't have much time before Ballern's forces would breach the city proper.

"We should have installed more traps."

"Come on," Alice said. "We can worry about that later."

Furi opened the door and waited for Alice and Jacob to enter before closing it behind them.

"Hello?" Alice called out to the dark room. No one answered. "With Theo and Targrove in Midstream, and the others in Bollwerk, there isn't anyone here. Or they're supporting the Titan Mechs."

"That's okay," Jacob said, pointing to a wall of ammunition for bolt throwers, Burners, and compound bombs. "Look."

Furi grabbed a bandolier filled with throwing knives. She pocketed a handful of Burners before grabbing a case of the compound bombs.

Alice took four coils of bolts for her wrist launcher.

Furi slid her glider off before detaching the smaller pack that had the symbol of the Shadowwing embroidered on its patch. "We shouldn't need these underground."

Jacob thought about how high some of those caverns were that he'd seen under the city. If all went well, there shouldn't be any reason for them to be up that high, but the last several weeks taught him it wasn't often that all went well. But in this case, the option to carry more bombs and ammunition outweighed the possibility of needing a glider.

Some of the corridors underground were narrow, and even the new glider packs could be a tight fit if they had to run. Jacob shrugged out of his pack and took a smaller satchel off the shelf, transferring multiple magazines for the air cannon along with extra clips for Alice's air cannon.

"Alice, if you need these, I have several."

Alice held open her own pack, revealing a tight arrangement of clips for the bolt glove and air cannon alike. "I think we're set."

Furi lifted a sword off the wall. It was old, and the blade had more than one chip in it when she unsheathed it, but it didn't crack or roll when she slammed it into a workbench. Furi nodded and clipped the sheath to her belt before dropping the sword into it.

"Here," Alice said, grabbing canteens and a leather pouch and tossing some to each of them in turn. "Dried Pill-Bug. I don't feel like eating, but we need to keep our energy up."

Furi took a handful of the salty meat and started back toward the door. "Let's go. There's more Ballern history in that library than in Ballern itself. If anything happens to it, I'm not going to be happy."

Jacob and Alice exchanged a grin. There were more than a few things they had in common with the Skyborn.

They left the workshop and headed down the street. An eerie silence hung in the air so close to the city center, only the distant thunder from the airships and the conflicts around the city perimeter echoed around them. There wasn't much to see in the way of a battle, other than the occasional body left crumpled along the way, and that was enough.

"I didn't realize they'd gotten this far," Alice said, eyeing a fallen Fel soldier as they passed.

"Scouts," Furi said. "Ballern does the same thing."

"Who would sign up for that?" Jacob asked.

"Some of them didn't have a choice in Ballern," Furi said. "Others, well, others believe what the monarchy told them. That they and their families will be bathed in glory for all time."

Jacob glanced back at the collapsed form, thankful he couldn't see their face. "Glory doesn't do much good if you're dead."

"It doesn't do much good if you're alive either," Alice said.

Jacob knew what Alice meant, and he agreed with her to a point. But he also remembered how they honored the Spider Knights in Ancora, and the entire city, both the Lowlands and the Highlands, thanked them for their sacrifice. And even Samuel, who Jacob knew didn't enjoy the ceremonies and status granted to the knights, seemed happier after those celebrations.

He wondered when they'd have celebrations like that again in the city. The Butcher had taken so much from them, and Jacob had little doubt there were parts of life in Ancora that would never return. Much like the soldiers lying dead on the streets would never go home.

"What did you mean that some didn't have a choice?" Alice asked.

Furi sighed as they moved to the edge of the street, walking in the shadow of some of the shorter towers as they angled for the Crown Library. "All the Skyborn have to serve in Fleet. That's just how Ballern has always been. Or, at least as far back as we have records." Furi frowned and shook her head. "And I don't even know if that was a lie. But the more troubled soldiers, those who were thieves and worse?"

"Like Jacob," Alice said.

"Hey."

"Yes, exactly," Furi said.

Jacob scowled at the pair as Alice let out a low laugh.

Furi flashed him a smile. "And it's not that they actually *were* troubled, you know? Some of them had simply spoken out about the monarchy, or its supporters, or worst of all, the queen. They were given a choice, if you can call it that. Prison, or become a scout for the fleet."

"Why wouldn't they just run away?" Jacob asked.

Furi looked back at the body in the streets. "Because *that* happens. Did you see their neck? The bloody X carved into it marked them a traitor. They didn't die at the hands of a Belldorn soldier. One of their own killed them."

Alice's face twisted up as she shook off a shiver. "That's terrible."

"It's also sloppy," Furi said. "Leaving a body where it can be found like that? Fleet may have been terrible in a lot of ways, but they certainly trained us in stealth better than that."

Jacob tried to imagine what that must have been like. Growing up on those docks, knowing that no matter what happened, they'd be serving in Fleet. No matter if they shunned violence or didn't have the capacity for it, they'd be forced to fight.

As cruel as life could be in Ancora, it seemed far more benevolent after hearing Furi's stories. The Butcher had been ruthless, which resulted in the deaths of thousands, but Parliament had kept his machinations in check far longer than Jacob had realized. Because if Fel shared its philosophies with Ballern, Ancora could have been far worse off than it was. And that was a sobering thought.

"We always have to fight to make things better," Alice said. "You can't fight for Ballern alone."

"What are you saying?" Furi asked.

"I'm saying we'll fight with you, Furi. Until you can go home and not worry about such terrible things."

Furi smiled at Alice, but Jacob choked back a rising pressure behind his eyes. Ballern was part of the Butcher's legacy too. And the same things that had crushed Ancora would spread across the sea under Mordair's hand. Alice was right. They had to help the Skyborn in any way they could, no matter how small the gesture might seem.

Alice tackled Furi to the street a moment before a bolt shattered on the stone where her head had been.

"Halt!" a deep voice boomed.

But the boom that followed from Jacob's air cannon silenced their would-be assassin. He crossed the street to the wide-eyed soldier staring up at the sky as he lay gasping for breath. Jacob recognized the sounds his chest was making. That horrible wet crackle that came before the soldier fell still, and his eyes unfocused.

Jacob raised the air cannon to the shadow in the alley, but before he could fire, they were gone. So what Furi had said was true. The scouts moved in pairs.

The rest of the walk to the Crown Library was spent in relative silence. Jacob kept his air cannon primed, while Furi held a crossbow in her hands. Alice wore the bolt glove and carried the smaller cannon. They didn't encounter any more of the scouts along the way, and part of Jacob worried that was simply because they hadn't *seen* the scouts. Not that they weren't there.

Regardless, they reached the plaza in front of the Crown Library. And what waited for them made Jacob's blood run cold.

"Hide," Jacob hissed.

They hurried into an alley, staring at each other in silence as the enemy gathered in the spokes of the courtyards, marching into an assembly. Jacob wasn't sure how many were there, but they couldn't get through them all.

"Jacob," Alice whispered. "There's no way out of this alley."

His heart dropped as he followed her gaze past Furi to a dead end. Jacob's mind raced, wondering if they could go back the way they came, but the soldiers had already moved closer to the street. They'd be seen.

He squeezed Alice's hand.

"We wait," Furi said. "See if they clear out. They aren't here to guard a library."

Alice nodded. "They're here because the exit from the tunnels is in the same square."

And that thought worried Jacob more. How many additional soldiers would be joining these in short order? He leaned his head against the wall as he struggled to come up with an idea that wouldn't get them killed.

CHAPTER THIRTY-FIVE

They'd barely been docked for an hour when Drakkar's call came over the transmitter. "Skysworn, we have an emergency."

"What is it, Drakkar?" Mary asked.

"Canopy scouts are reporting a significant force in the mountains coming from two large caverns. We have confirmed and are moving to engage."

"No, Drakkar. Jacob and Alice took Furi to the workshop. They're going underground by the Crown Library."

Drakkar's transmitter cut out for a time. "Understood. Samuel and I will return to the city and find them. Rin and Tatsu will lead the Dragonriders against the newcomers."

"If they do not answer their transmitter, they may already be underground," Smith said.

"Drakkar, hold position," Mary said. She switched frequency to Archibald. "Warship One, this is the Skysworn."

"Speaker here."

"Canopy reports heavy movement in the mountains east of Belldorn. If you're coming that way, you might want to engage."

"Understood. Have you confirmed the sighting?"

"Speaker, this is from a trusted source."

"Confirm the sighting, Skysworn. You know our procedures."

Mary cursed and switched back to Drakkar. "Drakkar, where can we confirm the sighting? Archibald wants additional confirmation."

If the Cave Guardian was annoyed at Archibald's request, he didn't express it. "Follow the beach to the east. It is impossible to miss."

"Evacuate the Dragonriders, Drakkar. Do you understand? I'm sending Archibald across the mountains."

The hatch to the cabin slammed closed as Smith stepped inside. "I completed a rough check of the systems. Minor damage that will have to wait. Chainguns are reloaded. We are as ready as we are going to be."

Mary nodded and pulled away from the docks, turning the Skysworn toward the mountains. "Full throttle in three … two …"

Smith leaned against the console, bracing himself as Mary threw the lever forward, and the Skysworn accelerated across the sky. The docks gave way to the city streets, which gave way to ash and ruin before they reached the sparse grasslands between the city and the mountains.

Mary froze when she saw it, and she didn't miss the stiffening of Smith's back. She pulled back on the throttle, and her hand hovered over the levers that would turn the ship around and take them anywhere but into the maw of what waited in those mountains.

She clicked the transmitter. "Warship One, we have confirmation."

Smith laid a hand on her shoulder. "No one would think less of us if we ran, Mary."

"The love of my life is in that city. Our friends are in that city. *I* would think less of us. Now get on the damn gun."

Smith squeezed Mary's shoulder before he headed for the gun pod.

Once, a long time before, they hadn't been the only ship that fled a major battle over the Deadlands. It was a dark day for those who lived in Pirate's Cove, and one that took years to rebuild after. It was the only time Mary had ever run from a fight, and it haunted her. In the years that followed, she had earned her reputation in full.

No one crossed the Skysworn without paying a price.

"I am ready," Smith said over the horn.

"Spin up the guns," Mary said as she eased off the throttle, letting the nose of the airship angle down. She slid one of the newer levers to the side, exposing the chainguns on the bow. Mary locked the trigger in place, and the rhythmic pulse of the gun pod joined the forward guns.

There was no warning in that moment. Only chaos as Fel's forces made their way through trees that had suddenly become splinters. Chaos as blood showered down as surely as the rains, and the organized march of their enemy broke into a panicked scramble.

But still more crawlers and troops and mining platforms exited the caverns. For every soldier they struck down, another took their place. But their progress had slowed as the disabled crawlers formed a roadblock.

"Ballistae, Mary!" Smith shouted.

She jerked the ship to the side, and one of those massive bolts glanced off the Skysworn's armored underbelly, missing the gun pod.

"Too close," Smith muttered, but she could see he was still firing.

They danced across the mountain ridge, circling faster than the ballistae could aim, until the forward chainguns ran dry.

"Smith, I'm out."

"I suspect I am nearing the end as well. I have more I can load for the forward cannons, but it will take some time."

Mary tipped the bow of the ship up and rode the angle of the mountain into a cloud bank. The Skysworn surged above the clouds before Mary saw it, a black shadow on the horizon like a floating mountain.

Archibald had held true to his word.

CHAPTER THIRTY-SIX

S AMUEL CURSED WHEN the plaza outside the Crown Library came into view. Somehow, he knew he'd find Jacob and Alice there, and his instincts proved him right. They were well hidden in an alley where a section of wall jutted out at regular intervals, providing cover from three sides, but not from above.

He glanced up at Drakkar, and the Cave Guardian signaled to land. It would mean abandoning their mounts, and Samuel wasn't sure if that was the best idea for what was to come. But when Drakkar held up a small gray case, Samuel grew far more certain.

The Spider Knight guided the Dragonwing to the roof of a tower. It would take time to get down if the Dragonwing decided to leave, but it would keep them out of range of the crossbows below.

Drakkar joined him a moment later. "How have Ballern and Fel gathered so many in the city center?"

"The tunnels," Samuel said. "I bet that's why Jacob and Alice were headed there."

"And it appears the Skyborn is with them." Drakkar rushed to open the case and pulled out the shell for a compound bomb.

"Are you sure about this?" Samuel asked.

"No, my friend. But we cannot fight them ourselves, and our friends have been spotted."

Samuel's stomach churned when he saw a squad of soldiers move toward the alley where Jacob and the others were hiding.

"This may force the surrender of the survivors and save the lives of our friends."

Samuel reached out and squeezed Drakkar's shoulder. "I can do it, if you don't want that blood on your hands."

"It is the same blood I judged Charles for, Samuel. This I must do." There weren't any more words as Drakkar clicked the igniter and snapped the shell closed. He heaved the assembly over the roof, and Samuel watched the slow arc as it gathered speed.

Horror crawled through his veins as he saw Jacob step toward the alley's exit. He didn't think, only screamed. "Jacob, take cover!"

He locked eyes with Alice a moment before she snatched Jacob back from the brink, just before the compound bomb cracked against the street, bounced once, and detonated in a fireball that broke stone and bodies alike.

"Crawlers are coming," Samuel shouted. "Look down the streets. Come on. We need to buy them time." He climbed back onto his Dragonwing, which mercifully hadn't flown away after the explosion.

Drakkar didn't hesitate to follow the Spider Knight, and Samuel hoped that was a good sign. He didn't know if he'd ever get the image of what he'd just seen out of his own head, and Drakkar had thrown the bomb.

A quarter of the soldiers had died in that blast. It was one of the problems with the compound bombs. Some were far more deadly than others. But in this case, grim as it was, Samuel thought it for the best.

"Surrender!" the Spider Knight cried out as he swooped low across the survivors. "Surrender and be spared!"

A crossbow tracked him through the sky before a collapsible spear punctured the soldier's chest. Another soldier followed the Spider Knight, only to have his back blown apart by the thunder of an air cannon.

Jacob and Alice and Furi were exposed now, and they moved with a savage precision that broke Samuel's heart. No one that young should be so good at killing.

Alice fired two rounds from a small air cannon, taking down another soldier who drew his sword. But it wasn't until the armored crawlers arrived on either side of the square that all resistance quieted. Belldorn soldiers leveled their crossbows and cannons at the invaders and gave them another ultimatum.

"Thank you, Dragonriders!" a captain called up to them. "We have it from here."

Samuel and Drakkar both landed their Dragonwings close to Jacob and the group, dismounting before signaling their mounts to return to the stables.

"I heard you were going underground," Samuel said. "We thought you might need a hand."

"I never thought I'd be so happy to see a Cave Guardian and a Spider Knight," Furi said. "Thank you."

"There is a time we must make sacrifices to help those who cannot overcome the poison in their own cities," Drakkar said. "I am here in that spirit, at whatever cost we must pay, so that the Skyborn may one day know the kindness of Cave."

Furi placed a hand over her heart, but didn't respond.

Samuel blinked at Drakkar. "What he said."

"We better go," Alice said. "Before any more of those soldiers decide they have decent odds."

Samuel trailed behind the group, keeping an eye on the enemy. They made their way into an alley and a dim corridor that had been hard to see from the street. No one waited in the shadows, perhaps because they'd seen what happened to those in the square.

Samuel glanced back once more at the carnage they'd left behind and then followed into the shadows.

✧   ✧   ✧

THE FIRST THING Jacob noticed in the dimly lit corridor was that the dead weren't only in the streets above. Ballern, Fel, and Belldorn uniforms alike littered the path. And he didn't need to see what his boots had slipped in to know it was blood.

As humid as the underground had been when they'd first visited it, the air was now thick with the scent of fire and the coppery scent of blood. The idea that a Carrion Worm might find its way into those narrow spaces made Jacob's skin crawl just as much as the dead at his feet.

They passed a choke point, where the corridor narrowed until it was only wide enough for them to walk single file. Samuel led the way, checking every shadow that could have hidden an enemy. But whatever had happened there had either taken the soldiers above ground, or deeper into the underground.

"Stay close," Drakkar said. "I hear movement ahead."

Jacob couldn't hear much of anything, but that might have been due to the bomb and the thunder of the air cannons. Still in the shadow of a wider corridor, they caught their first glimpse of the lost city beneath Belldorn down the adjoining tunnel, and the stronghold Ballern had built in a pit of dead.

Someone groaned just outside the corridor.

Alice leaned forward and frowned at the soldier, a cut oozing blood on the side of his face. "I know him. He was in the prison with Furi."

Furi stepped around Alice and gasped. "Beck! Beck, what are you doing here?" She grabbed him under the shoulders and dragged him back into the corridor.

Beck's eyes unfocused before they locked on the Skyborn. "Furi?"

Jacob crouched down to check the man over. A wide bruise had formed at the cut on his cheek. Jacob didn't see any other cuts or wounds, but blood stained the entire hall. "Looks like he got hit in the head. And hard."

"Why are you wearing a Belldorn uniform?" Furi asked.

Beck smiled and then winced. "Guards said we could fight if we wanted." Something crackled in his breath. "And I wanted to, Furi. If you were out here fighting, I needed to fight too." He coughed, and blood poured from the edge of his mouth.

"Beck?" Furi asked as his eyes rolled back. "Beck!" she cried in a hoarse whisper.

Samuel grabbed Beck's shoulders and turned him to the side before cursing. There, on his back, were the broken shafts of three bolts.

Furi lifted her hand and stared at the blood. "Beck, no. No."

But by the time they laid him down, the Skyborn was no longer breathing. No longer seeing the tears that coursed down Furi's face as she leaned her forehead against his. No longer suffering in the war his leaders had thrust onto his people.

Jacob looked away, barely able to stomach Furi's quiet sobs over her friend. This is what Charles had tried to stop. This is what everything he'd built had tried to prevent. But in the end, it had stolen him away too.

Armored crawlers moved across the marshy earth in the cavern beyond. They might not have had a way through yet, but they'd find one. More than one had been disabled by a javelin trap, but those were far deadlier to the soldiers who encountered them.

Jacob knew they needed to cut off the beachhead to stop more from reaching the underground.

"We need a Titan Mech," he said. "We need to get outside and stop them from getting under the city."

Alice wrapped her arms around Furi and held her.

Samuel took the small box from Drakkar and opened it, silent as he lifted two compound bombs and Burners free of the case.

"Samuel," Jacob hissed. "If you set those off in a confined space …"

"It'll kill every last one of them," Samuel growled as he clicked the igniters and locked them into their shells.

The only warning the Ballern soldiers had was a small splash before the bombs tore open an armored crawler. The tall ceilings weren't high enough to avoid the blast as a fireball raced across them some thirty feet up and rolled down into the rear lines.

Jacob dragged Samuel backward before the flash reached them, superheated air trying to steal the oxygen from their lungs before he heard it—the cracked steel and the falling stone.

"Stay against the walls!" Drakkar roared.

There was nowhere to run in the merciless black that followed, the dust and debris choking their lungs as surely as it blinded them. They stayed huddled in the deafening silence. Then the sound of pebbles crashing echoed in the muted corridors.

Movement still sounded in the distance, and Jacob had little doubt some of it was made by survivors. As the dust started to settle and voices rose in the confusion, other shapes took form in the growing light, hulking forms that pushed through the marsh like a ship's wake in the ocean.

"Carrion Worms," Alice whispered.

Screams followed.

"We have to go," Samuel said. "Have you ever seen an enraged Carrion Worm? We have to go, *now.*"

Jacob had. He remembered the attacks in the ruins of the Lowlands. Remembered the speed and the devastation they could inflict in moments. But he also remembered what an air cannon could do to them. He racked the slide and held it at the ready. The others followed Drakkar as the Cave Guardian ignited a lantern that looked more like a lighthouse in the distance.

Jacob trailed the group, keeping his eyes focused on the broken stones on the ground and behind them as best he could. They needed to get to a Titan Mech. If they could close the entrances to the underground, what forces had made it below Belldorn would have nowhere to go.

The corridor finally grew light, and they broke into the alley, trailing dust and debris as they went. Much of the square had already been cleared, but a handful of Ballern soldiers stared at them from their bindings.

Jacob clicked the transmitter in his collar. "Skysworn, are you there?"

A short burst of static came back before Mary's voice. "Jacob? Are you safe? There are reports of a collapse near the southern battlefield."

He raised an eyebrow and looked at Samuel.

The Spider Knight gave an awkward smile and a shrug.

"We're by the Crown Library."

"Still?"

"It's … a long story. We're heading for a Titan Mech. We have to seal the tunnels closer to the beachhead."

"No, Jacob. Stay inside the city. Whatever you do, stay inside the city. We're pulling back the Dragonriders now."

"Why, what's happening?"

"Find someplace with a view and stay safe." With that, Mary disconnected.

Alice's gaze traveled up the Crown Library. "Come on. We can see most of the city from the top floor, and we can defend it if anyone attacks the library."

"Yes," Furi said after a deep breath. "If the truth about Ballern is inside those walls, we have to keep it safe. The Skyborn have to know the truth."

"I'm sorry about Beck," Alice said.

"I am too, but he wouldn't want us to stop. He ..." Furi's voice cracked. "That he would fight with Belldorn ... Alice, you have no idea how much he hated Belldorn. It gives me hope."

"Time to go," Samuel said. "Now."

Jacob looked to the east, following Samuel's gaze. Shadows eclipsed the mountains, and a great darkness rolled toward Belldorn.

CHAPTER THIRTY-SEVEN

"WARSHIP TWO, THIS is your Speaker. Move to the south of Belldorn. Anything beyond no man's land, kill it. Warship One will drive Fel's soldiers from the mountains."

"Understood."

Archibald moved to a second transmitter, changing the frequency to the Lady of Belldorn. "Porcupine, this is Warship One, over." Archibald knew Lady Katherine's would be the only Porcupine listening on their current frequency.

"Archibald, I'm here."

"Lady Katherine, we are moving the warships together in a pincher maneuver. If you center the Porcupines in a dagger formation, we can cut straight through the city and into Ballern's carrier."

"The strikers will do more damage than we can sustain."

"Not if you remain between the warships. Just be careful about those flank cannons, yes?"

A strange humor sounded in Lady Katherine's laugh. "Of course, Speaker. We'll try not to shoot you down. I'll have our brigs provide cover above and below."

"Only above," Archibald said. "It's not safe below the warships. You have ten minutes. Don't give them a chance to realize what we're doing."

"We won't. And Archibald?" The Lady of Belldorn hesitated. "Thank you."

"Don't thank me," Archibald said. "Thank the Princess of Midstream. I wouldn't be here without her."

Gladys blinked at the Speaker. That wasn't entirely true, she knew. He'd already sent one warship ahead, and the Titan Mechs had arrived before them as well. But as the Lady of Belldorn thanked her, sincerity in her words, Gladys started to realize Archibald's intent.

"Of course," Gladys said. "I would never abandon an ally."

The smile on Archibald's face was something between a proud father and a devil incarnate. She'd said what he hoped she'd say, but Gladys didn't think Archibald understood how transparent he'd become. And her awareness of his ambitions would be enough to stop them should they sour.

It wasn't long before the warship crossed over the beach near the mountains, and Gladys saw what had come to Belldorn. She gasped at the scorched homes and collapsed rubble of what used to be the northern edge of the city. Buildings that had stood for centuries lay crumbled or burned to ash.

And what marched from the mountains was what had been described beneath the Bay of Sorrow. They might have thought all those forces had been lost to the collapsing tunnels, but there had been more. And there had been more than one tunnel. Large machines not so unlike the Titan Mechs rolled on treads, bearing down on the city's defenders.

"What are those?" Gladys asked.

George leaned forward, looking out the window. "Old mining equipment. They used to mount drills on those, didn't they?"

Archibald nodded. "But they did not look like that. Look at the drill mount. Where the shoulder would be on a Titan Mech, they have ballistae mounted."

"I don't see a way for them to reload those," Gladys said. "How much damage can they do with two bolts?"

"A great deal, I am afraid," George said.

"Those are built to survive a cave-in." Archibald rubbed his hands together. "They could tear down buildings, or run over Belldorn's defenses, with little threat of damage."

"Then we have to stop them, now," Gladys said.

Archibald looked down at the desert princess. "If you do this, there's no going back. We will have declared war on Ballern as surely as Belldorn has. And more fighting could come to Midstream. I leave the command to you, Princess."

Gladys didn't flinch. War had already come to Midstream. She didn't look to George for advice in that moment. The steel in her eyes didn't flicker as she spoke a single word. "Fire."

Archibald spun to face his bridge. "All forward guns, focus on the airships. Chainguns, churn the earth. Bombers, aim for the drill plat-forms."

The orders echoed through the halls of Warship One. And death came on streaks of fire.

There are visions so terrible, so violent, that no matter the heart and determination of an enemy, they'll retreat as fast as they can, broken. Gladys was well aware of that, as she was sure Archibald was. One of Belldorn's Porcupines joined them in the bombing, chewing up the rear of Fel's ground forces. Gladys held that in her heart as Archibald gave the order to cut down every retreating soldier in range as Fel's soldiers tried to scramble back into their tunnel. The bombs they dropped on top of it collapsed the entrance, cutting off retreat.

But the cannon fire from the flanking Porcupine crumbled the mountainside, sending an avalanche of stone and earth to crush everything below. Gladys watched in awful fascination as a crack thundered around them, and the mountain folded inward.

"The Porcupines created a fault line ..." Archibald whispered.

No one spoke as the side of a great Dragonwing Mountain sheered away, plunging into the narrow pass between the mountains and the Bay of Sorrow like the dagger of a god. Water exploded in a towering geyser as the collapse breached the water table, and a whirlpool formed in the Bay of Sorrow as an unimaginable volume swept into the undersea tunnels.

Nothing would survive it for more than a few terrified minutes.

Gladys let out a strangled cry as she realized what had happened. They would never know how many lives were lost under the bay, and somehow the lives that same tragedy saved in Belldorn did little to numb the horror.

Archibald slowly turned back to the table and pulled up the transmitter. "Northern ground forces neutralized. Focus all fire on Ballern's fleet."

There was a quiet moment as the airships drifted over the city, closing on the cluster of shadows on the horizon. But as they crossed the halfway point, Lady Katherine's orders sounded over the transmitter.

"All cannons, fire at will."

And the sky burned.

✧   ✧   ✧

JACOB STOOD AT the top of the Crown Library tower, staring out at the Crystal Sea. Alice slipped under his arm as they watched the horror unfold. The Dragonwings had done their job, sowing chaos in the skies, scattering Ballern's formation as the two great warships from Bollwerk and three Porcupines took up a formation of their own.

The attack had been sudden, violent, and horrifying. Destroyers and supply ships alike drifted into the sea like ash from a great fire. The burning shapes of Emerald Needles followed some of them down, still hacking and pulling at whatever sailors they could find before they met the same fate in the waters.

Some of Ballern's ships had retracted their red banners, trying to deploy white flags of surrender, but it was far too late. Even those that managed to raise their white flags burned from the unending volley of cannon fire.

The power of the Porcupines was formidable. The power of three of them combined with Bollwerk's warships was terrifying. Jacob had little doubt those ships together could burn a city to the ground, end the war with Ballern … at the price of every soul who lived there.

"They're running," Alice said, pointing off to the northwest.

Jacob watched as the strikers fled back to a carrier. He wondered if Archibald would chase that behemoth down as it drifted toward the horizon.

"A worthy adversary in those strikers," Drakkar said.

Samuel harrumphed. "I hate those things."

Flaming debris continued to fall from the sky as most surviving ships retreated and a handful fought on. Pockets of soldiers still battled in the city, while others surrendered.

"This is a turning point," Jacob said. "In the war with Fel, this changes everything."

"What do you mean?" Alice asked.

"We have to go to Ballern. We don't have a choice now."

Furi sat on the stone ledge of a nearby window. "We never had a choice."

Alice took a deep breath. "I know. But I can't help but think this is what Mordair wanted all along. He's overpowered Ballern without having to fight them. Kat won't leave her city unprotected, you know."

"I don't think Archibald will either," Furi said. "Maybe we're wrong."

"Mordair showed cunning with those tunnels. And the Butcher may have failed in Ancora, but look how much it cost our city. Kat and Archibald are going to be careful."

Jacob hugged Alice closer. It wouldn't end while Mordair was still alive. Of that, he was sure.

CHAPTER THIRTY-EIGHT

JACOB SAT BESIDE Alice and Furi in Theodosia's workshop. There was an awful silence in that room, punctuated by Furi's occasional sniffs as she composed herself. Jacob knew that kind of grief. It would come and go, triggered by the most random things, and only time would lessen it.

"Decades of peace since the Deadlands War," Smith said, sagging back into his seat at one of the workbenches. "Gone in a flash."

Mary nodded but didn't say anything.

"I always thought it would be Charles who broke the peace," Drakkar said, turning a pewter stein in his hand. "His gift for weapons was unparalleled. But now I see those same skills in Jacob, and I worry for the legacy he will leave in the end."

"As long as my friends and family are alive, I don't care," Jacob said.

Rin tightened his fists. "Steamborn and Skyborn working together, forming an alliance. We are *everything* our leaders feared. The key to a new age, but I fear for the coming storm."

Jacob remembered the first time he was called Steamborn, and it had been with the same disgust people used to call him a Lowland maggot. The Skyborn were no different, forced into the slums of Ballern to suffer the same fates as those in Ancora's Lowlands.

"Stormborn," Alice whispered, sitting up straighter.

"What?" Rin asked.

"We're something else now. Stormborn. Steamborn and Skyborn

united."

A shiver ran down Jacob's arm.

Furi undid the buckle on her pouch and raised the patch Alice had given her. "And we already have a symbol. The Shadowwing."

Rin held out his hand, and Furi passed her pack to him. He studied the abstract wings framed in a red octagon, jagged edges forming the outline of a gentle creature. "I don't like the red. It reminds me of Fel."

"But it stands against everything Mordair is," Alice said. "This is our future. An alliance that cannot be broken by time and distance because we've already seen the worst our cities have to offer."

Furi took her pack from Rin. "Get used to it. We're Stormborn now."

Rin blinked before a slow smile crawled across his face. "So be it."

"A united front from old enemies," Drakkar said. He gathered a few more steins and passed them out to the group, filling them with a bubbly amber liquid. Done, he returned to his post at the workbench. "I do not suppose you would have room for a Cave Guardian and a couple pirates?"

Smith and Mary both raised their drinks.

Furi grinned at Drakkar. "We have room for anyone who would stand at our side."

Drakkar inclined his head before raising his stein. "To the Stormborn."

The drink had an odd flavor, bitter yet not entirely unpleasant. A hint of leather and fruit hit Jacob's palate, and it was not nearly so harsh as some of the things he used to sneak sips of when his dad wasn't looking.

"It's going to get bad, isn't it?" Furi asked.

"At least we're with friends," Rin said, smiling at Furi. "And we have a chance to do something for the Skyborn. I would risk much for that chance, Furi."

Samuel put his stein down. "I still owe Mordair for what he did to the

Spider Knights. I'm just here for revenge."

Alice scoffed at him. "We know you better than that."

"I've known you for a week, and *I* know you better than that," Rin said.

Drakkar leaned forward and slapped Samuel on the back. "You put on a good show, Spider Knight, but we all know you are a good person."

Samuel looked like he was going to say more, but then relaxed against the bench instead. "Anyway, I'm coming with you."

"We lost more than Beck today," Furi said. "Some of those ships would have been crewed by Skyborn. Some of them won't want to see what really happened here."

"Kura's done good work," Rin said. "Kura will help find those who aren't loyal to Ballern. And now? With the queen dead? I think we may have more allies than ever before."

"Even if they've been told Belldorn assassinated the queen?" Mary asked. "You think they'll see through that?"

"Some of them will. Time will tell how many."

"It's going to look awfully suspicious that the queen died right after Mordair appeared in Ballern," Alice said. "That has to help."

"I don't think we'll know until we get there," Mary said. "Get some rest. We need to decide on a plan of action, and like Rin said, I think Kura is going to be crucial to anything we do in Ballern."

"Is Archibald chasing down the rest of their fleet?" Rin asked.

"Eva doesn't think so. The warships and Porcupines are just off the coast, and after that last maneuver, most of the remaining fleet appears to be in a full retreat."

"Mordair has already moved against Ballern," Smith said. "I do not believe we have the time to await Archibald and Kat's decision."

"What are you saying?"

"I am saying we should plan to return to Ballern. Speak with Kura privately and see what can be done to rally those who are not loyal to the monarchy."

"We can come with you," Rin said.

"Perhaps. But perhaps it would be better if you returned to Canopy to inquire about their willingness to send Dragonriders across the sea."

Rin frowned. "You mean, take our mounts with us?"

"Yes. I believe it could be done with a large enough warship, could it not?"

Rin rubbed his hands together. "It's possible, but the feed and care would not be insignificant. And the ship would have to proceed at a slow pace to avoid losing any that decide to explore our surroundings."

"All issues we can address, if you are willing to stay behind for now."

"I'll return to Canopy. But I can't promise I'll wait for this entire plan to come together. Ballern was my home for a long time, and the Skyborn mean a great deal to me."

Furi held out a hand before pulling it back. "I'll talk to Kura, Rin. But I think there might be something we can do in the meantime."

Everyone focused their attention on Furi, as she detailed an idea that raised more than a few eyebrows.

CHAPTER THIRTY-NINE

MORDAIR FOUND COMFORT in the chaos that followed the assassination of the queen. The Red Hand had proven her worth several times over, but he had to admit the execution of the queen's guard had been a work of art. Both an execution of stealth and a distraction for his own hand.

Joining the leaders of Ballern at the royal table to describe what had happened had been a stroke of luck he had not fully anticipated. An archduke sat to either side of him, while the rest of the table consisted of four viscounts, two baronesses, and a handful of priests.

These were the true faces behind the leadership of Ballern. These were the levers he could use to change the face of the monarchy. Or crush it. The corruption in Ancora had been useful, but Mordair's spies had uncovered something *far* more intriguing in Ballern. Almost every noble in the city had one crippling roadblock to their ambitions. A queen they wished dead.

Even if they suspected Mordair of the assassination, they'd take advantage of the opportunity to forward their own ambitions. It was possible they'd try to control Mordair and position him as their new pawn, but that was a game they could never win.

Jonas, the Archduke of Willett, raised his hand in a call for silence. "Viscount Allerton, you speak of treason, and yet the queen suspected you of undermining her rule."

The pale man with wispy hair almost snarled at the archduke. "And whose fault at this table would that be, Jonas? You've long sunk into the filth of the Skyborn at the cost of the royal line."

"Providing a space for our *soldiers* to live is not filth, you fool. It's good sense."

"Have we been reduced to insults and wit?" a woman, the Baroness of Auxley, asked from the head of the table. "We have heard the story of what happened in that room. Is there any one of us who could not have hired that assassin?"

No one answered.

"My point exactly. Many of you suspect Mordair's hand in this, but the death of the queen forwards the plans of almost everyone at this table *except* Mordair. It threatens his sanctuary after having to abandon his city."

"He is still an outsider," Viscount Allerton said. "And outsiders cannot be trusted."

Mordair leaned forward. "I'm not sure if this helps, but the guard appeared to know the assassin. Called out a name as he died, though I couldn't make it out."

The Baroness of Auxley nodded. "Then none at this table should be trusted. I call for the title of Steward to be granted to Mordair. He is a king and has an understanding of the intricacies and sensitivities of ruling a people."

Mordair hid the smile that tried to crawl across his face. "I cannot possibly accept such a generous offer."

"Then accept it temporarily," Viscount Allerton said. "I don't like it, but until we prove what has been done, the role must be filled."

"Did the queen not have an heir?" Mordair asked.

"That is a complicated question," the baroness said, but offered no elaboration. She turned to the archduke named Jonas. "Have the black throne set at the corner of the queen's seat. Mordair will be our steward until the matter of succession is settled. By the Great Machines, we have lost enough ships that we may have need of his fleet. So treat him with respect and with the hope he provides to us. All in favor?"

Every royal raised their hand in the end, even those who showed an initial hesitation.

Mordair laced his fingers together and leaned back in his chair. "I accept."

CHAPTER FORTY

JACOB AND ALICE returned to the Skysworn with most of the group. Even Rin stayed for a while before returning to the stables. They needed rest, and while they had a plan for what to do next, Smith recommended they sleep on it.

At first, Jacob had thought the tinker was crazy. How could anyone sleep after a battle like that? But it felt like no more than a few minutes from the time he curled up in the bunk with Alice to the time Samuel was shaking them awake.

"Jacob. Alice."

Jacob cracked open one eye and squinted at the Spider Knight. "What?"

"Dinner."

"Already?" Alice muttered into her pillow.

"As soon as Furi sends the message."

"The message!" Jacob said, sitting up too fast and cracking his head on the bunk. "Oww."

Alice kissed his hair and then slid out past him, straightening her dress before pulling her hair back. "Is she in the cabin?"

Samuel nodded.

Jacob slipped his boots on and rubbed at his face before Alice grabbed his arm and dragged him to the ladder.

"Let's go!" Alice said, and the level of alertness in her voice was entirely annoying.

Jacob yawned and started up after her while Samuel followed them both. They made their way across the deck and into the cabin, where Furi was seated in the captain's chair, Mary and Smith by her side. She held the letter out in front of her, now translated into a series of code.

"Did you send it?" Alice asked.

"Just getting ready to," Mary said.

Furi glanced up and smiled before reaching out to put her finger on the communicator. She moved it with a deft hand, sending short and long signals out that rose or fell in pitch depending on how she shifted the hammer.

Jacob stepped closer and read the note over her shoulder. It had been a mad idea, using the stolen communicator to broadcast a message, but they'd worked together on the letter before going to sleep. He could see some tiny changes in the text, but most of it was what the group had decided before they rested.

Alice wrapped her fingers between his own, and they read. Even now, after reading it so many times, it gave him chills.

```
    This is a call to the Skyborn of Ballern. The queen
was assassinated by the monarchy and the King of Fel.
This is not the end of our city. This is only the begin-
ning of the truth, a truth that has been hidden from you
for far too long.
    The Children of the Dark Fire have poisoned the roy-
al line. And there is proof of it in the libraries of
Belldorn. Texts that were printed in Ballern only to be
banned from our city by the very hands that corrupted
our monarchy. Steel yourselves for the days to come.
    The King of Fel killed thousands in Ancora, and he
will do the same in Ballern. We lost family in Belldorn,
but it was due to the King of Fel and the monarchy it-
self. Do not be blinded by their lies. The Steamborn and
the Skyborn fight on.
    Join us. Together, we are the Stormborn. And none
will stand against us.
```

Note from Eric R. Asher

Thank you for spending time with Jacob and Alice! I've been blown away by the reader response to this series, and am so grateful to you all. As you may have guessed, we aren't done with the story quite yet! The next book of Jacob and Alice's adventures is called Stormborn.

If you'd like an email when I release a new book, sign up for my mailing list (www.ericrasher.com). Emails only go out about once per month and your information is closely guarded by a ravenous Pilly.

Also, follow me on BookBub (bookbub.com/authors/eric-r-asher), and you'll always get an email for special sales.

If you enjoyed Skysworn, please consider leaving a review on a platform of your choice. Reviews can make a huge difference and help make sure we get more Steamborn books.

Thanks for reading!
Eric

Coming in 2022. Preorder today!

Stormborn

The Steamborn Series, Book #7

By Eric R. Asher

Books by Eric R. Asher

Shop ebooks, audiobooks, and paperbacks at ericrasherstore.com

The Theme Park at the End of the World

The Steamborn Series

Steamborn

Steamforged

Steamsworn

Skyborn

Skyforged

Skysworn

Stormborn

Stormforged

Stormsworn

The Vesik Series
(Recommended for Ages 17+)

Days Gone Bad

Wolves and the River of Stone

Winter's Demon

This Broken World

Destroyer Rising

Rattle the Bones

Witch Queen's War

Forgotten Ghosts

The Book of the Ghost

The Book of the Claw
The Book of the Sea
The Book of the Staff
The Book of the Rune
The Book of the Sails
The Book of the Wing
The Book of the Blade
The Book of the Fang
The Book of the Reaper
Dreams of the Forgotten Dead
Garden Gnome Graves

The Vesik Series Box Sets

Box Set One (Books 1-3)
Box Set Two (Books 4-6)
Box Set Three (Books 7-8)
Box Set Four: The Books of the Dead Part 1
Box Set Five: The Books of the Dead Part 2

Mason Dixon: Monster Hunter

Episode One
Episode Two
Episode Three
Episode Four

Want to receive an email when one of Eric's books releases?
Visit ericrasher.com to get started.

About the Author

Eric is a former bookseller, cellist, and comic seller currently living in Saint Louis, Missouri. A lifelong enthusiast of books, music, toys, and games, he discovered a love for the written word after being dragged to the library by his parents at a young age. When he is not writing, you can usually find him reading, gaming, or buried beneath a small avalanche of Transformers. For more about Eric, see: www.ericrasher.com

Enjoy this book? You can make a big difference.

If you've enjoyed this book, I would be very grateful if you could take a minute to leave a review on the platform of your choice. It can be as short as you like. Thank you for spending time with Jacob and Alice.